James Lawless is an award-winning Irish novelist, short story writer and poe who was born in the Liberties of Dublin. He is an arts graduate of University College Dublin and holds an MA in Communications from Dublin City University. He has broadcast his work on radio and writes book reviews for national newspapers. His awards include the Scintilla Welsh Open Poetry Competition, the WOW award, a Biscuit International Prize for short stories, the Cecil Day Lewis Award, a Hennessey award nomination for emerging fiction and an arts bursary award for a study of modern poetry. Two of his stories were also shortlisted for the Willesden and Bridport prizes and he was an award winner in the Colm Tóibín Short Story Awards (2020). His books have been translated into several languages.

His work has been commended by, among others, Jennifer Johnston ('has a mighty thoughtful and penetrating capacity to make you gasp and rage and then burst out laughing'), Declan Kiberd ('invents a new way of seeing the world'), Michael D Higgins, President of Ireland ('His love for words and form is at all times discernible'), Carlo Gébler ('gives deep literary pleasure'), the Hollywood actor and writer Gabriel Byrne ('I highly recommend him'), *Sunday Independent* ('Possessed of a lively, fleet-footed style that brims with intellect and poeticism, Lawless, an award-winning short story writer and poet, is an author who we should perhaps start taking more seriously').

The author divides his time between County Kildare and West Cork, and you can read more about him at https://jameslawless.net

ALSO BY JAMES LAWLESS

Novels

Peeling Oranges

For Love of Anna

The Avenue

Finding Penelope

Knowing Women

Poetry

Rus in Urbe

Noise & Sound Reflections

Non-Fiction

Clearing the Tangled Wood: Poetry as a Way of Seeing the World

Contemporary Book Reviews

Children's Stories

The Adventures of Jo Jo

PREFACE

As human beings we tend to hide our real selves. We are afraid to express our darkest thoughts. Words we use are frequently just lottery letters fortuitously trying to hit on meaning and ambushing our minds in Whorfian perceptions of reality. All the world's literature in English is derived from twenty-six letters. (In the Talmud God is about to create the world through the word when the letters of the alphabet descend from his crown and plead that he create it through them). Think of all the combinations and permutations of twenty-six spirits flitting about in all directions like a child's cardboard cutouts dangling from strings, allowing for occasional white space—the universe of void. The slightest ruffle of air makes them dance. A stronger current from a door opening makes them chatter. But a gust of wind makes them individualise their speech.

Leo Lambkin, an unfulfilled married man in a childless marriage and the, for want of a better word, protagonist of *Letters to Jude* is an ageing solipsist preoccupied with his mortality but who can be equally as blackly *Homo ludens* as *Homo tragicus*; and this is a novel primarily of the spirit, tragic and comic, an individual's quest for things of the soul where the institutionalised world has failed us. The method is through the elasticity of language. The writer and characters play and interact with it to mould their own creation. And Leo in particular does this as a forager, not for his ancestor's berries, but for illuminations as, in the quotidian odyssey of his life, he tries to lasso each new observation into a meaningful and hermeneutic discovery.

Every word uttered puts a limitation on the vast content of one's mind. In between the two darknesses of birth and death we fail to learn who we are. Nor do we even, for the most part, allow ourselves to enquire. We are tied up in all sorts of baggage and pseudomorality, and many of us go to the grave in a state of terror or bewilderment.

Dreaming gives the brain a chance to act on its own. The conscious mind cannot create art and, as Montesquieu points out, 'the best and most pleasing writing is that which excites in the soul the greatest number of simultaneous sensations'. Truth can be relative as it depends on whose lens you are looking through. A single author can no longer indulge in the luxury of being omniscient, and James Francis becomes a character complicit in his own novel, as critics and a reader and various other voices are interwoven into the narrative.

A novel, if it is worth its salt, should throw light on the human condition. The truest art will be that which refuses us the neatness of the finished thing. Our best selves, our most complex selves, are not our social selves. An artist's job is to try to release the infinite potentialities of language, to chronicle our often nameless longings and daydreams of our secret selves. He or she plays with language in order to test its power. But he organises more than words; he organises experience, the felt life. Art is superior to science as it is not restricted by logic. But what was there prior to speech from which language derives? *Letters to Jude* is as much a work of applied philosophy as it is of fiction, dealing as it does teleologically and eschatologically in the breaking down of the body—as exemplified by Leo's growing ailments, and by the inevitable annihilation of the world which started with the word, and as marked by the disintegration of the letters.

Some critics argue that the technique of writing known as stream of consciousness is artificial. But all language is artificial, and letters are mere symbols. Our syntactically accurate sentences are more counterfeit than any stream of consciousness. Additionally, they are limited and only reveal a fraction of what is inside our minds. Stream of consciousness gives language a chance to break free from its conventional fetters and frequently works by word association and similar sounds which spark off thoughts in enrichingly diverse tangents: eye/I, relative/relation, coffin/coughin', etc. The free range of the mind should not be imprisoned like battery hens.

The modern Odyssey is internalised. Man's actions are no longer necessarily physically heroic but in his dreams they can be, and dreams are important in that, like reading, they create images, anarchic at times and uncircumscribed by wakeful convention, thus adding to our insights together with the half-wakeful, half-oneiric states of our semi-consciousness. And the act of writing about a non-heroic character such as Leopold Bloom, as Joyce (whom I claim as my literary progenitor) did, could paradoxically be regarded as a heroic action in itself when one considers the effort he put into the making of *Ulysses.* Emotions, only partly articulated, must bubble up from the prose. Stream of consciousness doesn't simply mean adding extra punctuation points to a formal sentence; rather, it is an attempt to capture the disparate elements, both rational and irrational, that make up who we are—all the pluralities that inhabit our minds.

For example, at a creative writing workshop we listen to a story or a poem, and during the reading all sorts of thoughts are going on—an unkind or flattering impulse perhaps towards the reader, and there our own unrestrained egos come to the fore in relation more often to the story teller than to the story he or she is telling. These powerful, mostly unexpressed, forces inside our minds are far stronger than anything contained in the squeaky little sentences that come out in formal utterances.

In our so-called civilised society we often suppress one another to avoid the anarchy in ourselves emerging despite maybe inwardly acknowledging that it is precisely this anarchy which ultimately presents the real truth about ourselves. Man is sometimes more irrational than rational, as Freud demonstrates. He recognises the limitations of literal language to express our inner selves. Our thoughts, as Bergson points out, go round in circles, but our language is linear and mainly on the surface of our being. We rarely give voice to our true and often irrational thoughts, the unsociable side of our selves, our inner core. Rather, we spend our lives subsisting behind a hierarchically imposed linguistic veneer clinging to one limiting ideology or other as our raison d'être, but really living in mortal fear and without ever becoming known to either ourselves or to anyone else. Hence we need art to unravel some of the complexities of our innermost psyches, to express the whole person trembling.

So how do you get to ultimate truth in literature? By breaking down a class-imposed alphabet system and searching for new forms of expressing ourselves—a film can often catch the truth of a moment without the resonance of a word. Logically and grammatically constructed sentences (what I am compelled to use now as exegesis) no longer suit the fragmented world of today with its interlinking global gadgets, and with all of us having two simultaneous thinks at a time, as Joyce would say. It can even be more than two thinks now: as Daniel C Dennett argues in *Consciousness Explained*, our brains are like parallel processors performing many different tasks at the same time. Or as Kierkegaard puts it—and this could be applied directly to *Letters to Jude*—'more and more becomes possible' when 'nothing becomes actual'. And this idea in turn may have been influenced by Hegel, according to whom language negates things and beings in their insularity, replacing them with concepts. Words give us the world by taking it away.

James Lawless
January 2022

The author wishes to acknowledge a generous arts grant from
Kildare County Council
arts service towards the completion of this novel.

Letters to Jude

Some terms/abbreviations used in the novel:

AISLING: A vision or dream, usually involving a beautiful symbolic or mythological woman.

JF: James Francis, the fictive author.

JLA: Junior library assistant, Crichton's nephew.

JUDE: Bernarda Rodríguez.

MARES: Nightmares.

NBB: New born babe, a baby spider.

PHAL: The phallus.

SAM: Samuel Beckett.

SFC: Stern-Faced Critic, also chief librarian Frederick Crichton.

SHEM THE PENMAN: James Joyce.

SMRT: The term for death as used in some Slavic languages.

SYC: Sympathetic Critic.

WBY: Willian Butler Yeats.

I

'The likeness of those who have taken to them protectors,
apart from God, is as the likeness of the spider that takes
to itself a house; and surely the frailest of houses
is the house of the spider, did they but know.'
The Koran

I AM LOOKING AT MY MOTHER THOUGH A WINDOW IN THE ACT of dying. She is lifting a cup of tea to her lips. The flash of lightning strikes and kills her. As the lightning strikes her it registers her picture instantaneously on the pane of glass. The lightning passes through a tree outside—the passing of her soul—and burns the tree down.

My Dear Leo,

I hope you don't mind my writing to you after such a long, long time, but my thoughts of you never faded. I just had to write when I heard of the sudden death of your mother. It must have been a dreadful blow. I knew how close you were to her. Freddie Crichton conveyed the news. He had my phone number from when I au paired for him, of my parents' home in Sevilla. When he called I was polite to him but I didn't tell him much of my business. He hinted at the terrible ordeal we suffered that night in his house. He was trying to get me to describe it as if he wanted me to relive the trauma inflicted on us by those creatures. He called them dogs. 'You know the way the dogs do it,' he said, making me feel most uncomfortable. I asked him did they ever catch the assailants. He said what would be the point of that? 'You know the cops here never catch anyone; they just spend their time asking the public to solve their crimes.' It was he who suggested I write to you. He seemed so concerned—friends that go back the furthest, he said, but I never knew you two were close. In fact I would have thought the opposite. Anyway age can mellow people and maybe that's what happened to him. He told me how you were shattered by the unexpectedness of her death—my poor, poor Leo—and that I would be like a tonic, he said. O, how he goes on. He tried it on with me you know more than once, but what chance did he have when my heart was smitten by you? However, he did mention your wife in very favourable terms. O Leo, I should not be talking like this, not now that you are a married man …

He remembers a pleasantly cool evening in midsummer in his prenuptial days with Lil. They had come from the theatre and were seated at the bar of the Royal Dublin Hotel. A man with a leering face—what disguise did he wear? A mask of *risus sardonicus*—unsteadily wriggled into a high barstool beside them. He gulped down a double whiskey and touched Lil on the back of her exposed neck. Was it accidental? Her shoulder, he remembers expecting it to recoil but no, it remained motionless and she said nothing but dangled the beads on her necklace and he could have sworn a fleeting smile crossed her lips. Had she known him? Was he from the play, he wondered, one of the cast from the *commedia dell'arte* of Lolita which they had just seen at the Peacock and which he enjoyed but which Lil found an awful bore? A little later he got off his high stool and falteringly ...

The Rhymer
There's many a slip
Between cup and lip

... touched the back of Lil's neck again near the clasp of her pendant—this time trying to make it look like an accidental brushing as he struggled with the arms of his white linen jacket—where did he think he was? In some hot colonial outpost and the cool evening outside? He embarrassedly caught my eye, that bald head lurking under its fedora where had I seen it. 'Sorry,' he said and his accent seemed familiar, coming half muffled from behind the mask and yet disguised enough to prevent me from pinpointing it exactly. I was about to take umbrage when Lil's hand went out to restrain me. 'Did you know him?' I asked Lil afterwards. 'Who was he?' 'Just a man,' she said.

... O Leo, I hope you are happy. There are so many things I want to tell you, and one thing in particular, which I don't know if I should ever tell you. Please write to me. It all depends on whether you answer this letter. Just look at it. I didn't even write in paragraphs, I was so nervous.

With sincere sympathy,

Bernarda.

Dear Bernarda,

Was it really you? Has Crichton done some good at last? (Although, why didn't he appear at my mother's funeral?) Is it possible? After all the years. Or is he trying to stir up trouble? He fancied my wife—he chased anything it seems in a skirt. He actually knew Lil before me when both of them worked in the Department of Trade before he moved to the libraries where he found his true metier, and he writes now in the media as a sternfaced critic. He was jealous when we got married and held a lifelong resentment towards me, so maybe his exhorting you to contact me again is an attempt on his part to break up or at least undermine the marriage. Who can tell? He was quite surprised, you see; he thought that I purloined Lil from him because you had left. He knew we had dated, and after all wasn't it in his house the horror happened. Of course he was never to know the sordid details. How could either of us have confided such a thing to him? And then you went away. He never questioned about your disappearance; he just presumed your time of learning English in Ireland was at an end with your fluency achieved (and what fluency: you grasped the nuances of Hiberno-English like a native to the envy of your fellow students). Did you get the teaching job when you went back to Spain? O but Bernarda, it is so welcome you are to me. You come like a shaft of sunlight through the gloomy mists. Thank you so much for your kind letter. My mother, yes it was so sudden. I was so unprepared. I dream by day and mare by night, my thoughts flapping like Painted Ladies ...

JF: If a caterpillar can become a butterfly, why can a child not become a ... ?

... Or how come when we immerse ourselves in water we can swim, but when we embrace the air we cannot fly? I seem to have lost my direction. Trying to reach out a spiritual hand towards burgeoning feelings as they agitate inside me, and coax an unarticulated idea from an embryonic egg. Sometimes I dream her back and I feel close to her. Like when she died, I felt this overwhelming pressure on my chest but then I found her Lourdes holy water bottle shaped like the Virgin, and despite my lapsed belief I held it to my chest and all pain eased for a while at least; all was calm. I feel we are all like little spiders seeking a matrix. I think if I really try I could commune with her. I sometimes sense a presence, a flutter of breeze or a leaf, a whisper. I see her image in the windowpane so beautiful, still young—she was only nineteen when she had me. I will to hear her through a melting cloud, an evanescent sound. I imagine I hear her voice faintly coming in from the labyrinths of the dead. Loneliness dissolves for a wonderful moment but then she is gone. Was it a lack of concentration on my part or not? I don't know. I walk a lot. I went down to the river this evening to see if I could find some energy. My eczema (the barometer of the state of my health) is bad. The weight on my chest returns. And time passes like the season's leaves. Such vague trepidation.

I stood on a grassy patch overlooking the river, neon light reflecting off the water, and I looked across at all the houses, all the little tungsten bulbs, and I thought of all the lives inside, all the disputes and copulations, and my own Wounded House—my own life—drowning amongst them, lost in the sameness ...

JF: Two rusting chains hang from either side of the porch of no. 28 Wounded House, chrome rail, grey steps, grey wall sloping inward.

... But you, Bernarda, of course I want to hear more from you. It has been so long. I thought I would never see you again. Not that I can see you now but ... I feel quite emotional. You ask if I am happy. I don't know if anybody is happy. We just try to keep our levels of misery contained. To go on no matter what. Don't you think that would be a heroic achievement when you consider the state of human destiny? I married, yes. It seemed the platitudinous thing to do as the years rolled by. People said they would like to see me 'settled'. What a dreadful word …

JF: Let's torture a word in a thousand ways.

… Lilith is my wife's name. Not all things are uncommon between us. But enough of that. I suppose Crichton told you I'm working under him now. He is Top Dog, County Librarian no less. I compute and file. O the enervation of employment! Bernarda, the night is drawing in. I must conclude, no, defer now. Lil is restless. She has thrown off the eiderdown. Her long left leg is uncovered. If I wake her now she will curse me. How easily some people sleep. She does not dream, or never tells me if she does.

Write soon.

Leo.

PS Some time has elapsed, perhaps an hour. I could not sleep. I had to turn on the lamp, under which dust particles floated like a constellation, and here I am now undoing the neat, little letter I had written you. I was startled. I felt an insect, a spider or something on my forehead. Lil groans. She is not sound. Toes touch accidentally.

How many hours to light? Thoughts teeming. What was our education encouraging us to think our own thoughts only to have society force us to think like everyone else? That, or be an odd ball. I must add to the letter, otherwise more mares. You may ask why I dream so much; there is no one to talk to or be talked to. O the crushing power of silence. Lil does not feel it, or perhaps feels it in me, and torments me all the more with her taciturnity. I am talking to you now but I shouldn't be burdening you especially with this first letter. Nevertheless, we, I at least, and perhaps you also, need to communicate with the living. We need to give one another daily reassurances that we are not falling from the tautened wire.

In the morning a spider in the bathroom sink was trying to find a grip on the ceramic. When I turned on the shower the spider was hurled by the avalanche of water towards the drain. It tried to grip onto one of the bars across the hole. The force of the water ripped off one of its legs, which got caught in the bar as the spider was driven down the gulch.

'Another one,' I shouted from the shower, 'or maybe it's the same one. Who can tell? It's the dampness that's bringing them in.'

'I told you before,' Lil said as she moved downstairs, 'I don't want to hear about them.'

'But do you ever wonder what happens down the drain?' I shouted after her. 'Do they drown? I mean this one, would it return to reclaim its missing leg. Do you ever think like that, Lil? I mean that the world is like that, like a drain, dark and slimy? Lil!'

It's strange but everywhere today one hears of men's insensitivity to women, that men grunt and women talk. But can one generalise? I feel I could burst for the want of a shared word or soul exchange. Lil knits and knits, each stitch a substitute for a syllable uttered as she designs moods into the atmosphere …

JF: She makes a purl of great price.

… O there is communication by recrimination. She puts dates on all my offences and files them away in her memory, and when the fit seizes her she throws them at me in litanies. And you ask if I'm happy. At mealtimes I feel each banged plate or door like a blow to the stomach …

The Seer of Suburbia: Lil speaks with pots and pans and door slams.

… I have permanent indigestion. Wash plate, dry plate, set plate for the numbered tomorrows. Perhaps if we had had children, but I don't know. I have gone on for too long. I speak as if we had been in touch always. Please forgive me. Since Mam died, I am just a lost soul. Good night my refound friend.

Dearest Leo,

How I valued your long letter. I am so sad for you, but you should not despair. Solicitude about past or future never pays. Our communication is so beautiful. Can I put a dot on the page for you to touch also? It is just that we are so far away physically. Our words fly like migrating birds over the sea, and we catch them, but the sea spray has removed your touch. Here is the dot. I shall pause a while now my gentle lion (remember that, how I used to call you Leo the lion?). I shall do something while watching the dot. This dot is you and will be touched by you. O forgive me. I have become bold in my solitariness. It is such a long time since we … since I … and here I am being as forward as ever. Are we more pure than the adulterers? The truth is of course, we tended to idealise (and idolise) each other. I still remember your words: You said I was a woman dressed by the sun with the moon as my pedestal and that my heart was as pure as the sand washed by the sea. You expected so much. Such a strong life force, that I still sense in you despite your present lethargy. But then when we were together, the real presence as it were seemed at times to disappoint (we had our little tiffs, your word, remember?). O but we were young then! I remember, remember with tears the Wood of the Black Glen. *Gleann Dubh*, wasn't that what you called it? You were trying to teach me Gaelic. *Gleann Dubh*, so much softer in its sound than the English words. O I loved your poetry and your darkness …

SFC: He used poetry to pull chicks.

SYC: No, that's not it. He allied himself with poetry, and as a consequence he was attractive to some women.

… But these mares you have. I know you will think me oldfashioned, but I really believe that religion can give one peace …

The Seer of Suburbia: Religion's anaesthetic.

… We all need some god. There are so many things happening; there is such evil about. O Leo, I have to tell you. I cannot keep it in any longer. The reason why I went away. That dreadful night. I have a little boy. You are a father, Leo.

My Dearest Bernarda,

You say I am a father. You drop the words so lightly from your pen. A father. That dreadful night. And I thought that everything was all right after the novenas, the fifteen consecutive novenas to the Grotto in Inchicore. Remember the night I nearly forgot; we were supposed to walk, but it was so late that I went on my bicycle through the dark valley of Bluebell, my little torch lighting the way, and I arrived just as the midnight bell chimed. And you suffered it all on your own! And what is he like? Does he look like me? O Bernarda, you should have told me.

But we will have to be cautious. Your first letter was intercepted. Lil is suspicious. We must abbreviate, use signs and symbols. Nothing must be clear. You must disguise your hand. I was thinking of making you a man, just drop the *a* and call you Bernard. But it is too obvious. She will have remembered a Bernarda working for Crichton. Henceforth I will call you Jude, my bluestockinged friend. But that fateful night. After that beautiful day in the Dublin mountains in the wood of *Gleann Dubh*. Remember the last snow of winter falling, numbing our hands as we cycled, pedalling upwards to the clear light, leaving the canopy of the dark season below us …

JF: Singing songs to banish the hag of winter.

… Poetry and wine. And the kindling fire. The smell still lingers with me. And the closeness. Keeping each other warm and cosy in our little wood, looking out on the timberline of the great white mountain across from us, and thinking the world pure. There was a Boy Scout, remember on a peak with flags, performing semaphore …

Yes, I remember. And then the night came. O I can't …

… and then the night came my dearest, let me continue for you—and then the night came …

… Disguise, you say. How can one disguise unless I write in the language of my ancestors, and who will understand me then? Jude, you call me Jude, a new Christening. I play around with the name in my mind, and on the tip of my tongue. I feel like a transpersona. Must I deepen my voice too? Ha ha! I'll keep the name. I like it, Jude or Judith, it's biblical, it suits me. The secret name fits in well with our secret world. O but Leo, if only the words had life; their blood is the wrong colour. If we could kiss from each other's balconies as lovers do here in the narrow streets of Sevilla. Our words come across the sea. I enclose a lock of hair just for … sorry, I keep forgetting … Our little boy's name is Uanito.

Dear Jude,

Perhaps you have a point. It is difficult to disguise. It is more important from your end, however. But we'll stick to Jude, at least it's androgynous; it may keep me out of trouble. Although perhaps I need not worry, knowing Lil flirted with Crichton and possibly still does under the guise of her many outings. But Uanito, tell me how he is? I really can't believe it. Tell me when his birthday falls, or perhaps you shouldn't, I don't know.

I enclose a little something for him anyway; perhaps you could buy him a football or a kite. Maybe you could send a photograph. And his health, is it good? O should I really know these things? But like you if only I could hold him in the flesh. You are indeed far away in the great land of Iberia but also the land of the failed Armada, a Spanish and Irish hope that went awry. In our history there were ominous signs which I tended to disregard. But now I touch the dot and all the memories flood back.

I have become inward of late. There are so few people I trust anymore. It's the way the world is; the way we've been conditioned; the half lies that we live through every day.

Last night, the Eve of Halloween, I walked through the valley. Just enough light from the distant houses to see my way. A tree with outstretched limbs looked like the Christ crucified. Lovers approached the bridge, finding courage in each other's heartbeats. As I crunched through the fallen leaves my advance was blocked by a young boy with his hand on a wooden structure. 'I got it in the canal,' he said, 'it's for the bonfire.'

Halloween: Don a mask, go trick or treat. All the masks should be taken off at Halloween. The wind made the trees sing a whispering air, haunting the starless night. Samhain: the veil between the dead and the living at its thinnest now. A bonfire was lit deep in the valley down near the canal. Car tyres were heaped on the fire and belching smoke choked the atmosphere. By the light of the flames I could see the shiny steel of motorbikes through the bushes. I heard a dog barking; no it was not a bark, it was a squeal of pain. I had a dog once when I was a kid, never called him any name other than Dog.

I remember the Halloween night I lost him: I was playing with him in a field: Dog was a cocker spaniel with a shiny brown mane. His ears flapped about and the brass studs on his new collar gleamed in the evening sun. We were down in the field by the canal playing.

AINM, FOCAL, ABAIRT

The Gaelic words from the blackboard that day in school were racing through my mind as I hid by a blackberry bush ...

JF: The devil urinated on blackberries.

... We were to make up a name and a word and turn it into a sentence in Gaelic. I couldn't think of anything at the time. I remember some pupils forgot the word or the order, and Teacher helped them by writing these on the board once more: AINM, FOCAL, ABAIRT. I kept saying the words to myself as if they were the sentences, slurring them together: ainmfocalabairt ainmfocal ainmfoc, to stop in mid word, feeling naughty but delighting in my first discovery of polysemy.

Dog sniffed about, tail downcast, tongue hanging out as he searched for me. I noticed how his chest heaved like Mam's did ever since Dad passed away. When he found me his tail lifted and wagged, and he excitedly jumped up on me. Possessive paws. We wrestled and rolled down the grassy slope towards the canal. Across the water I could see several big fellows. They wore chained leather and had spiked hair. They were standing by the bonfire passing flagons around.

Suddenly, I felt a hand tightly over my mouth. I was wheeled around to face a creature in purple spiked hair. He produced a shining blade. Dog leapt on him and bit him on the hand, and he ran away screaming, 'I'll get your fucking dog for this.'

In the early darkness me and Dog headed homewards. Children, some with starlights, passed me on the street. They were dressed in masks and witches' hats, and old adult clothes. Already they were calling to houses, collecting fruit and nuts. On the way we met Freddie Crichton, who was heading in the direction of the bonfire, which was blazing by this stage.

When I got home I didn't tell Mam about my experience. I didn't want to make her chest heave. She was drawing a picture of herself with me under a cloak in a garden with many coloured flowers. I loved writing notes; it was a game between Mam and me. We would leave them lying around the house rhyming occasionally and sometimes we'd draw a little picture.

I got no ecker, Mam.
I ate the bread and jam.

And she would write things like:

Where does the wind blow?
Down in the valley O.

That night Mam mentioned the Bible, about the man with two cloaks, and she wrote:

If I had two cloaks,
I would keep one,
and use the other to shelter my son.

We ate curly kale, barmbrack and played snap apple, and coininthewater. Then I dressed up in a mask and old clothes. Mam was anxious.

'Only our street, mind.'

I accompanied some children as they tricked or treated. It was exciting to feel the paper bag swell under the weight of the assorted fruit and nuts given to us by neighbours. It was quite dark now, and the small group of children, as they made their way, blurred into the streetscape.

Freddie appeared and pointed with delight towards the blazing bonfire by the canal. Dog, who had run out the front door after me, crouched down and made a low growl as bangers went off.

'I'd better bring him home,' I said. 'The bangers frighten him.'

'I'll thee he geth home,' Freddie said and his lisp showed, 'I have to go back to get my mathk.'

A rocket exploded in the sky over the canal. I ran with the other children towards it but we kept a safe distance from the bonfire.

Flames were jumping. Hands waved in a sort of ritual. Large flagons were raised in a toast. Some of the drinkers started hollering and dancing around the fire.

'Did you bring Dog home?' I said to Freddie when he reappeared.

'He broke away from me and I couldn't find him.'

We searched or at least I searched. Freddie with his mask on, after a halfhearted effort, said he'd better return to the group. I looked behind the bushes where we had been playing. I whistled the familiar note for Dog to return. But there was no barking, no sound now, only echoes of my own sound. I retraced my steps though the streets. I asked other children if they had seen Dog, but nobody had seen him. When I got home I had to tell Mam what had happened. We went looking, the two of us, through the dark streets, but there was no sign of Dog. Later we put his picture on shop doors and on lampposts but all to no avail.

In school I wrote:

AINM, FOCAL, ABAIRT
Dog imithe Tá
AINM FOC

When I get home Lil is out. I sit by the open fire watching its gold vermilion disintegrate into itself. O Jude, these reveries? Lil knows nothing of them, too busy what with her bridge and her hundred practicalities. Besides she passes off my dreams as unmanly. You know I overheard a telephone conversation she was having—she has no shortage of words when it comes to her friends—but the talk seemed so far away, as if it were coming from an ethereal world. Am I going mad, Jude? Please keep writing to me. But should I ask one already burdened? Uanito. If only I could see him. Perhaps someday.

My dear Leo,

Your poor dog. He never came back. Gone without a trace. And Crichton, was it deliberate? Was he really not able to find the dog? And what could have happened to him is too frightening to contemplate. Anyway it's in the past now (but who am I to talk with our past still haunting me?).Your little something purchased a white football for Uanito. You asked why I went away? After the Grotto novenas I hadn't the heart to tell you of my pregnancy. You were so sure it would work, the prayers, that is, to the Virgen María and traversing through that dark valley on fifteen consecutive nights, supplicating to be as pure as her. But that wasn't the real reason. The real reason was that I was so traumatised, I did not think you would want to know about a baby born in such circumstances, even though it was from you. I felt dirty, contaminated, O not by you, *mi cariño*, but by their eyes strobing my nakedness as if they were doing the deed, and I was merely the handmaiden and you the instrument. How could you love something generated in such a manner? So I went away rather than tell you, back to the home of *mis padres*, where Uanito was born. I had this thing going through my mind, a poem of Southerne that we learned in the English class in Dublin and which stuck with me for its cruelty:

Be wise, be wise, and do not try
How he can court, or you be won;
For love is but discovery:
When that is made, the pleasure's done.

And that I thought was the way it was with you and all men. Forgive me. I was prepared to bring him up with the help of *mis padres*, who, although elderly, were loving always towards me, their only child, and I never wanted to go back to Ireland ever again. That experience rocked me to my foundations. I felt safe in *España* and no longer safe in your country. I had nightmares about that night, as I am sure you also had, those mares. I felt such shame. But then I read of the tragic manner of your mother's death. In fairness I would not have known only for Crichton. And then I saw it in all the newspapers, an international incident in its unusualness: dying like that, electrocuted by the lightning …

Leo: Why had the lightning rod not disarmed the gods?

… and her image preserved in the glass; it was a talking point throughout all of Sevilla, and of course I pretended I did not know who the lady was when people asked me, knowing that I had been to Ireland. They think Ireland is like Spain with moving statues and all sorts of religious things; however, they don't know the dark side. But your mother—whom I did meet, remember, on a number of occasions—I found to be a lovely *señora*, full of caring for you.

And you, *mi cariño*, have made your life with Lil. And that is good. You must look after her. She is your wife now and she needs you. Opposites can attract …

JF: An apple and a plum can make an interesting pear.

… You must give a loud shout like the roar of a lion. You know the path to the stream of living water. I nearly lost faith. I did lose faith for a while after the Grotto prayers failed. But it has come back now. I read Santa Teresa and San Juan de la Cruz and I am resigned, and Uanito is a good little boy. I am teaching him English which is as good as his Spanish now. The Dublin idioms he takes to with such facility. It must be from you he gets it—something from deep down but also from an Irish boy, a diplomat's son, whom he has befriended. Religion gives me strength, the words and the rituals which we are very strong on in Sevilla.

Be careful, Leo. I don't know why I am fearful for you. With your mother gone perhaps. One can overdo things; the mind can crack: that extra grain that tips the scales which nearly happened to me, and remember that in the Lord's sight the whole world is only a drop of morning dew falling on the ground.

Dear Jude,

O why did you go away that time? Why did you have so little faith in me? I thought we had finished with each other after that horrific experience. I thought you no longer desired me. For days after, you will remember, you would not let me touch you. So I withdrew as I thought that was your wish. And a son! You should have told me straight away. But now I understand it was the defilement, the enforced act that needed coming to terms with. You begot us a son no matter what the circumstances. It is an occasion to rejoice. I am trying to retrace since my mother died. And now you appear, you whom I thought I would never hear from again. Yes, that night traumatised me too. I berated myself umpteen times for being such a weakling, for being so meek, for complying with what they demanded. How was I even able to get it up with all those eyes leering at us? But I really thought they were going to kill you. That guy holding the knife to your throat pressing it, drawing trickles of blood. What choice did I have? O it was not the way it was meant to be. I was never the same after it. But unlike you, I have lost my faith. What good were all those novenas, even though I was the one to suggest it in the first place, trying to make it to the Grotto before midnight on foot as the superstition demanded. (Was it my cycling on that last night that disqualified me?) But you never told me. I was not to know …

The Seer of Suburbia: Condoms were not on then.

… But don't let me rock what gives you strength. As regards Lil, I try. I do look after her as best I can despite the vacuum inside me. O Jude, you should not have abandoned me. To try to tell you what I am or was about: I was perusing an encyclopaedia the other day and I came across Imabari, a famous cotton textile centre in Japan. Never heard of it. How many things and places unknown to my individual soul …

JF: *Omnia mea mecum porto.*

... How many Imabaris? We are all just snippets ...

JF: Snippet snappers.

... or like the dew you mention, dispensable insignificances, trying to carve a mark on the rough crust of the universe. That is all we can hope for, a little mark. Any more is presumption. The world is losing itself. We have lost something of great value. We are like Nero fiddling in a false refuge while the outer walls crumble. The temple is being torn asunder, and it will not be built up again. Let's go back, back to the chrysalis, to the tadpole. What happened then? First water then life then life in water then land then pollen then life on land then animal then ape then manlike ape then apelike man then man then machine then war then man kills man then earth then worms then bones then fossils then ... Why am I trying to go back? Because we are worse off now than what we were millions of years ago? We are not what we were. In three ways: man kills man, man cheats man, man dissimulates to man. How far back can you trace your ancestry, Jude? Find your roots. American black African slave Irish potato famine, go back further, travel through the mists of time through childhood infancy womb mother father great gran gggg, make occasional stops like a train at a station, back back medieval tribal cave. Homo erectus, Homo sapiens. Wait, stop there, zoom in, calling HS my earliest known ancestor. Let's not go to the hominids, too difficult to decipher. The darkness is complete except for one white circle beckoning me, welcoming me in. I've got you in my lens, HS. I see you walking through the wooded land. You are like a man at a fancy dress party. I expect you to unzip at any moment; that is what man has done: he has jumped out of your skin and left the pelt to rot. O I have lost contact, Jude. He has gone. Come in.

I went to the zoo on my own the Sunday after that mare. Lil had no interest. I went to see the gorilla. He looked so forlorn in his life imprisonment, no privacy under the constant gaze of humans.

Despite the sign not to feed the animals, they pelted his pelt with bananas. The eyes looked out from the blackness, pleading for some sort of understanding. But the spectators soon grew tired. He wasn't putting on much of a show after all, and they went to view some other caged 'beast'.

Put on hold, Jude, HS is coming in. He is walking handinhand with another of his kind and three young ones. The young are carrying plastic bags. They are stopping outside a cage. They are looking at some animal inside the cage. It is naked except for spectacles and a bald head. It is cowering in the corner. HS's young throw in some nuts, and they laugh as he reaches out for them and consumes them, shells and all. There is a plaque on the cage which reads:

HOMO INBECILLUS

Ancestor Homo sapiens. Depraved offspring, selfdestructive animal, highly dangerous to its own species, threat of extinction. Best isolated from its own kind. Shows neurotic tendencies. Before the fifth global war among the species inhabited most climes in terra firma but hadn't sufficiently developed intelligence to inhabit Luna or other planets.

HS and his clan soon tired of watching the withdrawn and weakeyed creature and they left him masturbating to the amusement of the black pelts outside the bars.

And now I am inside a pelt walking with HS. I am zipped up but I can't find the zipper. How do I get out? Where am I going? HS seems to understand my dilemma. He beckons me to follow him. We are wandering. Different climes and times flash by my eyes. The clock has stopped. The candle flickered its last. We are in a dark world without time. We are halted. We are in a black country on a mountain. I am among a tribe of perhaps a hundred black pelts. The young are playful and loll about while the adults wander or forage or just sit in a misty timelessness. Suddenly a shout is heard and there is shrieking and running about. HS and I hide in thick shrubbery and watch the adults fall as they are decapitated by black and white men, wielding long knives.

I feel the pelt loosening, the zip is undoing itself and I am being whisked back to my own study. Another strange feeling, Jude: I feel my handwriting is becoming more and more like my mother's in its elongated sloping, and instead of going forward I feel I am going back closer to her. Even as I write to you now I feel I am a little boy doing homework while downstairs Mam is preparing the evening meal. But the transient feeling of security is quickly shattered by a banged press.

Dear Leo,

Little spider is rambling along the page as I open and furrow channels for her, like potato drills. She walks through the lanes of letters without stepping on one. She turns and heads back to the beginning (you may say you are returning to your mother; I think I am returning to you) up the main street, until she lights on the letter L. What does it mean? Maybe she's pulling your hair …

Leo: *Tomando el pelo*, your words I remember, the hair pulling the leg.

… So I don't think I have abandoned you. Don't think like that anymore. Everything makes its signal: the window flap bangs until the latch is tightened, the soft wind blowing up from Africa. It was Uanito who said the other morning that the pig was screeching under the grill (I've grown fond of rashers since my time in Ireland). And he did a drawing when I asked him. It was of a lion eating a lamb. He worries me sometimes, Leo. Can one parent raise a child … ?

JF: It takes a *clann* to raise a child.

… And the circumstances of his conception? In the womb they know, they receive signals from the mother. O I wish you were here to reassure me. Mamá is fine but she is getting old, and Papá, since his retirement, is growing very forgetful. I don't wish to burden them. I live in a separate apartment now not far from them and yes I have secured a teaching job in Sevilla. I like it enough. I like the children. But I keep my personal business to myself.

Maybe you, like Freddie Crichton on a pretext, might be able to visit me sometime or maybe we could visit you. I don't see why not. How many yuppie wives go on holidays without their husbands … ?

JF: What is a flower …

… Baby's Breath …

JF: … but a number of petals to a yuppie?

The Seer of Suburbia: The penalty for bigamy?

Reader: What?

The Seer of Suburbia: Two mothersinlaw.

… No need for a big house. All one needs is a little space for the mind to expand. But I can't help thinking of you. I need someone to hold. At night looking out at the great big moon all alone up there in the sky in its splendour I think of the intense brown eyes of the deer that we saw in the woods—remember that evening as it darkened on the mountain?—piercing through to the soft pleasure dome of the doe.

Is God ashamed of this?

Hey Jude, don't be concerned. Don't worry about god intruding; he is much too busy like our author JF …

JF: When my writing is done I have only leftover energy.

… Besides what can we possibly be doing wrong when we are not even touching? We are only sharing words. That is all. I just turned off the radio. Emotional, sentimental music was playing. It makes tears well so easily, like something unresolved inside myself. How can we accept clichéridden songs so readily and on the other hand exact such originality from our poets ... ?

JF (*wielding a James Perry nib and sporting a Fred Perry shirt*): Music for weeping is like a tale without a tongue.

Reader: Why is he weeping?

JF: He has been cut in half.

Reader: Accident?

JF: His wife went away and he is weeping to heal his wound. All the little pebbles jagged being thrown, wounding and tearing the skin of our world making us bleed and brood as if the little pebbles were all that is. Throw the little pebbles back into the sea; banish them forever; don't let them distract the soul from its eternal task.

... Lil has gone to bridge. She phoned—a smattering of guilt?—for being away so long ...

Did you go out for some air, she asked.

No.

Why don't you go out for a walk? It will get you out of yourself?

I don't want to get out of myself. I want to go into myself ...

JF: He commits himself to solitary melancholy.

... The last letter was weighted like a little baby. I would have loved to have seen Uanito like that. NBB is still here, adult spider up from the drain again looking for its baby. Very dark now, before the incandescence of artificial light. I should lie on a stone slab in darkness to decompose. The vulnerability of one's ownness. I'm concerned about you, Jude. We must try the telephone, though that can be lonelier with distant voices, clipped time, and one never knows who could be listening in ...

JF: Can't beat the flesh.

... Some strange things, Jude: in the garden a pink rose is growing from the white rose bush as if nature is playing games with us …

Cub Scout: Snatch the bacon.

… What can it portend? A gallless year among the oaks …

JF: Acorns rule. Oak eh?

… Something is not right.

JF: Nature encompasses all things.

O Leo, No matter how hard I try, I will never be able to shake off the way our little boy was conceived. It had to be that time, for there never was anyone else but you. Freddie Crichton came onto me you know the old lecher—maybe that's the reason he probably thought I had left. Had a fascination with what he called my swan's neck …

Reader: He liked Lil's neck too, did he not?

Leo: All women's necks from behind.

JF: He had some neck. Wouldn't get away with that in Japan.

… I mean he never found out what really happened. He was out as you know at the time, and the intruders' devastation, remember we tidied up almost as if we were the guilty ones, as if we were somehow responsible for messing up his house. When you think of it.

Reader: That night did you not report them to the police?

Leo: I did of course go to the garda station but nothing came of it, and the perpetrators vanished into the darkness whence they had sprung. And I was fearful to pursue it and for some time after I felt I was a marked man. They knew me, their eyes through their masks would follow me through the streets where I walked.

Jude: O my God how young and innocent we were then. But I wasn't afraid of Freddie Crichton and it was just a pass after all which I felt was all he was making. I was too young for him and he kept friendly with me despite my rebuttal. But those creatures, Leo, they made my skin crawl. Who were they? And you goaded by them, the voyeurs as they salivated from the peepholes of their balaclavas. They were not burglars. They did not look for any money in the house. It was like they wanted some form of lewd entertainment at our expense. We had returned flushed and happy from the mountain, remember, feeling all romantic and having something beautiful that was between us shattered by them when they burst in on us and forced you to … O Leo, that night terror will never go away. Only it was you who was coerced to do it, I would have thrown myself in the river long ago. I thought by returning home that the memory of such a horror would eventually fade away. But no, and Freddie Crichton has resurrected it even more so now. And our Uanito, I teach him about your country in case some day … and I give him all my love, all the love that is that I can muster in the circumstances, but he was not born of love.

I'm looking at the dot. I feel it so strong, so strong, the feeling building up all the time. Like someone whose ears need to be popped. I'm deliquescing into … softness … gentle … Your hand … artist's hands, I remember your fingers long and slender. Leo, I feel close to you. Our minds can make us close. I'm floating. Don't go away. That night you and I and them, all glaring … eyes. What depraved people, making me turn like an upturned broom and they, pointing their knives at us on the orders of the masked man in the shadows, as if we were participating in some grotesque farce…

Yes, I remember the drool of saliva sliding down from behind his mask.

…That was then, that time, instead of the way it should have been, O if only now I could feel the pale softness of your skin over me. Walk in the ways of perfection. I want you to do the same, so we will have our common denominator … whooooo … I implore you to lead a life worthy of your vocation.

Hey Jude. O for your sunny clime. Here comes our daily rain over here as regular as All Bran. Met a man who was singing the

'Song of the Rain'. He loves the rain, he said. Every time it rains he sings. He is from Africa.

We should make dummies of ourselves to avoid life's hurts like the Asian spider Cyclosa makes a dummy of itself, parcels part of his prey in silk until the same size as itself and then strategically plants them in the web …

Reader: Why does a spider not get entangled in his own web?

JF: Because his oleaginous feet don't stick to sticky strands.

… And spidereating birds go for the decoy instead of the real thing. The last of your last letter was very arousing. Here's love's old song again. Remember when we first heard it. Maybe it was a nocturne by the field. I remember it well; it wasn't love's old song, it was … I forget, a Spanish song: *antes de morirme quiero echar mis versos del alma. Guantanamera*, yes that's what it was.

Jude: And the other song …

What other song?

Wishing I was lying in the arms of Mary. Remember?

… Whatever. NBB dances on the spots on the dots on the full stops eight spider power hesitates before settling on a capital. Wait, she is arriving at your dot and bypasses it and settles comfortably on the last full stop. Your dot perfectly round is growing, becoming a tight cavern. I think of you on your own, such a waste flowing lonely like a river and I *Homo erectus*, banished to a lonely cave. Where is the dot? The page, the words, the letters flow as if with their own lifeforce, exclamations, commas hold back then a reaching out, carried with the flood. NBB scarpers to a corner as fast as her eight legs will carry her. That's what makes her an animal; an insect has only six …

Reader: What are centipedes then?

JF: Arthropods.

… What then is man? How tidy she is with her little brushes attached, cleaning as she goes. She sets the program—*me* missing, short on ego. NBB *in a shuí* at the keyboard …

JF: Like a keyboard warrior.

… then gently dancing on the letters, directing my course, driving me on. She is watching. She can see me from every angle. Maybe she is the weaver in purple …

JF: Colliding atoms are the weave of the world.

… Arachne who wove the love acts of the gods. She is looking at me. Look at her. O man. She is weaving it all into a beautiful tapestry to enrage the gods. She has made a picture: a comely barefooted maiden in such a light white robe, soft delineation of curves so loose so easy for her gown to flow away. She is stooping down to lift the cover off a casket. Another picture is taking shape: the girl is kneeling, unveiling an erect phallus. She is being flagellated. Next picture: the girl is dancing in bliss and the gown is shed and she shows her beauty to the sun and sky. But wait, what is this? Another picture to show the previous picture being destroyed and Arachne hanging from a rope. O Athena. The rope is loosening. It is changing into a web. Arachne is turning into a spider. She is looking at me now. O Jude, you have sent me Arachne. That is why all the siblings come up the dark drain. They are looking for their matrix: sheetweb, hammock, redback, what a family and button, no sign of the black widow, the brown widow yes. And outside the smaller ones climbing the grass stacks lifting their swagbellies and being carried away by the wind on silken strands back, back to the mould.

Dear Jude, I am back having to leave off for a while because of exhaustion after that experience drawing up like the spider's thread from the deep well of my subconscious. As regards Crichton, he was always like that, encouraging Chinese whispers …

JF: We walk about in a jungle of whispered words.

… His nephew JLA is exactly like him with his cauliflower ears and premature hair thinning, a chip off the old block, a mimicman getting up to clandestine things with young female recruits in the basement behind the old library stacks. Crichton already had that reputation and always gets away with it too. The girls are enticed there, believing they are going for bibliographic induction and never complain, especially the country girls unfamiliar with the city, fearful of losing their jobs. So enough of him.

My pen was out wandering today expressing impressions along the street. A man approached. Hush pen, lie down, I said, and I quickly hid the pen under my coat as one would hide a weakness …

JF: A pen could stab a philosopher.

… Took myself to a hill on the outskirts of the town and witnessed hundreds of birds perched like black fruit on the leafless trees, and they took flight at the sound of a gun and made their messages with letters in the sky. And as I headed back, I saw my home, Wounded House, from afar, which perhaps could have been filled with joy and us. A bleak house growing bleaker as the autumn passes, its walls oranging with the falling leaves, black slates giving way to mouldy green. A long grey water stain down the gable end. No kindred spirit near, fading into the mist, sinking into timelessness. Is that the way we are going, the way of all flesh and all mortar … ?

Reader: Leo should paint his house.

JF: Motivation is a brush.

… In the distance the blurred muted colours of autumn. Silent leaf fall, a stillness in the air like death. Back home a leaf came down past my kitchen window. It did not float; it jumped suicidelike as if it could not take any more of this hanging around and drying out and changing colours or waiting for some storm to push it down. May as well jump and speed up the whole accursed business. Who is to know the difference between a jump or a fall of a leaf? Later in bed I was awakened by birds squawking: panic in the heavens. Hundreds of birds flying in disarray in the dawn sky, like black specks of paper. Is it an omen?

Reader: What is Leo doing?

JF: He's waving to a lover who can't be reached.

What is wrong, Jude? I am writing to you from the library now. It's weeks since I heard from you. Did you fail to disguise the letters sufficiently? If Lil intercepted them, she never let on. I must hear from you. Write in code or whatever way you wish. Write an upside down language, like the Walpiris. Speak—what's it called? Tjiliwirri. Mix up everything. I will unravel it. O why are you so far away? We could learn Silbo and whistle to one another. We only need to devise the code for the private part (public without L).

You talk about spiders. Last night in bed I dreamed I appeared in a leonine leotard. Lil's shoulder was cold giving me the cold shoulder. The scroop of her nightdress—a gift from Crichton who still brazenly bestows presents on her, including jewellery and pungent perfumes, sometimes delivered like fan mail in the post on her birthdays and at Christmas and which she, without the slightest hesitation, accepts.

Reader: A necklace?

O yes. But the nightdress, the silk, from what source the silvery threads? Mr and Mrs Lambkin. And there was the spider plucking her thread on the ceiling before the light went out. She is changing the pedipalps. When you think of it with human males the phallus has very limited use, only two really. I mean the pedipalps can be used to handle food or as a sense organ. If we train our prehensile toes and fingers …

JF: A bum can close a door.

… why then can we not train the phallus to perform other tasks? WPAU. Wash Phal after use. Put it there, Phal, shake. How is the lingam? Hold my knife for me there, Phal. Or maybe it could balance a tray. Three legs improving. A guy could give a girl a lift home on his crossbar. And look at Shiva, a paradox: simultaneously ascetic and sensuous, yogic and ithyphallic. Doesn't sag when dusted as the cleaning lady exclaims in the art gallery. Use it as a straw to drink through its eye. Even the bull's pizzle was used as a flogging instrument ... The silk is unravelling as the geometric orb is being caressed, all undercover, left to wonder ...

The Seer of Suburbia: Lil does a bit of undercover work.

Reader: What, she sells tents?

... What got me onto this? What I am really saying is that Lil sees no use for Phal other than as something perfunctory and mechanical. Not anymore, not that she was ever into things sensual with me anyway, but then I thought that was her, that of course after you left and with the years things die inside you.

Reader: But what about the nightdress that Crichton bought her? I wouldn't have stood for that. I would be angry.

Anger is an emotion long lost. On my way to work I saw the morning's dew shine on the silver web, freshly made. If only I could go into myself and produce words like silk.

In the library I heard the sharp voice of an elderly spinster speaking to the diffident and nasal junior library assistant.

Twist in the Tale, is that a collection of short stories? asks the spinster.

I eh ... eh ... tee ... a eh ... er ...

What? I can't hear you.

Yeah ... em ... em I tink it is, is it?

Is that his latest book?

Eh ... em ... yeah ... I tink ...

What?

Yeah ... eh ... I tink it is, is it?

How did he get the job? Crichton of course. Funny when you think of it, we're all born with a tail. Some of us, a rare few, can actually recall being born, such as the Sterne man. Grows back into the buttocks, fishy, swimming sperms like little fish; we are tadpoles floating about before the change. In the beginning was water. What the ... did that old spinster want? Not much good to her. Here comes the poor boy who can't afford to travel. He devours travel books from the library and wanders to exotic places in his imagination, contrasting with his real predicament.

The Seer of Suburbia: Like Jimmy and his magic patch.

JF: Or a man on his way to the turd world. And here comes the red tart sheltering from the rain.

Reader: Who is she?

JF: There she is, her shapely legs showing through her red coat on her circadian odyssey. She's coming from ...

Red Tart: ... Cross Guns Bridge. Say there was more than guns crossed there. Get your knickers in a knot, all the wasted seed on the grey canal wall dead and still as the water. Phibsboro trolleys abandoned from the supermarket like babies' prams interrupting the flow of traffic, a good thing that, spluttering slow movement, angry faces of drivers, god love them. Boland's bread van stopped on a double yellow line where you're not supposed to park at all at all. Blushing boy in the middle of the road at Doyle's corner picking up the fallen bread, runs with the wooden tray while cars swerve to avoid hitting him. As he picks up the sliced pans off the road, hostile horns blow. Lights turn green. Kill the bastard, he's an inconvenience. The traffic moves in its eternal flow. A wino with a rough chin standing by the old Bohemian cinema smiling, thinks it is the best show he has seen in a long time. He lifts the bottle to his lips and toasts the human race.

A drop of rain beginning to fall. In to shelter in the library adults only, nice carpets soft on the feet and quiet after the din far enough back from the road in a little oasis of green temporary relief, that's what they're all after, relief, let the conifer outstare in the shadowy run in. Sleepylooking librarian seems familiar, doesn't get enough sleep or enough of something. Stamping someone out: stamp out philately or quicksand; where did I see that? On a wall near the Basin when I was doing the business the other evening, remember asking the fella what philately was. Philately, for fuck's sake, he did tell me afterwards. Would say he was handsome the librarian in his prime, a little past it now maybe with pink spots on his skin and a natural flick of grey that some pay a fortune to highlight, slight stoop in the shoulders, the books I suppose have him like that, takes his glasses off more often that he puts them on—now I reck him.

Thank you, Leo, says a borrower, an oul one on familiar ground worse for wear. Leo the lion, doesn't look much like a lion to me, never gave me his name, I do remember he did have that little lost world boy quality, not like the roaring lion you see at the beginning of some of those Hollywood films. The lion they used, someone told me, was from the Dublin zoo. All that way, imagine. Tare an' ages there's that little mark peeping through the back of his hair? Many men are like that; the back of their hair will not lie down. The same with their other apparel. The way of it. Would be out of business if it warren that way popping up at the least provocation, must be embarrassing for men at times. It's not a bald patch he has, no, the mark is more like a sore or a wound which I remember now, god yes the mark, it is him the lonely night walker. Still, nice brown eyes, casts an odd glance in my direction. Feel he's undressing me. Wonder what he's thinking. No, it's a look of recognition, embarrassed, see it in the way he's bustling about uneasily, afraid perhaps I will expose him, cost him his job. Some of these bookish ones have kinky tastes. But not him. He wasn't willing for a shilling …

JF: The world's cheapest prostitute.

Reader: Who?

JF: Centaur. She offers round the cock services.

... Disgruntled looking younger male assistant beside him. He wants to be out there in the world and not just left cataloguing or whatever he's doing. Has a sour look about him. Wouldn't fancy him at all. If you had to do it with him you'd keep the eyes closed tight. A gentleman of leisure with a dogcollar at the round teak table reading the *Irish Times*, shaking it noisily as if he's looking for attention. Occasional glances at my legs, must be a leg man. The libido is strong in here. Generated by the heat from those heavy iron radiators. Take off the red coat, getting the eye from the young assistant resting his gaze on my breasts. Men and their little penises so small compared to a woman's breasts which incorporate the whole world. Funny the way everyone wants to know what lies behind the covers, in my case the dress with the spring paisley which none of them remark on or remember in their haste to negotiate their way in. Whether it is a book or a dress, it's all the same, always wanting to strip bare. Why do we want covers at all? But then they get fed up with you when they know everything about you.

A bit of blue sky at the tall window. Out now, I make my way down the North Circular Road past Mountjoy prison. What abuse are the screws getting today? Did the business with one of them once, down by the canal, confided like he was in a state that the animals are ruling the jungle, he said and he wanted out, the poor fella, needed such relief he was on the verge of a breakdown and he cried he did when he came. Past the Mater Hospital, remember being in there once with a troublesome varicose vein, didn't want anyone to see it like in my business. The arrogant doctor had no time for me, looked down his nose at me, didn't want to treat me at all. Down Eccles street choc a bloc with cars into Dorset street the last of the streets with the small shops and twenty-nine traffic lights. Is that a record? I know from all the times waiting. Loitering with intent as the guards do say.

Evening drawing in now. Lampposts lighting up, a bit more rouge, lift the leg, have to make my way to the quays, don't want those English bitches getting on the beat before me. Always turf wars with them. Hate walking past that Simon hostel. All those queer oul fellas banging at the steel door, part of the esplanade, steel balls and a cannon there where the soldiers play football in the daytime. Old Kings Bridge being replaced by new bridge …

JF: A pontist measuring voussoirs and soffits.

… all the rusting of the metal gives a bogbrown colour to the Liffey, you'd have to go up to the Strawberry Beds to see the pure colour. Who will bring me to the Park tonight? Usually someone in a Ferrari or a Lexus; certainly wouldn't lower myself to the smaller cars, too awkward, would do yourself an injury, couldn't swing a cat in them. Hate lack of class, hate that, the gruffness, how much straight out. Depends what you want. Up to the Furry Glen. No apartment. Would cost a lot more, although it was nice to stay in the Montpellier that rainy night, the clean sheets with that nice man—of the soulful eyes like a poet not knowing then he was the librarian. His words were like music. He said he was a man who wandered out alone at night, a lonely man seeking the beautiful in shadows …

Reader: It was Leo.

… One who hears the whispering of secrets from the wind, one who burns with an inner intensity that can never be satisfied. One who is an endless seeker? Jesus, how I remember his words. Could've listened to him all night. He raised me up from the drab world. And it took me an age to warm his shaking body, my shining white prince.

Reader: Why was his body shaking?

JF: Because of Roman guilt.

But he couldn't do the business no matter how I coaxed him. He was afraid of being disloyal to his wife. He thanked me for my company and paid for the room and the drinks and walked away.

But night is falling fast. Cars moving at a slower pace now as rain begins to fall again, heavier this time. Will soon get the rheumatism out in all weather. Soon won't be able to satisfy anyone. O to do this job in a hotter country like Spain or somewhere. Spain now, that's a place I'd love to visit. This accursed city …

JF: The city is a laboratory of the human psyche.

… a strumpet like me, we're alike, we're one and the same, raped and plundered by the same selfish hordes. We can't fight back. We just wait. Here comes a shining silver Ferrari slowing down as a late sun peeps out after all the rain like it's mocking us.

II

Communing with the Dead

I PEER THROUGH MY MOTHER AT THE SCORCHED STUMP OF what was her beloved cherry blossom tree. If only she had made it to the spring who knows but the warm winds could have kept her going. What good was the thunder roar coming in its wake? It should have preceded the lightning. It would have given her warning, although she would have accepted to have gone that way, instantly, like a firing squad, she would say. Isn't it great for those fellows supposed to be traitors or army deserters to be given the luxury of an instant death. Get rid of me quick, she used to say as she cared for my father in the slow agonising throes of cancer (not that I knew much of that as she shielded all that from me). She did not want to be dependent on any one: *Cabhair ní ghairfead go gcuirtear mé i gcruinnchomhrainn* was a favourite quote of hers—*no help I'll call for till they coffin me*, from her beloved poet Aogán Ó Rathaille, a poem she learned at school and never forgot. She was rebellious like that, but how ironic that she never got to make that call. I feel close to her now like maybe the way I would like to have been when she died ...

The Rhymer
The dead who are dear
are always near.

Reader: So Leo became an orphan.

... We are all orphans in different ways. But I think if I really try, I could commune with her. I have sensed a presence, and feel that she is watching over me and makes signs to me when necessary. She used to encourage me so much in whatever I might have wanted to do. If there was a way to break through from the ethereal world, she would find it. I look at her in pain in glass, so young, so beautiful with her auburn hair and dark brown eyes.

A strange feeling: to pursue or retreat? A voice, weak from lack of practice:

My son.

Mam, is it you? Are you all right?

Yes love, for I am unchanging, but you I must watch over.

I have often felt your presence, Mam.

I am always here, love. Sometimes far, sometimes near. But here all the same. Perhaps I could explain it like a radio wave.

You always loved the wireless, Mam—Joe Linnane.

Yes.

Sometimes you would have two stations on two different radios at the same time, remember?

Yes.

I do that now occasionally with RTÉ One and Newstalk, catching two thoughts at a time ...

The Seer of Suburbia: If you keep watching the news you will think the world is coming to an end.

... Mam. My loneliness has dissolved, like a heavy weight has lifted, it is no more. I feel confident.

Concentrate on what is important, love.

How does one know what is important?

Abandon what is trivial.

I held back the trivial question, fearing it would hinder the larger thought.

It is so short, the process, so many miss the meaning.

What is the meaning, Mam? Mam ... She has faded like the radio wave, but it is wonderful to have made contact ...

Reader: Was she really there?

... She will be back. Looking out on the garden now the sparrows are chasing away the blue tits to feed from the nutbag ...

Letters Page, *Irish Times*: Is there anything I can do to get my tits back? H. Winterbottom (Monkstown).

... No different from the human gangs scavenging in lightning raids on young children, taking their food and change …

Jude: O those gangs. Mortal dread.

… A robin looking for food through the white winter. She is there all the time, the robin I mean in the garden; it's just with the other birds migrated, she is more noticeable now …

The Rhymer
What little throat
has framed that note?

… The garden is her territory. She bounces about and fearlessly comes quite near the kitchen door. Bad luck to kill a robin, her Christred breast, got they say pulling the thorns from His Head, always emblazoned on Christmas cards. What a cocky bouncer she is. Confiding towards man. Female paler than male. She comes from the hedge every day and goes to work. What cheerful warbling. Birds were the first and sweetest twitterers. Defends her territory fiercely, red rag to a bull. Are we any different? Here comes the cat curiosity killed. Let's mob him. Signals are given like a ventriloquist performing his act. Blood in the snow. Red breast in white pinpricked carpet.

I think of you, Jude.

My dear Leo,

You write inspired like an evangelist at times, but the main construction is your own. Your last letter came alive just as your mother did. It was a holy night, the power of which dispelled all evil. What telergy to penetrate the dead world, met half way coming the other way? Remember the psalm: 'Wilt thou shew wonders to the dead? Shall the dead arise and praise thee?' You should sing the Kaddish: 'May the One who creates harmony on high bring peace to us,' or you could recite an Irish *caoineadh*, remember you told me about that, but that is a lament, is it not? You need joy, you need to celebrate your mother. You don't want tragedy. You don't want gloom. You want sunny days. You want people to wear gay summer clothes. Or maybe that is me wishing. But what a powerful mind your mother had. Not all minds can commune. But those gangs, Leo, scavenging on the young children. Could they be the offspring of ... ? O, they will never go away.

But let me tell you about Uanito. He was interested to hear of your observations about the robin. He knows the rhyme by heart, which I have taught him in English:

The north wind doth blow
And we shall have snow ...

The poor robin. I did not tell him about her fate at the hands of the cat. Are we right to keep such things from our children, as your mother sheltered you? Should we protect them from reality? Will it be tougher for them later to accept that nature is red in tooth and claw—remember that phrase of yours?

O Jude,

The morbid feelings. My mother to leave without a final farewell, without one's house in order, leaves the mourner which of course is me bereft to wander through the world alone seeking fulfilment from shadows and fantasies. And yes I am an orphan, a grownup orphan. We are all looking for someone to hold our hand to quell the loneliness when death calls ...

JF: Death comes as a stranger from a foreign land.

... Have you left others to die alone? ...

SYC: Bertrand Russell's wife left him because she could not or would not commit to the intense bonding which might have eased his terrible loneliness.

... You're talking of cosmic loneliness. It's all about fear. There are no Houdinis up above or wherever. Nights of wakefulness spent tearing away the skin and flesh, to come to terms with the skeleton. Imagine you are an xray machine and you see your loved ones as skeletons, creaking about with their long bones, walking graves. When the flesh is gone, all bones are the same. So much for our individuality. My mother never took me to a funeral when I was small or let me touch a corpse. It was like somehow she was hoping I would be one who would not die. That I would not be marked by death. But now in my manhood intimations of mortality descend on me in torrents as if making up for lost time and for which I am so illprepared. So, Jude, perhaps you should prepare Uanito in a gradual way of course but for the inevitable which is our ultimate annihilation ...

JF: Death like poverty may be responsive to intervention. Google funds a company to find a cure for death.

... Sorry, I am being gloomy. It's good you are teaching Uanito the nursery rhymes. You never told me his response to them, a child's interpretation. Will I tell you a story about Johnny McGory? Will I begin it? That's all that's in it. Maybe Uanito will have some insight into McGory.

The temperature is dropping rapidly here. Minus six last night. A freezing fog shrouds buildings and people in an unreal setting. Folks huddled in thick coats pass me by like ghosts, unseeing.

I walk through the dark valley with all the memories of you and I going ...

Reader: Where are we going?

The Rhymer
We're all going amarauding

which we will not rue
we'll take a couple of chalices
And a slave or two.

Reader: Let me leaf through you before I read you out loud.

... through it, the dark night of the soul to the light of the Grotto believing ... believing in some miracle. Still if my mother can commune. I can't see the river but can hear its sound, the little waterfall falling, falling like the murmuring of souls ...

The Seer of Suburbia: Why do we like the flowing water of a waterfall and become demented when a tap drips?

... Not manmade. White horse whinnies. Ghostlike. Is he afraid of the dark? Just enough light from the distant houses to walk without trepidation. Silently remote. The world blanketed and quiet. Smoke adding to the haze. No human passing; all entombed in their semis.

One exception to the quiet. As I approached the wide trunk of the Crucifixion Tree with its outstretched limbs, a leatherjacketed male suddenly appeared. I was temporarily startled. I thought of the past for a moment, of those house assailants who had been dressed in leather too. But I regained composure quickly—show a hesitation and you could be knifed; show nonchalance and you pass each other like ships in the night.

Today I have no work. The library is closed for revamping. I have a liein. What is lovely? It is lovely to have the bladder empty, the sheets warm and hear the early car tyres crinkle on the ice and know that you don't have to be part of it ...

The Seer of Suburbia: A car and a bus had an argument.

... I hear Lil talking on the phone downstairs and I pick up the phone by my bed.

JF: The Lambkins have sacks of phones.

... The conversation is between her and Crichton. She thinks I am still asleep. Most bizarre to hear Lil so vociferous. Normally taciturn but after four or five 25cl glasses of Cuba libre she has been known to wax lyrical. Sometimes carries the aftereffects into the morning.

Crichton: I wanted to ask you in my exofficio capacity as … I wonder if … some questions?

Lil: You want to feast your eyes on a nipple as is your wont, admit it little boy. Call over to see me sometime when himself is out. Nibble on a nipple. All you chainsmoking critics, you were not suckled enough. Come here you little balding middleaged pseudooracle with your lantern jaw. Nibble at the nipple and you, like Fionn Mac Cumhaill sucking his tongue from the salmon, will go forth with the milk of knowledge, unadulterated truth, to penetrate uh (*belches*) excuse me, to penetrate—you always liked that word, didn't you?—to penetrate the carbon and caffeine of your life.

Lil … I … was wondering …

Wonder wonder little star, how I wonder what you are. O my husband is the stargazer.

Perhaps you could tell me a little … about him since he ahem married that is.

A little, yes. He rises at night and rises in the morning. An upright gent is my hus. He flashes light interminably through the night …

JF: Leo was always fascinated by light. Even as a boy he delighted in the torch at dusk giving his face in the mirror a ghoulish appearance. Later it was the romance of candlelight and the light of dying embers. Faint light, gas light, oil lamp light which threw shadows and illumined without blotches, not like the allseeing naked electric bulb.

… He asks for this and I give him that. That's me all over. He would talk the legs off a pot. A Thoth, a scribe, a scribbler, a threeword sentence maker. At last you think light out, sleep but then the light goes on again. And sometimes he looks at me as if he'd never seen me before. Are you looking for something else? I'd say. I groan and dread the exhausted day.

And what is your attitude to your husband's ... eh scribbling?

I give him no encouragement. I say neither yeah nor nay. I am more interested in real world living than in Leo's meanderings. My job lies in descarifying and deodorising rather than deciphering or decoding. But he does offer to help sometimes. He dries till his fingers hurt, but he will not bend. I have to bend.

Ah, yes.

Enough of that, Freddie. He is corresponding with this literary freak.

I see.

Yeah. Seems to imply that there is some rapport between them that does not exist between us, going back to his premarried state.

How do you know this?

I caught glimpses of some of the letters when he was otherwise engaged.

Could I see, perhaps?

You mean you want me to steal some of his letters?

Well, maybe borrow.

What good would it do?

We could explore the rapport he is supposed to have with this person.

O Leo has always been like that though, ever since I knew him, always hankering after the unattainable. I might as well be talking to the wall as talking to him. Don't think that I don't know about the filthy innuendo, about the dot.

The dot?

Like they were doing things.

Despicable.

You're one to talk, Freddie.

Am I?

But this Jude …

Jude you say? Is it a woman?

Male, female or the other, strikes me as someone frustrated. Yeah maybe someone unfulfilled.

And how does that make you feel?

Let them keep at it without a menopause. The frustration of all the innards comes out in the letters, climaxing in print, ha could you credit it. But I don't know. They say one out of a hundred would do you as a mate.

Would I have done you as a mate?

Now now, Freddie. Marriages are impairfect and you have to give each other a little rein. Leo is highly charged. Let him scribble away; it comes to no harm, once it goes no further. Do you really still like me, Freddie?

Always will, me oul china.

Maybe Leo is seriously ill, I don't know. Can be hypochondriacal at the best of times. He knows by now I refuse to listen to his whingeing but then he won't talk about the serious ailments, so where do you go? Strange like that, shy about the body parts. I remember we came across a nudist colony on a holiday in Greece way back in the early days. I didn't bat an eyelid. I mean in a hot country you have to expect things like that, but Leo spent the whole of that night talking about it, analysing like he was writing a thesis. What was he saying? I can't remember the half of it. Something like nudity destroyed the erotic because it left nothing to the imagination. Jaysus, I ask you, not that I have children, mind, but wouldn't it be an eyeopener for Leo if someone brought him to a maternity hospital.

So you and he don't … ?

None of your business now, Freddie Crichton. Are you going to write all of this up or down? Is it a review you are preparing or something? I have to be careful what I say to you.

I have to write a review of Francis' book. You can trust me, Lil. You know that I'm always on your side.

Are you?

Didn't Leo steal you away from me?

Maybe he did for all the good it did me.

Are you not content?

Maybe that is the female role, and not to be always striving after airy fairy pies in the sky. Our role is to survive from one moan, in my case Leo's, to the next. But your presents are always welcome.

I am glad of that, Kooshycoo. Remember I used to call you that? I still carry a torch for you.

And for how many others? O I know your ways, Freddie. But my worry with Leo is he has so many longings that no human will ever fulfil or at least that I will never fulfil in him. I hear your nib scribble, Freddie. You're still taking notes?

Yes.

Jaysus, everyone is writing things down these days. Can one not just utter a feckin word without … ?

Sorry.

And *your* wife, Freddie, who passed away, what was she like?

She had a kind bottom and a large heart.

You must've driven her nuts.

She thought I was a pig.

A pig?

Yes.

I would've thought you had a similarity to some other animal which I won't embarrass you by naming, but not a pig.

In her mind I was a pig, a boar, an outandout misanthrope who digs for warts in people and welts and piles.

Piles?

Yes.

So that was why after a year she divorced you.

Yes. Well, she said I had dark ways.

Ah, you poor dear.

Dear Leo,

I await your letters like manna and yet they are strangely unsatisfying. We need something else, something more tactile. Could your seeds be windborne like a plant's? I am bold to say such a thing. The mistletoe seed which I got in the market in vain hope is also sticky, rubbed into a tree by a bird, a parasite just like me. I'm feeding off the offal of your marriage table. O if you could be carried like the seed of the Virgin's Bower. I am protea. I will open when I have been scorched by fire. Is that what happened that dark time as the night owl was hooting when I was scorched by you? So burning may produce some good like the burning down of the furze we saw on the mountain. O Leo, I have no one to accommodate me. I should draw milk from the milk tree.

I tested Uanito about McGory. I first told him about the cold, cold night in Siberia when two men were sitting under a wall and when one said to the other will I tell you a story, and this is the story he told: it was a cold, cold night in Siberia …

Mamá, he said.

What is it, Uanito?

Was Johnny McGory one of the men under the wall in Siberia?

Maybe he was.

Who was the other man?

A friend of Johnny.

What happened to him?

He was burned in a fire.

Who burned him?

He burned himself.

How, Mamá?

He went too close to the flames. What's burning, Uanito?

The flame, Mamá.

The dinner was not entirely burned. I had quite forgotten, I was so carried away ...

Reader: Was it a German shepherd's pie?

... We played dinner shapes in English. Mammy chip baby chip Daddy chip gone. Potato snowman, carrot boat. Held imagination until they were consumed. Shed a tear for the disappearing snowman—the snow which he imagines and has never yet seen except in picture cards.

I will close now, Leo, because a sadness is descending upon me with the darkening evening. When the dark is deep, the hurt is lonely. I am making do in my new *piso*. It's compact and on the second floor near the *Jardines de María Luisa*. The Chinese lantern which I purchased throws poor light. I feel *muy sola*, although I am not far from my parents' home. O will we meet again? I am anguishing for the ack of love, L ...

Reader: JF, the author, seems to be having trouble controlling his infantry. They lack discipline.

SFC: The problem with the letters is that Mr Francis cannot type properly. He circles the *i*'s to gauge ego frequency.

SYC: Egotism is i-sore. He complains about having to type and how he would love to have an amanuensis, but then he talks about someone who hewed out a novel with his left foot.

... Sorry for the interruption, Leo. Something coming across the airwaves. Enclosed a little fragment of mistletoe and already kissed and touched by me. O I do not want to waste away like the candle in the cupboard. Forget me not at Navidad.

Jude,
the pure of impure heart.

Hey Jude,

Take a sad song and make it better. At least you are not as cold as I am in Hibernia. Hibernate with me in Hibernia, the land of the wintry weather. The candle burns and the fire is blazing; the radiators are so hot, they cannot be touched. Yet I shiver. My feet, my bones have no warmth. Hot drinks are no good; the cold is coming from my soul. I have the flu marks of the artist: rashes, hypochondria, hyperactivity and a lighthearted morbidity. It's as if I have come out of the icy sea. Brrh …

JF: The coldest place in Ireland.

Reader: Where?

JF: Birr.

… I am delighted to hear Uanito is coming along so well. Maybe some day we shall meet when he is bigger. Can he count? Thank you for the mistletoe. I could not bring myself to k anyone else but you under it. I put a moist kiss on the final dot; may it never dry.

I was reading for so long that a spider descended from my spectacles. Lowering itself by a thread to alight on the word that I had lost. Arachne interrupting? She needs to be given a start. I took off my glasses and swayed her from side to side of my desk. There is a photograph of James Stephens, the writer, in the newspaper. The spider is trying to get inside his breast pocket. Now she has disappeared, hiding in one of the full stops. Leave her at it; she will not distract me.

There has been a great increase in selfabuse since the advancement of AIDS. Is it really abuse of the self or love of the self? How to ascertain? Greater honesty today in such matters at least. A corresponding increase in fantasy fecundity.

It is late. I put my pen down, resting that tongue of the intellect. A beautiful darkhaired girl with fuliginous eyes in a loosefitting white dress appears before me. She is prodding her ongue through her ips in a most eductive manner …

SYC: There go the elisions again.

SFC: The root cause of the problem is that Lambkin is a prude, a prurient one at that. Notice every time there is an erotic piece, an ellipsis occurs. He is afraid to say what he thinks is a dirty word.

SYC: No, he is trying to conceal it for fear that Lil …

Reader: Who is he kidding?

… She is loosening the belt of the white dress. The silk falls silently to her ankles. Such beautiful curves and firm reasts, and rect tipple and the ongue and ips, her hair is loose and shining, she comes forward and unbuttons the jama, she takes rect Phal … eyes transfixing. It is Arachne.

The door of the bedroom opens. Lil storms in. She is brandishing a whip. Trickles of blood flow from the perpendicular stripes. Seems to turn Arachne on the more …

JF: The blood quota in movies is restricted lest it appear to reel.

… The harder the whipping the more she goes down on … O, Lil is enraged. She pulls her away and tries to strangle her with the rope. Arachne gasps and then disappears *mar toit san aer.*

O Jude, I tell you because you understand me, such beauty—you yourself would have been attracted. But the next morning Lil is up and singing as she works. She asks me if I slept well knowing well I didn't. I told her I was dreaming again. She went on laughing in a strange, macabre manner …

JF: It is Leo's condition to fantasise through his life.

Jude (*singing*): Any dream will do.

JF: As pleasant a way as any that is to say, once no one bursts his bubble. Yes, dreaming by day suits him fine that is until night comes and all his dreams are used up and they become mares and he tries to keep them at bay to outstare the darkness.

… And here back in our bedroom I spy her, my spider, and beside her on the bed a small fragment of silk.

JF: Beds are more treacherous than fields of battle.

Dear Leo,

Elo You d.o.m. I am jealous of your telling of that fecund fantasy. But could it have been a succubus? Nonetheless it had me oist and anting. O to melt into the crystalline blue of sea and sky under a warm sun with you. In bed you say you and Lil are holding hands but not holding minds, something we ought to do …

Leo: Before bed I undress the mind, lay its apparel softly down, slide in gently so as not to ruffle its soft down.

The Rhymer
I have a brain to rack.
Hold me but don't hold me back.

… Your spirit like a cloud escapes through the fingers, floating away to another country. Through the orange groves of Sevilla or the Mediterranean blue or the snowpeaked Sierra Nevada floating or rocking on a rackety train through the night, seeking faces in the lighted glass (what I do in the dark evening returning from work on the autobús and sometimes thinking of your mother in the glasspane in Ireland).

You ask me if Uanito counts. He is fine up to twenty, okay in Spanish, but in English he goes twenty-nine, twenty-ten, twenty-eleven. O Leo, the time is short. I am torn in so many ways. It will be daylight soon. Let us give up all the things we prefer to do under the cover of dark. WWJD?

JF: To the estate of Jesus Christ of Nazareth all royalties due.

SYC: The highest loyalties are paid to football teams.

Dear Jude,

Lil's hoovering is deafening nascent thought. Leaves a vacuum. Cotton wool, no, where are those strong wax earplugs made? In France. There, a more relaxed hum. So many machines: neighbour's car aggressive rev washing machine electric drill drilling the road, drilling the brain.

Glad you share my enthusiasm about Arachne (it was hardly the other that you mentioned). Those Greeks very broadminded; last saw her as a white curvehugging miniskirt lifting as the long thighs moved. O to share the sensory joy and fragrance of Seville with you ...

The Seer of Suburbia: If two took a half they could share a hole.

... to listen to the erotic flamenco, to image the guitar as a woman's wide hips, to see the house of your ancestors and Arab eyes lustful and lustrous blackening against the white of the sun.

I look out my window through the pane of Mam and I see two thieves walk with a hatchet and a lodgepole pine tree which they have stolen from the nearby copse. The spirit of Christmas.

JF: Perhaps I should tell you a little story set around Christmas time ...

Reader and all the company: Please do.

... Long ago and in a faraway clime there once was a little boy, and a handsome boy he was. He lived in a cottage in a forest with his widowed mother. Poor they were, as poor as poor could be, as their ragged clothes and bare cupboards bore testimony. They had one cow, which gave milk, and some hens, which gave eggs. The mother made a little money by selling eggs and milk to the forest folk who lived in farflung outreaches of the great forest and she would come home after a day's selling very tired.

The boy made his own toys which he did from wood with his pocket knife and the toys came to the notice of the forest folk, who admired them for the skill and artistry in their making. The boy, thus encouraged, fashioned more toys: little animals, squirrels and foxes and images of children, which were meant to be his imaginary friends to share with him the joys of the forest. The forest folk began to give presents of bread loaves and salted butter and small amounts of money in exchange for them.

In winter, a week before Christmas, a heavy snow fell and the forest looked as pure as a poem. Frozen crystals hung on the trees like diamonds when the rays of the sun burst through and one could make out in the snow the different footprints of the animals of the forest.

The boy's mother did not come home from selling that evening and the boy with great worry on him set out to look for her. Darkness soon fell and the icy cold caused the boy to shiver in his ragged clothes. 'Mam, Mam,' he cried. And his voice echoed through the trees, dislodging some snow from the tops of the branches of stately pines. But no sound could he hear save for the hooting of an owl …

Jude: O the owl, Leo, that hooted that night.

Leo: Always the omen.

… The boy had no fear of losing his way despite the darkness enveloping because he knew every inch of the forest as well as any animal. The snow fell in great big flakes like white ghosts through the blackness and melted into the hot tears rolling down the boy's cheeks. 'Mam, Mam,' he cried again, but the only sound he heard was the wind in the trees.

He wandered on and on by the light of the stars and the moon. Suddenly he came across human footprints, the light bootmarks of his mother, he thought. He followed them, excitement growing in him and he called once more, 'Mam, Mam'. And this time it was not the wind or the owl he heard but a human voice, the voice of his mother. He followed to where the cry came from and he could just make her out. She was sunk in a snowdrift in a hollow of the wood.

How to get her out? He used his knife to cut a fine long branch and stretched it towards his mother because he knew if he walked on the drift he would sink too. 'Hold on, Mam. Hold on,' he shouted. His mother clung to the branch …

Jude: The wood, Leo. The cross.

… and the boy pulled with all his might. At first there was not a budge, but then after another great heave his mother came free from the snowdrift. She was blue with cold and her teeth chattered and her hands were lumps of ice. The boy took off his jacket and put it round her …

Jude: The cloak, Leo.

… and half stumbling carried her home. They soon had a fire blazing in their little cottage and the mother looked proudly at her son and he looked at her with great love in his eyes.

Leo: She is in her room, her back is to the door which is slightly ajar. She is dressing. I could change my mind. I could turn away or I could sculpt her into my dream, fashioning her into my desired likeness for her. Not the form no, not the form to capture her in her prime, that glorious beautiful woman at her moment when she is ripe to woo a suitor …

Jude: Or be wooed.

… Who could be her lover? What age, what generation, what century? What period of history? Here she is in my world, her hair slightly curled and shining, and her dark brown eyes like the deer of the forest …

Jude: O yes Leo, and on the mountain.

… Moulding one's mother into a form. The picture of her in her twenties capturing her beauty. I see her standing, smiling, holding her bicycle, her High Nelly, and the little boy on the child seat plump and happy with a tuft of hair standing up on the back of his head like an Indians' feather …

Reader: You?

... The gold of childhood, where is it to be found? In one's own youth or the youth of one's parents where one could cocoon oneself securely in a sepiacoloured world, a solace for the dark times. My mother's body. Porcelain like the ballerina statue on the mantelpiece. She is being transposed from flesh and bone to marble, no, not marble, that is cold, but to a soft malleable art material, to form an image that is warm and comforting. She is undressing with her back to me about to step out of her skirt, the slit in the door just affording a cutoff vision, a partial view: all we can ever hope for, all we can ever see of the world, the picture of a mother is the picture of eternity. What we can glimpse of it on the edge of it. Is it death that stalks her at the doorway? No, but at the window. Death is at the window waiting for her to look out. To see the storm coming. But she will never hear the thunder. Only the lightning in its sudden, savage swoosh ...

The Seer of Suburbia: The dead return when their departure is sudden.

... I see her now full of the summer joys of youth: mater matar madre máthair in her woollen onepiece bathing costume, green with black diamonds, heavy with brine after the bracing waves, her breasts showing in their fullness. Does she know I am peeping through the keyhole seeing her from the back? But it is all fortuitous. I am not a Peeping Tom. It was by chance that I mounted the stair and found the door ajar. Perhaps I should have turned away. But I will fashion her in my image—a terrifying concept—her cheekbones will be high, and her brow wide. My father, what did he behold when he saw her in her bloom? I will never know. Six I was when he passed away. I did not kill him. There was no Oedipus thing; there was no chance for that. I hardly knew him. Although when he saw my pencil drawing etched innocently in an unwitting heuristic quest at such a young age, trying to find my mother through the graphite when I had seen her that time, he snatched the page from me and tore it up and threw the pieces into the fire. He never said a word. Just frowned. Never mentioned it and I wanted to ask him to explain, but next thing I knew he was dead. So it was just me and her, the woman and her boy, her only boy, the apple of her eye, who would care for her when she grew old, but she never grew old and the boy languishes and tries to bring her back, to resurrect her, to tell her that he intended to take care of her when she would become frail, that he would protect her, that she would not perish in the snowdrift or when the lightning struck. With his indestructible tree, his cross, he would rescue her and bring her to safety. She would not be a wandering waif but would spend her days at home and secure with her son to care for her. The milkwhite fear would be abated, and she would smell of seawater and seapebbles. But this sculpture that I create with my adult mind is incomplete. Like me, fulfilment cannot be found, but she will never corrode or decompose as long as I keep moulding her, eternally making her new, and as long as I keep communicating with her, and she will never age. She will always be young and beautiful in the image of the glass, and when I hear the light footfalls on the stair, I will know it is her.

III

The moth flies inwards towards the light.

Dear Jude,

What was I going to say? A dreadful thought to have had a thought and lost it. Let me walk backwards to find it—*l'esprit de l'escalier.* A fierce commotion from the TV. Lil is addicted to soaps, a bombardment screen, Shem the Penman called it, man's eye and ear tainted by it, destroying the inner life, reel reality palimpsest on reality …

SYC: The screen tells you everything except what you are.

… We see the instant images pushbuttoned or remotecontrolled from an armchair but we don't see the photographers standing in the rain …

The Seer of Suburbia: The oily streets slicked.

… In the Botanic Gardens today there was a man digging, trying to uproot a dead tree stump with just a spade. Having had a surgical removal of a molar root, I know how the earth feels. Some things don't change …

JF: You can stick a wet thumb in the air and feel the winds of change.

… Horticultural students taking notes huddle closer together in winter …

JF: Midwinter weather: wind, rime, wet earth.

… Myositis, m y o, don't forget it. Man needs memory …

The Seer of Suburbia: Memory oozes out of him.

… Sun suffusing the bare tree engendering an orange glow blending with the silver cloud, the illusion of the sky lengthening the pretwilight winter evening. But she is sinking fast into the west, leaving us with darkening branches and the squawking of innumerable birds. The dawn redwood planted in 1948, a common birthday with Mr Francis. Looks like it's only coming into its prime.

Reader: What does Leo Lambkin look like? We haven't been told.

SYC: Should be in the *Oxford Discs of Literary Characters* … Lambkin, Leopold, main character of novel *Letters to Jude*, despite opposition for the lead by Freddie Crichton, his superior in the Library Service …

Reader: Didn't halffancy himself.

… Written by the highly quirky but original writer James Francis.

Reader: He's not a writer. He's not wearing tweeds. What of Crichton?

SYC: Crichton is a man now who always, despite his lessthancomely features, liked the limelight. Liked to show off a bit in his flashy Ferrari. Always trying to attract the ladies. Overcoming a childhood lisp, he is proud of his orotund speaking voice. Can change his accent at will. A lover of subterfuge and *commedia dell'arte*. Fond of making oracular and sometimes spurious moral pronouncements.

Back to Leo: Complexion: fair. Eyes: brown. Height: medium. Married state: mainly unfulfilled. Sex: rare. Wife: Lilith. Distinguishing features: suffers from sporadic seasonal outbreaks of eczema on face and private areas characterised by itching and sometimes pain. Blood discharges suggest a more serious problem about which he is too embarrassed to talk. Occupation: librarian. Interests: delving peripatetically into the quotidian, the absurd, the mystical and the erotic.

Judas, Jude the obscure, no, Jude, Judith/Bernarda Rodríguez. Complexion: sallow. Eyes: black …

Reader: No such thing as black eyes.

JF: Tell that to a boxer. There was a girl in an *aisling* of Dennis Potter's whose eyes looked black at least on the TV, but bruise the thought.

… Height: 5' 6". Marital state: unmarried mother, unfulfilled yearning, son Juan affectionaltely called Uanito, somewhat precocious at times in his bilingual utterances. She is mystical and apocalyptical. Interests: quite conversant with the Bible and the works of Santa Teresa and San Juan de la Cruz, likes to quote, also preoccupied rather guiltily with the libido which she shares in illicit correspondence with Leo Lambkin (see Disc 2, L. L). Born Seville.

Leo: Jude, have I lost you? The interrupters are getting worse. Tiredness setting in, must rest. The dead tree stump still stands in the garden, a resting place for jackdaws. I rub the dot.

Dear Leo, Uanito is sleeping now as I correct copy books in his room, the ceiling light extinguished, a gesture to him. I work in black and white by table lamp; his dreams and my reality merge when the light turns to shadow and we are one.

Dear Jude, how I envy your closeness to him. I was in a bookshop the other day and noticed that quite a few Bibles were bought, which was never a thing with Catholics here in the past, resigned to receive their doctrine from the pulpit. Why the change? Is it a wanting to get to the original source of things to find their own meaning? Dissatisfaction with the institutionalised church, which doesn't satisfy the longings of the spirit. Whatever the soul is, the institution is its opposite. When one leaves an institution one is able to give oneself back to oneself. Poor sermons not enough sustenance in them but also not addressing the longing for the mystical, the proverbial, the poetic and the intellectual challenge of trying to unravel some of the more cryptic passages, a lesson to the learned perhaps.

O Leo, I understand. I do like the job of teaching. I am grateful to have it. I like the children especially—all the strange little utterances they come out with, but like you perhaps in the library it binds you in its restrictions.

One two three O'Leary four five six O'Leary seven eight nine O'Leary ten O'Leary catch the ball. Remember you used to sing or half recite that to me infuriatingly like a mantra whenever we'd be together so I know it off my heart. Who was O'Leary? A friend or maybe a relation of McGory? Wait, is that you, Leo, coming across the waves?

JF: The institution shackles the soul from free enquiry.

Leo: McGory is pushing O'Leary out. We hide our real selves. We are afraid to express our darkest thoughts. We never learn who we are. We do not allow ourselves to probe. We are tied up in all sorts of baggage and pseudomorality and we go to the grave in wonderment. Will I tell you a … one two three … about Johnny … O'Leary … What? Snot. Will I tell you how to live? says McGory.

What's your … your? asks O'Leary.

Johnny.

… sch … school? Where do … do you … ?

St Mels.

… live?

O Leo, what are you about? I must end now.

My mother is laid to rest. Driving through fog, cars like ghosts with dimmed lights lancing the sable clouds as I drive by instinct through the netherworld.

Eight legs walk under a coffin which digs into the shoulder as we go up the hill carrying the cross of Calvary. Worried about leather soles easy to slip and they came tumbling down. Must shoulder it to the cemetery too where traumatised people walk. Squelching feet avoid heels of porter in from stout porter.

At funeral shake one hundred and seventy hands and twenty-three fingers sorry for your … thank you … good to see … she had a lovely … and little pain, if we all could … One hundred and fifteen phone calls terribly so … tears well … a lovely … Red roses on wet coffin cushioned by straw grey stony soil a devil to dig the devil down there pump used to draw water …

The Seer of Suburbia: The season with all its rain is pushing up the flowers on the graves. What state of decomposition are the bodies of the loved ones at?

... all the soil piled on the neighbouring grave; hope they don't come to pay respects today. Funny that, how they talked about the great view the corpse would have facing the mountains ...

Jude: Your mother could see the Dublin mountain, our mountain, Leo.

... Too much drinking, hangover, blessed Mary ache in head, moderation in everything achieves nothing other than mediocrity. Housebound by the storm. A feeling of debility, virus or toxins trying to burst through the epidermis, facial skin inflamed. I am shedding silent salt tears like the salt doll wanting to return to the sea and dissolve into an infinity of water, or maybe it's the stars melting into the constellation ...

JF: Voyager II flew past Uranus and gave humanity its first close look.

Reader: Did you know Uranus rotated?

JF: Miranda is nearest to Uranus although she was bombarded in her early days.

Reader: How come there is so much wind blowing through Uranus? Are you not deflated enough?

JF: The reader has wit.

... With Lil it's the earth. Provide good cheer. Does the snowdrop down or come up? Death is the only thing worth thinking about ...

JF: The Greeks don't like the D word.

... The handwriting has paled. The only certainty. Feel your brow, thin disguise. We are just padded bones. I opened a book from the old basement stacks, when Crichton had left with the stockingtwisted Kerry novice, and inhaled the notunpleasant smell from the yellowing pages, like a mellow tobacco ...

JF: He was one who hoarded things, things that his wife wanted to throw out, mustysmelling things that dated him. Moth balls.

Catch the motes of dust.

... The book I read is recalcitrant, Jude. If I put it down it jumps closed causing me to lose my page. Everything is so transient, another page, another book. *A New History of England and Great Britain* by Professor Meiklejohn, twentieth edition, 1904. I went forth into the night and met the shadow of myself advancing ...

O Leo, don't let me grow apart from you so much that our shadows will not meet.

... Back to myself now. Saturday has come. Don't forget your Lemon's Pure Sweets. Travel through floods and high water for them. Sorry we don't stock them, no demand. They're your only man. Who is your man? A queue forming, stocking up for Christmas. Has Uanito his pillow slip up? Or is that the custom in Spain? Ask him what is the first tree in the greenwood?

I went into the city to see the lights to sample the tinsel to hear the piped music of yuletide, to fondle the knickknacks and hear the hawkers shout their wares. Superficial you may say, Jude, but life teems with many icialities. Better than the grey dull nothingness of semirural gloom or the wasteland of suburbia. Let's listen for the sounds, when the bells stop ringing. With love at Christmas, and some left over to thaw the ice of the New Year. Hush, I can hear the snowdrops growing; they are pushing up.

My dear Leo, Uanito is all excited. He is looking forward to Christmas when he says we'll get out *la cosa de Jesús*, meaning the crib. The *pobrecito*. He asks me where his daddy is. I perhaps should not have told him but I told him he was in Ireland and ever since he wants to know everything Irish, all the rhymes he is fascinated by, and I have a Dublin accent when I speak in English, the Irish ambassador's wife told me at the school. They seem to have taken a shine to him. Everything is a joke to him; he latches onto that word *cosa* for everything. I teach him all the Irish customs. I loved the Irish Christmases when I worked over there. I can't get him to sleep at night. He kisses me with frightening force and asks if Papá Noel is his daddy. Then he gets a fit of the giggles. He talks of Johnny McGory as if he lived next door. What is he? The beginning and the end. Christmas is coming the goose is getting fat, you sang that …

Leo: Not now, even turkey not the same, too many vegetarians heard them squeal.

The Rhymer
Eeny meany miney mo
Catch a nigger by the toe
If he squeals let him go
Eeny meany miney mo

Racist rhymes learned nesciently in childhood. Must come from one two three four five I dreamed I caught a fish alive.

JF: Wholly mackerel.

… Leo heart of lion, the Lord himself will give you a sign. Will you climb the mountain a new you?

Dear Jude, the elements erupt to announce their presence for Christmas. Torrents of rain, outpourings, emotional floods. How lost we are in this signposted world. The piped music pumps out the seasonal tunes coercing us into happiness. Happy holiday. Christmas Eve and memories well, forlorn forsaken, feel the barrenness of the land and I think of the barren womb of Lil and know that happiness can mean luck. I hunger for and thirst for the spirit that has left us swamped …

JF: The spirit that quickeneth.

SFC: Pull yourself out by your pigtails.

… by the consumer myth. I know I longed for it but how soon it tires. Sacrifice gives way to indulgence …

JF: Like Cleopatra queen of denial.

... We wish you a ... we wish you a ... and a happy ... Plastic, plasmic voices coagulate on tape: wish everyone a happy kissmas, joy to the world.

Christmas morning. What's that down the end of my bed? Nothing but long toes. Are we in the land of the living at all? Remove the padded flesh. What do you see? A skeleton jogging, creaks and hinges, joints and femurs. On his way to ... bald skull. Hard to know who's who by their bones.

Turkey that was once alive moving wings for. Give us a wing, mister. Will you have a bit of breast? A breast man; tear off a leg; comes away easily. Another form of cannibalism no different from the planecrash victims in South America who ate human flesh to stay alive. Look at your skin: cracks and crevices and goose pimples. All the same when roasted. Some tribes believe that by eating the body, you receive the spirit of the dead one. Take this body and eat, drink my blood. One way or the other. Flesh departs, deep down into holes, rots to leave the bone. On the third day of Christmas, turkey stripped to bone. Still Dog used always find an extra bit. All animals we. Where did the last bit go? Down the red lane. Clearway, to let Dog see the rabbit ...

The Seer of Suburbia: He still misses his dog but not that short stumpy pampered pedigree of the brindled colour coming down the street now with the rasping bark just like his mistress.

JF: A crowd gathered to listen to a moving story about a moving statue. Being demophobic, Leo stood uncomfortably. The statue was not allowed to move inside, so it was moved outside to move where an ecstatic man spoke to the statue, and when he was moving away he patted it on the head.

... Dangerous dark night between Christmas and *Oíche Nollaig na mBan*—Louisa May Alcott's Christmas. Picking at leftovers, bones of ... bits of ... times gone ... twelve nights, the Gallitcantzari are about, be on guard or they will carry you away. Burn the big log, hyssop the door and keep the black cock inside. Cockadoodledo. Where to find a black … We approach not just the end of a year but the end of a decade, say a decade, ring a ring a rosary. We'll not fall down with the plague. Let's hope it's a good one. Not much future in the future. Bash it with the present tense. Each one must decide himself the order of things. Ding dong dell, for whom the bell … goodnight sweet ladybird, sleep steals.

Jude, sorry must have dozed. Three nights now without sleep. I lie with my hands folded like wings to protect my heart from the world's onslaughts. Can't turn off the mind, like a radio left on all night with the volume down. Ancient Gaelic triads, three days and three nights, three wishes, three things good about a woman, three things that cannot be done. Christian proselytisers CAPITALISED on it with three leaves of shamrock, fourleaved clover good luck superstition frowned upon. Could there be four in the one? No proof for the three wise men. Pater, Mac, Espíritu Santo. Could there be a daughter? That is a sin, a sacrilege. Just asking, using my mind, no harm in thinking. Three nights' dizzy spells, too much alcohol. Dizzy spells turning into momentary blackout, blockout, frightening in that you've no control when it comes like the involuntary physical jerk in the leg or arm during consciousness or semiconsciousness, supposed to be caused by the heart stopping for a second. Dancing water in sink, little beads of light, dazzling, dizzy; see speck, no it's an illusion.

I pulled a cracker and got a skeleton. *Memento mori.* Ho ho bones of turkey. Hush, Lil stirs, write in darkness.

Ding dong day dawns the same old … New Year's weather day same as yesterday last year dull grey no change then Sam same again all changes are manmade.

Anyway Jude, happy New Year, open beer new resolve resolution, be resolute. Count down to changelessness, count in decades swinging sixties naughty nineties, naughty nighties naught night ní … ná …

Dear Leo, let me tell you my dream. The day before I went to see Uanito's teacher I had a dream about black polish in a school. I had brought it with me because my scuffed shoes were dirty, intended polishing them in the toilet …

JF: Only act if shoe pinches.

… when the polish disappeared. Bits of black polish along corridors, stains and smears. *El director de la escuela* accosted me. Yes, it was mine. I said I didn't know how it went missing. He looked at me as someone strange. I don't know how it went missing. What does it mean?

O Leo, thrill me with the lilt of your voice and your wealth of words, only the latter for me alas. Let us send each other disks for when we lie awake in darkness to hear a voice other than our own drone to break the silence.

All that talk, writing about bones and skeletons and graves, you must believe; we are more than tarsi and that passing of blood, please see a doctor; don't be embarrassed; they are trained in such matters. You must believe the Lord will breathe life into the dried bones and fill them with his spirit. The bones will rise up from the grave. The Lord will pad them out with flesh once more and they will walk in a new land.

Dear Jude, I am recording this on a disk for you as I wander lonely in a crowd (I have become a true *flâneur*, but allow for interruptions). The crowd are gathered in a field. They are watching a man striking a minute white ball with a stick in the direction of a minuscule hole earmarked with a flag. But the ball has its own volition and sets off towards a copse, taking in a sandpit along the way. Eventually after much ooing and ahing from the crowd, the ball lands in the hole to thunderous applause with ominous thunder up above also, and umbrellas resurrect …

JF: To traverse the land of Dot without an umbrella is a form of hubris.

... and the crowd moves on like a giant beetle up the field to another hole. I caught a man in the crowd scratching his back with the point of his brolly.

O Leo, Uanito says someone in his class thought he was great. Who is great? He is not great, he said he only thinks he is great. No one is great, only God. Yesterday he wound up the blue plastic statue of the Virgin (like yours) and then it played the Bells of the Angelus .. .

JF: Wee paws for the Angelus.

... slowing near the end, slowing but not halting, heaving its final notes like a last gasp. I dreamed to fulfil his dream for postChrirstmas. Three dwarf santas at the window. Uanito ran to them in red outside imaginary snowflakes the real thing. Mainly a sweet party, drew many to the door, some for heat, down but not out. Father present Christmas. Tripod for video camera. Good show for epiphany: *el Día de los Reyes Magos. Aguinaldos para todos.* It is the day you asked when Spanish children receive their presents when they leave not pillow cases but shoes out not for Santa but for the *reyes magos* to fill. Complex tourist destroying Spain. What was that phrase you taught me?

Titeann an dúchas amach trí chraicaenn an duine.

Leo was that you? Did you say that?

Leo: Say it I did but my preoccupation is carnal. Is there a correlation between breast fondling and penile stimulation? Can it be measured? Any surveys on this? Shed the seed. Let new life spring from the dead branch. A shudder of intimations grips my soul at odd moments of the night and I cling tightly to my wife, her blond hair silky from shampoo. Lil is sighing. Must turn out the light, birth and waste orifices beside one another, birth from decay extra glow from dying embers. Wasp's or is it bee's dying sting? The temple built up again. Let the dead bury their dead. And the polish, you wanted to impress anybody associated with Uanito. You wanted to look well, that is all and it going missing simply means you were unsure, nervous. I saw a solitary woman visiting a grave near Mam's, her belief in talking to a stone …

JF: Hack it out of the tedium of your life, create the sculpture, chisel it out of the stone that binds you.

… withered flowers gone to seed; plastic flowers in glass globe. Big moments and small honour all; some stones more important than others. Here lies Mr and Mrs Pebble not as important as Mr and Mrs Rock …

JF: Some pebbles have to be stoned to get boulder.

… Dig up again in twenty years. Oak coffins last longer. All the same in time. Time, ladies and gents, last drinks before … coughin' on way, all on way behind it. Solidarity. Crocodile tears some. A dogcollared one had arranged to weep at Mam's funeral but didn't get around to it.

JF: When you cry at a funeral it's yourself you're feeling sorry for.

Jude: O Leo, cry me a river.

Leo: The bell tolls at the gate; a new soul enters, another soul queues outside. Death is busy this season …

The Rhymer
Death is a bee
who doesn't miss a tree
and the old weeping willow
is laughing at me.

… My thoughts and ideas, Jude, come from the world of men, not from the silence of the soil. Selfawareness and selfknowledge, to know thyself, how many have the humility to succeed in this? Deluded life, wasted life, little knowledge of others, presume to know all, knowing nothing, no.

Noises in the night heaving, wailing, echoing, summoning up lost souls—the sound from the fridge freezer. There is nowhere noiseless anymore. No nook or cranny. Yuppie planes lowflying, the new birdsong. Who owns the sky? We live in a place where no one knows silence.

I flash the flashlight for a flash of inspiration. Three men pissed by torchlight in a white bowl; one man two men three men and his dog politely pissed in a white bowl …

Reader: Who were they?

JF: Mourners. The weight of their piss was like stampeding horses in the lavatory bowl.

… Silver jets like swords crisscrossing in a duel. Direct the jets to the side to reduce sound effects, so as not to waken the slumberers with our wakeful members …

The Rhymer
If you tinkle where you sprinkle
Be a sweetie and wipe the seatie.

… The mountain climb was tough on the calves, picking comfrey leaves to chew as I walk. The landscape is our pharmacy. I returned there, our mountain, remember, Jude? How does an old and feeble man live high up on the mountain? What is growing old? …

The Seer of Suburbia: Growing old is a sentence you have to endure for a crime you did not commit.

… A sentence Mam avoided.

JF: Growing old is losing the present to reclaim the past.

… Anyway, Jude, remember the cottage. We called to him. It was like he had grown into the mountain. He was part of it, one with the wild gorse and *fionnán* and grouse and pheasant and soft bog and hard rock. He has returned to the earth as the trees do and become compounded into turf in aeons of time. I am here again years later in the early morn when the matted dew like cobwebs lodged in the furze. A bird flew out from a bush. The spirit of the old man on the mountain. The old man died because he fell out of people's consciousness. He felt his death was wished for, and he obliged. The mountain with its ancient burial stones predating Christianity, and across a little lake and a hollow, the rock of the Mass in Penal times. Does the chalice still lie below? Pagan and Christian burials blending into datelessness. A place removed from modern man's litter, sheep droppings same as time immemorial …

JF: Leo was walking with the sheep, a llama among them to make robes for the Inca kings, when a flock of men disturbed him.

… A lark sang and flew from the *fionnán* flight dipping trilling titlooet and then lou lou here comes more; what an exaltation and all free. I was about to whisper when someone shot in the distance: two young fellows. What have you in the bag? Pheasant, woodcock and snipe.

A house hewn out of rock. Live like a hermit on this rock. I will build Cephas. Let me go on a little further to see the water flow down the mountain (remember it?): white froth on green rock like life itself it goes on through the straight and narrow over the big rocks and small pebbles gurgling its song as it goes, breaking into separate streams only to join as one again further down. I love to go awandering. Who would dare to wash dirty linen here?

A bright halfmoon dipping in and out of a darkening cloud. I go about in silence fearful or maybe respectful and the birds remain quiet in their bush …

SFC: The serpent hisses when the sweet birds sing.

… and sheep and cows keep heads downcast. I look on a star and think of another world. *Soineann agus doineann.* What was the weather like? asked the meteorologist. A dolly mixture. If you don't like the weather, wait a minute. It's taking up. Brother sun, sister moon appearing simultaneously in the bluedaysky. We showed ourselves at Epiphany mass. Some saw, some heard, some heard the saw, some saw the herd. I saw an old man with silver hair purpled under the light of the stained glass window. The blue Virgin looked over him. *Venite adoremus*. Find God. May he find me as I go on my way. *A Íosagáin*, help my unbelief …

Jude: The catechism, Leo.

… Only made matters worse attempting to give omniscient rational answers to impossible questions. Like trying to empty the sea with a small shell.

Jude: If you don't believe in god how can you say hello in Irish, your language, Leo?

… Should make allowances for. Wise men. The meal is over, who will dry the tears from the cups … ?

Reader: What's Mr Francis doing?

SFC: He's giving his writer's card to someone looking for a toothpick.

… I look through my lazy right eye and see a woman with her head under a bonnet on bended knee; the more she bends the more I see. Apologies for stain on right of page, Jude. Fly crushed to death. How long dead I cannot say since turning new leaf. It must have been flyday when they made the paper, flypaper now. Writing on recycled paper to save a tree. All trees should be called *nobilis*. Recycled thoughts. Will anything be original anymore … ?

JF: Who is thinking my thoughts now?

… When I'm writing my diary or notebook, not in the grandiloquent style of Mr Francis, but in the quieter, observational way perhaps of my quotidian thinking, I sometimes feel I'm communicating from my brain to my heart or maybe vice versa. It is like different parts of me at a given time act as an audience to another part …

O Leo, let me be that other part.

JF: Expressions not from the heart do not enter the ear.

… I put a map of the world on the wall of my study. See our land as a central dot of the universe, ideal centre for world missionaries, equidistant from the four corners. What else could it spread, so small? Its literature. Look at the dot in a global context to counteract provincialism and insularity …

Reader: But we can only live in one place. So what does it matter?

… The mind knows no limits; no frontiers for it. How many of our dots would it take to fill the vast tracts of Russia? History will have to be retaught; too many smug theories and dates out of date. I have opened a little door that was rarely opened before in my mind …

JF: When is a door not a door?

… It gives heightened awareness, but I cannot close the door, and the thinking goes on and on through the wakeful night, waiting for the milkman with his Dawn milk …

JF: When it is ajar. Ha ha.

… Mild day end of January coatless people walking about wheeling a pram baby out—*Half an hour I'll put her down and give her five ounces …*

JF: What are baby's last steps?

… Instead of joy I feel a melancholy shudder at the touch of spring.

Jude: Be joyful, Leo. It is the time of the melting of ice in your country.

The first dan the lions.

Yes, and the first grasshopper, and the first swallow of summer. Our little boy came home from school on this January day. He has seen five Januaries. The blue satchel is laid down and his jumper is suspended from one arm as he gapes at the children's channel and sees an animal change from elephant to bird to rabbit to crocodile to rhinoceros to … How many skins will his youth put past? His centimetres will never measure the same again.

He will be fine, Jude. Life going again, more prams and babies as we come out of the death season. All the dead leaves fermenting in the canal making a thick gravy and the graves left behind. But a grey canopy of sky is trying to suffocate the evening and the dead are still haunting us like trees showing new buds ...

The Seer of Suburbia: Actually calyx, leaf whorl before bud formation.

... still bearing dead branches nonetheless. What was that on the news? Burglars apprehended in shootout. Could it have been them, Jude, still doing the rounds? O the chance of that, we are so alarmist. I understand your fears. Do you remember the burly fellow in the balaclava pushing you down? I recall the scar on his hand, And the one with the clown's mask lurking in the corner of the room like he was a guvnor or a voyeur, commanding me with his strange accent to do it ...

O Leo, the horror.

... Night and darkness once more. Venus going down on Mars. Wind brings warmth, unnatural as I shed the blankets with thought silently tormenting. To whom to talk? Would you scream going into the abyss? I am so scared, no, forsaken, that's the word. How can I come to terms with my dot? I am just a fly waiting to be crushed and be no more. Is there more? There must be more, but what? I must try to contact Mam again. Quieta non movere. Please Jude, talk to me about death, an encouraging word. What is really beyond the grave? It's such a torment for the doubter.

The Rhymer
The dead won't harm a hair on your head
it's the living you have to dread.

... O to have the blind faith of our fathers. But no, who wants to be blind? Be deaf to all doubt. *Dubito ergo sum.*

Jude: Do you not believe, Leo?

No, but I touched the robe nonetheless. How can you know something and believe it at the same time? Man is an orphan. He has lost his way. He needs help. He does not know his ordained path as the tortoise does. The things it says in the Bible, so much truth, so much myth. Lot offering his daughters, or they lying down with him.

Reader: Leo himself seems to have lost his way.

JF: Let me tell you a story. Pull over a chair, sit near the fire. Warm your hands and cock up your ears. Once there was a young man who dreamed dreams and saw visions. However, the dreams or the visions were never completely clear. He only halfsaw the future, halfgleaned the truth. But only God he believed at that time could see the whole truth, so he was a halfgod. And the halfgod looked upon the world with a sapient eye. He smiled when he saw people oscillate or doubt. He smiled when the autumn winds undressed the trees or when he heard the cry of a newborn babe. He smiled when a cloud burst. What is a cloud after all but an amorphous thing which takes the shape of the viewer's mind and becomes its soul and heart. These things he knew but he was not satisfied and he said to himself if only he could grasp the other half of truth he would then be a god.

When spring came, in his effort to grasp the other half of truth, he went closer to nature. He watched the foliage return to the trees and the young buds bloom. He watched the little lambs gambol in the green meadows and listened to the birds rejoice in the warmth of spring. All these things he understood but he knew there was something missing, there was something else. Ah, he exclaimed, it is man himself who provides the answer to the other half of truth.

So the young man set out to where there would be many people and he duly arrived in a great city. There was a lot of beeping of car horns and clashing of sirens, roaring of engines and cries of vendors. The young man also sensed many conflicting smells in the city: unwholesome smells, a strange mixture of oil and gas and smoke. He saw many strange things: buildings having no shape or form without space shooting skywards as if grasping for air and vehicular traffic which covered the streets as far as the eye could see making the ground invisible. And the people, ah yes people, there they were in their droves rushing in all directions of the compass. Never before had the young man seen so many people. Where were they all going to in such haste?

So, not forgetting his purpose, he decided to follow some of them. He shadowed two young ladies who were too engrossed in conversation with each other to notice him. Their rate of walking was as fast as their talking and the young man had to keep close at their heels so as not to lose them in the crowds. They entered a large department store, looked at a few sundry items and came out a different door. They slowed down outside another store but were satisfied this time just to look in the window and then move on. Thy entered yet another store and just when it appeared to the young man they were about to purchase material, they replaced the garments and walked out yet another door onto the street again. When the young man got outside he realised he was back where he had started, that is to say the street whereon he had first decided to shadow the girls. The girls, still rapt in their conversation, then entered the store which they had first gone into using the same door. The young man felt no urge to follow further. His eyes were no longer sapient. He felt rather muddled and knew that he had been going around in a circle. He took in the city one more time. Twilight had fallen and the other half of truth seemed more obscure and further away than ever …

Reader: So what happened to him?

… He grew up as one halfknowing?

Leo: The silence of Wounded House. All asleep except me. Lil will groan when I go up but the silent moments are rare, and precious too, and have their place as much as speech. Silence to hear your own heart beat to open the front door …

Reader: Does Leo not have a key?

JF: He is knocking at the door of Insight.

… and see the moth fly inwards towards the light just as I veer, to feel your thoughts emerge from the chrysalis of yourself, to wonder where the wild cats are sleeping, to feel age creeping and capture its transience, to feel the hunger and think of the mind to awaken refreshed as an empty shell.

A liquid morning, raining cats and dogs, rained dead frogs once, yes and rained meteorites too yes in Limerick once. Spiders' legs will fall. The earth, the heavens, what lies beyond the canopy? Watching the sky to see what lurks through the bruises, leaving us tormented by the striptease of light, dimming our eyes from seeing ever fully.

The wind blows warmth from the south. Nature is standing on its head. No snow or ice or bracing cold air …

The Rhymer
Half air, half despair

… to greet our dawn. Block the ears and hear no rumblings. The silence of certitude or oblivion.

Jude: Not a secure age, *mi león*. Locking up *mi piso* at night, I saw someone, a shadow under the street light lurking. I slammed the door shut and prayed. O Leo, memories flood back.

Uanito has started to eat paper, specialises in corners, eats the foldedover corners of copies, what you call …

Leo: Dog ears.

… He is very restless at night. Sometimes he comes to me and curls my hair in knots; other times he shouts in his sleep. When I ask him about it he is reluctant to admit, a pain in … *estómago.*

I said to Uanito I had caught a chill—*un escalofrío* (using the English word). We're having chilli con carne, he said, that will make you better …

JF: Her forefinger and thumb caressed the long stem of the wineglass, ascending and descending and ascending again.

… What I miss most, Leo, is physical contact with you; the letters have made the feeling like a craving despite the passing years. Your handsome face, eyes shining, that dreamy look; to hold, to feel your painted member. All I have is paper pages, dead leaves. Come June of the blossoms and the warm sun. I have not gone into the sun. I can't go into the sun without you. Spain, where the powder blue sky melts in the matt blue sea. Come into me. The dot. I will go back to the early pages. O let me say a prayer to Santa Teresa. I am like an owl in abandoned ruins. I go through the deepest darkness. Make me a lampstand for a lamp that never got its turnon. I will decorate its shaft with flowers the shape of almond blossoms. The incubus is in me. O Leo, I hold the Bible with one hand while the other … It is the Wicked Bible or maybe the Wifehaters' Bible. It is not blasphemy, it is the loneliness, and yet I am surrounded by parents and people and guilt. O rise up and come to me. I am as dark as the desert tents of Kedar. Come like the wild flowers and bloom upon my breasts …

JF: The cheapest special effects in movies.

… I am the mare; let me excite the stallion. O if you could come and stay until the darkness disappears, until the morning breezes blow. If only we could reach Androgyne together, …

The Rhymer
A baby called Enda
could be any genda.

… each of us a half of Shiva or Baas and Asperah or any two. You ask me about death because you have been in its field. Such thoughts will not pass but will lessen in intensity …

The Seer of Suburbia: The only death is Time.

… As regards physical death, it cannot be avoided, so that leaves the spirit; we need to study it more and more. O Leo, it is difficult to have control over our lives when our languages are mixed up. The only common language now is the laughter of children. Our people are scattered over the earth because of Babel. We must not lose sight of our humility. Even those houseinvaders, those creatures who … we must forgive them but never forget them. Bury the hatchet but mark the spot. Pour out the bowl of wrath. *Basta.* I am becoming biblebacked, too much pouring over. I enclose a fragment of Gethsemane: *Orchis maculata*, spotted by the blood of Christ. We must uplift. In Jude 16 of the Murderers' Bible: 'There are murderers, complainers, walking after their own lust.'

Dear Jude, walking after their lust you say. Today I saw eternal blue. Perfect buttocks in blue jeans (and I thought of you jeaned and bobbing up and down on your bicycle as we ascended the road towards the wood on that momentous day, the day of Saint Patrick). Such delicious shape, such curving hemispheres undulating uphill projecting denim hugging in the climb. A car stopped in the middle of the jam to watch. I did not hear the horns of the growling motorists until the blue rhapsody had disappeared. And then I felt my head which I had forgotten for a moment …

JF: When the brew of the night meets the cold of the day.

… I have a head—*ragairne na hoíche aréir—delirium tremens*, mixed the grain with the vine hadn't my measure, poured too generous a finger. I was footless. I hadn't a leg to stand on, still travelled on foot, too many wheel deaths. Saw a car impaled on a railing in the Phoenix Park. Was the driver impaled too? A steel rod straight through the windscreen.

Don't fret about Uanito eating paper. Did it myself. Better than gum, both from the tree; other animals eat twigs; his ancestors ate clay …

O Leo, I am bound to you.

JF: Sit under the fig tree if you are bound, that will free you, a peck of ipecacuanha there was but she was virtuous, and literature delights more in vice.

Reader: What of Lil then?

JF: Leave the lion his pride. She thinks that if you live cerebrally, you are wasting your time.

Leo: Funny how cerebral preoccupation can make one appear so physically awkward, so stupid as it were.

And what about, says Reader, all the emphasis on phallic symbolism and sexual release? I mean it's positively pornographic.

JF. Jack Meoff.

Reader: Who?

JF: The name of the pornographer. The phallic preoccupation is simple objective enquiry in keeping with the existential probing tone throughout. Besides Phal is a character in his own right, like the toe or the foot or the ear or the belly in other works. As regards your second point: sexual release, it is simply a response to the deep loneliness of these characters, one of whom is apparently seriously ill, which partly explains his thanatomia, that coupled with his mother's death and her appearing as a revenant. I mean if you yourself I mean … *obscurum per obscurius*, I could quote to you from the parable of the vinegar.

What about, says Reader, the adulterous liaison between Jude and Leo?

No touch, an unconsumed menu.

Reader: But what about the June promise?

Hypothetical as yet. Read on. What does the Bible of sixteen thirty-one tell us? Thou shalt commit adultery: 'Yield ye your members as instruments of righteousness unto sin.'

Reader: What? Could you threepeat that?

Many men have had epistolary dealings with women, intimately too, and still retained the marital bonds intact.

Reader: What?

It's all to do with hearing. Who hath ears to ear? Are you a wifehater?

Reader: I think you are holding the wolf by the ears. Leo is too handsome to be taken seriously, god love him. But you can see the worry of death, or is it of life, in his dark eyes.

Phal: If you were to speak through another organ …

SYC: Hasn't said a word yet.

Phal: The tongue is silent when Phal speaks. Why elect the tongue to speak? Can the ear speak, and the tongue listen? Or piss through the nose. Why should I have to pass all the piss? Breathe through the eye of Phal. Talk through your arse. The snake hears with its tongue.

IV

'The writer will be judged only by the resonance of
his solitude or the quality of his despair.'
Cyril Connolly

All digging digging digging, preparing for spring aerating the beds wherein will lie flowers of different hue and cry. Warm winds warm the seeds to generate faster. Shed the warm seed on the warm earth. Start the cycle over again …

The Rhymer
Get the trike for the babe
and the bike for the child
and the bigger bike for the next in size
who will leave his bike to the one behind
and so the cycle continues.

… Samsara. Mind as fertile as the soil. When I die will there be a suttee? How arrogant. But still if they have it in some cultures. Lil no way, but you, Jude, I hope you would not be foolish enough. Sorry to mention. Imagination running away with me. Not too different from ancient Celts though: plied the widow with alcohol, passed her around before the final Frank Sinatra.

I speculate how I am still alert after the night's insomnia. It's like something paranormal is driving me on; an extended dream or rather mare, a whetstone to the senses that drives me relentlessly. Even alcohol does not dim my sharpness. It's as if the mind has transcended all the mortal fops, I mean props. But the longing, Jude, it never goes away. The *anhelo*, is that the word you often used in Spanish, or perhaps the Portuguese *saudade*? We don't appear to have a word in Anglo-Saxon or Gaelic for hopeless longing.

I saw a picture, a photograph in black and white in a travel magazine of a lithe girl with her back to me, dressed in shorts and a vest and a widebrimmed hat and beautiful dark plaits cascading down to meet her rucksack, hands in pockets enhancing her shape. Will she turn around? If only it were you, Jude. A feeling of lost moments washes over me at the darkening hour, a realisation that young romantic encounters are gone from me, the excitement of a look or a gesture. The girl with her back to me conjures up youthful longing as up the mountain she treks …

Jude: As you and I did.

… Yes. Such longing for something beyond myself, beyond my own mortality, touches me to the core, never young no more. Crockety age waits at the corner with wheels and crutches and bionic devices. Turn around, fair maiden, and look at me. I hope you don't disappoint with a hag's face, a bakkushan, and that you are as comely front as behind. Do you look at the world questioningly like me?

When Lil came in I took out the china to cheer her. We had four china cups depicting the four seasons. I accidentally let the summer cup fall. A crack appeared. As good as broken, said Lil, we will have no summer. She was rather put out. I hope it is not an omen.

O Leo.

I walk by the Basin. Benches along the Royal Canal bank. Wooden laths ripped out of them. Vandalism or maybe for firewood. Wino sitting muttering on empty base, two bottles at his feet. Ah steel benches up above, now that's more practical, less aesthetic though. Woman with a distorted face leadchugs a reluctant dog …

The Seer of Suburbia: A dog is a backward god.

… A lot of old people near the Basin. Gulls squawk around a tree that grows out of water, wellwatered roots, the roots that steady, the minute island manmade. Elderly woman feeding ducks. What changes? Therapy. Grey dull light not cold. Dublin's grey city, a pall of smoke hanging over like a giant genie stagnant in the air. Short woman passes, thrusting, trying to walk faster than her natural gait; she's going somewhere. Big man approaches but I know by the nonchalant way he carries his shoulders that he is nonthreatening. Grey slates and paths. People go by carrying plastic bags with cheap advertising, same with Tshirts. Do they get royalties? The shopping bag, a thing of the past like the vermin jelly. Was that the Red Tart going towards the North Circular? Too far away to see in the darkening day. I should wear my glasses when I'm looking out, things are blurred otherwise …

The Rhymer
My eyes are dim I cannot see.
I have not brought my specs with me.

JF: Last time Leo was driving he thought it was fog at the windscreen but then he realised he wasn't wearing his spectacles.

… Vanity otherwise. The other is wise. Speckyfoureyes, a thing of the past too the namecalling or maybe just growing older …

Reader: Are you shortsighted or longsighted?

… All I know is that I can't see without my specs, and that's the long and the short of it. Away from trafficsnarl. Juggernauts, masters of the world, trying to bring the earth to a vehicular standstill. What signals are the gulls making to one another? They make circular swoops low near watersurface. Greenheaded ducks impervious, such a calm floating appearance they give, all on the surface; underneath legs straddling like mad in pursuit of crumbs. We are all the same. A swan appears, must have been hiding somewhere. An old man sleeps on a bench, tear falls from eye, a page falls from his newspaper. What is written on the dustbin? OBEDIENTIA CIVIUM URBIS FELICITAS. Happy city.

At the public standup lavatory no facilities to WPAU. The tall man with the long foreskin aimed his jet on the naphthalene balls and shook his phal so long and hard that it was positively barrassing to peehole and I made my X as fasticud.

Who is this that just passed by? She carried a grin of nonrecognition; recognised the hips. Ah well.

I walk on the city pavement slab; don't touch the lines, bad luck. Adjust pace to walk in the spaces. All citizens know that. Memories from childhood when we played 'beds' with shoepolish tin …

JF: He needed black shoes for his library job interview to go with his grey suit so he dyed his brown shoes black but they turned out just a darker brown.

The Red Tart: I dyed all my underwear black and look how I turned out.

… full of clay, land in the square, hop skip and jump. Push the tin with the shoe polish tin, lands on line, out you go. Whose turn next? What's reeling in the cinema?

Itinerant man and woman sitting on the side of the road forlorn as they stare blankly into a void. Their despair strikes me only when I see the pram with a baby in it abandoned in the middle of the road …

JF: The pram that was the Trojan horse.

Jude: O Leo, the *pobrecitos*.

JF: Some truths only the stricken know.

… I dare not interfere, dagger looks. The library at last. How are things in there, Andy? I say to the janitor. A lot of friction, he says. Someone looking for the work of Edgar Allan Pole. You man Poe, I say. Could be sitting on it, he says. And how are you? Sharp and alert for the day's proceedings, I say. Can you read the runes? Just check the futhark and Mick's your uncle. I've a bone to pick with you, says Crichton.

Reader: What was Crichton doing?

JF: He was after manhandling a girl among the stacks and was returning to give out his daily guff.

Reader: He's a micky dazzler.

Crichton: Last Friday you were noticed by your absence.

Leo: No bones about it. I sent in an aegrotat. What's bred in the bone will come out in the flesh, feel it in the bones.

You're a descendent of Ham, says Crichton.

Ham: I can't be cured.

Reader: Andy, you know Leo well?

Andy: I've seen him come and I've seen him go these twenty years.

Reader: And your impression of him?

Andy: He keeps thinking he's going to be bleedin remembered. He speaks as if he wants everything recorded. I remember something he said, for the life of me can't think of it now. O a great man. What do we bleedin want to remember or record for? Why do some want to leave their little mark to say they were here? I ask ya. O I just remembered, another thing, he can never abide a collar button closed; always has his shirt open at the neck with his tie slightly crooked, like as if he was inviting someone to straighten it like. I heard a woman calling his style what was it O yes a studied carelessness, that's what it was so it was.

Crichton let his passport fall out of his pocket: Frederick Crichton height 5' 9" stooped headhair long gone, wig putatively of his pubic hair covering ears and portwine birthmark on his neck, eyes nutria, hairveins splitting through bulging pink cheeks.

As I head homewards after work I see an old man walking on three legs in the twilight capturing the wind in his coat. A lot of young ageists about with no time for him as they nearly knock him off the pavement in their headlong advance. On what will we be judged, Jude, or will we be judged at all? Is it all a cod? What if there is a god, and he's big into the physical? I mean he is entitled to his preferences, and say, low on literature, big on the *beart* and low on the *briathar. Homo faber, Homo ludens, Homo sapiens, Homo sexual …*

Reader: What about the working man?

… *Homo ergaster*, sorry. This man's work is more valid, he will say, because he drills or because he has dug many gardens, or this woman because … but this man, this social parasite pushes nothing but a … Couldn't turn an ox. Let him walk backwards for the rest of his life …

JF: When do you count backwards to go upwards?

Reader: Let me see. No wait, wait. When do you count upwards to go … ? The backstroke.

JF: Backwards to go upwards?

Reader: O I've got it. At a rocket launch. Now riddle me this: when do you count backwards to go forward?

… As the day darkens darkening fears make me shudder. I must try to contact Mam again. She may counsel me. Was it last night's alcohol or something deeper? I am a deep lonely well. People coming and going, shadowy exteriors, far removed from the well. I saw the comely maiden again gaze from her oriel window. She gave me the glad eye as I passed by. Ascending the lampless lane, the grassy verge above is black with three sentries standing guard; dogs or wolves? Only bushes …

JF: What is it with English writers that keep beating about the bush?

… mindtricks. Fear stalks the unfamiliar. Not as bad as the man who mistook his wife for a hat. What is your greatest fear, Jude? Mine is the fear of being dependent on another. The last time convalescing …

Reader: Was it the blood discharge?

SYC: He won't say, maybe later.

… tied up in a hospital bed and I cannot open the knots. Better get up I say. No use lying here. Better to tell the truth somewhere else. My cries are unheard. There is nobody about …

JF: Counting years in BC.

… The nurse's starched skirt swished as she hurried by. I am on my own helplessly …

Reader: Leo can be too whiny at times.

... tied in knots. Scream like the man in the iron mask must have screamed. It would be nice to die for a while to hear one's plaudits if any uttered and obituary read. What would they say? Must achieve something to be talked about and then the sort of person you were. They will say this man was afraid of his own mind and the body's debility, pinning him down, stuck to a spot.

I opened and closed after me the door of the tombhouse. Words and reassurances longing to hear. I asked Lil to speak to me. Any old word at all will do, I said, just to acknowledge that I am here. But no word came from her and the pressure on my chest felt so great that I could not lie in bed any longer. How some people can live within the silence of themselves, but I could not. The conversations with my mother when I was a boy made me take communication between people for granted, and I never thought in my adult life I would cry out at night for the want of a human word, a sound, an echo. I wandered out into the garden. I knew what I was doing—ruining the morrow before it began, but at least it was not suffocating out here in the cold night air. I looked up at the moon unmoved.

Reader: And what is *your* greatest fear, Mr Francis?

JF: That I will be just a painter of moustaches, a stirrer of porridge.

Reader: Perhaps your influence is not ripe enough for the age that's in it.

SYC: Like a ploughed field ready for the seed.

*

THE SNOW HAS COME, VERY WATERY, WILL HARDLY STICK, STILL untrammelled in the sheetwhite fields passing purifier air fresher sky bluer smog pushed behind the blue canopy for a while nature normalising or is it snow in California rain the desert of Arizona manmade traffic jams. The irony of fast sports cars stuck. The snow is blamed, lodging on the traffic light futilely changing its colours. A woman in her automobile does not move and is weeping …

Reader (*sarcastically*): None of the traffic light colours suit her.

… She is trapped in her vehicle because of the gridlock. O to fly through the air on the gossamer thread and follow the ancient silk route. Time for divine worship.

Reader: Why do you go to mass?

Out of fear, to feel secure, I'm afraid of death and the pagan contradiction of our Christian school motto: *Malo mori quam foedari …*

JF: It's better than ham and eggs.

… I read the poetry of John Donne during the boring mass. When I was done, we were shouted at to shout out the responses. Some highpitched voices of certainty, some muted voices of doubt or disbelief. Some semimumbling of coercion: *And some parents expect their children to be baptised when they …* The plate is passed around. *We will sing, we will sing out loud*, the voice thunders. *Put your hand in the hand of the man who stilled the …*

O Leo, sing the world into existence. Sing out the name of plant and animal. Recreate the land through song.

Does he know the whereabouts of the water holes, I wonder?

Who?

The dogcollared one. Their whereabouts are revealed in the songs. If you don't know the song you could die.

O Leo.

Ammatyerre.

What?

The aboriginal language. The plate comes to the blind man who feels the serrated edge of the coin and he knows its value. Look over there, that's JF writing notes …

JF: The rubber tube of the fountain pen perished from too long alying.

Reader: Mr Francis is quite witty.

SFC: One wit more and he'd be a halfwit. His effort at humour is a joke.

... Worshippers of Isis promised immortality, perished in Pompeii. How will we perish, Jude? O will I have to submit to dreaded certainty to understand the triple spirals? The problem is this that ... no it is that this ... what's this that is? The problem is. I hear something. Which of the four hundred thousand sounds was that ... ?

JF: He spent his whole life talking about sounds. So that eventually when he did find quiet, there was nothing to talk about.

... There is something coming through on the hammer, anvil and stirrup. It is a faint voice:

To go to her house is to approach the world of the dead. You will never return to the road of life.

Is it you, Mam?

I am concerned for you, my son.

Mam, what must I do?

You must listen to your own spirit.

There are so many things I would like to know the meaning of. I try to write.

The record of the word.

And the writer?

The keeper of the word.

And what is the word?

The expression of the tongue.

And what is the tongue then?

That which whips the air.

What is the air?

That which breathes life.

What is life?

Waiting for death.

What is death?

The beginning of …

Life, of course. Why of course. Your voice is growing fainter. Don't fade away. Is your life beginning? What is man?

Man is the broken rung on the ladder.

What should I value?

Silence. Everything will flow from it.

Silence, Mam! When you talked so much in life? Is that what is meant by the silence of the grave? Are you still there? Mam, don't go. You talk in aphorisms. Where is your humour, if life is beginning for you? You always had humour. Hail Mary is lashing down. Where was creation born and where does it lead? I don't believe in the death of God, but how can our words reach his? Will there be an interrogation after life? Should we not eat our dead relatives, so they will no longer be sad? Better than worms doing the job …

Reader: He's acting the maggot.

… Why give them the feast? I am a mortal playing near the immortal sea. I must go through the waterfall of tears and leave those earthly drops to dry up and descend into the cavern of yellow light …

SFC: Lambkin has a weakened grip of reality. I always suspected it. He is psychotic. He was the *suspirium puellarum* in his day as if that gave him extra privileges, and quite strong when he was dealing with the ludic element, but an overrated actor nonetheless.

JF: Raw reality is just a compost heap.

Jude: Who will rise from the compost heap?

… Time tempus tiempo. How do you beat time?

JF: 84,600 seconds. Does that not mean anything to you?

No, why? …

Then you don't know the length of your day, my boy.

... *An tam ag sileadh uaim*, the subtle thief, more an erosion than a thieving when you learn music, a gradual wearing down like the sea wearing down the shore: detrition. Must have contrition first, sorry for what and to whom? Confess to an ear in the dark box, all ears outside. When do you kill time? He's killing time. When you walk on two legs at noon. O if we could run along the backward line of time, along the long road back and start all over again ...

Reader: Where is Leo?

JF: He is hiding in the womb of the house with cottonwooled ears, shielded from the slings and arrows of the fastforwardworld, but sheltered most of all from Temptation.

... Jude, console me, your doubting Tom, and that little spider *Tegenaria domestica curiosa*, where has she gone?

Mi cariño, my dearest *suspirium puellarum*, come and listen to me. Your letter and ramblings are as long as an ancient papyrus roll. And such a beautiful hand, italics, a new pen a new stylus? Such accurate serifs. I love the curlicues in your signature. O but I see the sadness in the downward sloping of your words. Such revelations. Do you type at all? Don't ever. Write on parchment from the woolless hides of sheep. Your writing has the celibate purity of a monastic scribe but your capitals are lightly drawn.

O if only you were in Spain with me, Leo, what is there that we could not do? I have a room and a lonely bed, a *ducha*, a veranda with shutters open to the blue sky and the sun. There is guitar music coming from a nearby restaurant and downstairs the sweet sounds of my language can be heard between a mother and a child—*Cariño, no llores*. Yesterday, *el sábado* I had a swim in the local indoor pool when the *madre* was minding Uanito. I looked up from the water as I swam on my back at the glass roof and saw the underfeet of birds sticking like suction stoppers to the pane (you see you have me thinking like you, observing). My black bikini *de rayas* wet with the pearly drops falling on the ceramic floor. My breasts heaved. I imagined you standing before me briefly briefed. The sigh, the caress, the way it should have been, voluntary and gentle standing erect pressing into each other's nakedness. What then? What pleasures were stolen from us? What we could have done. I am so bold on paper, but was always a little bit bolder than you. We could have started with page one of the *Kama Sutra* and not stopped till the end, listening to the music and language of my people. *Amado con amada.* Do I eat you up like the black widow? No, for I need you for other days and sweet Spanish nights. Ignore the cracked cup. Throw it out; it is just superstition. We will have our summer together. *Nuestro verano en España.* O I feel so cloistered …

The Seer of Suburbia: From the cloister she looked up and saw the sky was reduced to a rectangle.

… I must go to eat. After Spain you must take me to Singar, Leo, to where Jesus is buried …

Leo: The Golgotha martyr.

… We must travel like pilgrims, wandering souls and see all the faces of humanity. I have read of a new potion with a spider. Catch the spider with its web whole, entrap in shell with heated oil and drink, my love …

SFC: Should one be inoculated against such soppy conditions like the smallpox?

… and you will be mine but only as long as the spider lives … Maybe your little spider was not a tegenaria at all but a saltigrade and jumped away.

O Leo save the spider, and she will build a web to catch all your bad dreams. Nature is the web where everything connects. But Uanito, I worry about him I wonder if he is developing at all. A *vecino* asked him when he would be six. On my next birthday he said I think. And the other day he wet his bed. I did not give out. I made little of it.

Leo: One of my most abiding memories of early school life was the smell of urine in the classroom. Hygiene was not good then. We have showers today of course. But in those days it was often straight from the wet bed and saturated pyjamas into school clothes …

The Rhymer
My mother and your mother were hanging out the clothes
my mother punched your mother right in the nose.
What colour was the blood?

… carrying the smell. No, no money. Always the way, money tight, morals loose, and the place reeked with it. I can still remember the initial soft indulgent warmth of the pissbed contrasting later with the bracing cold air of the raw morning. How hard it was to get up, stuck to the sheets. The whole day marred and marked as you carried the pong.

SFC: Do you smell it?

Reader: The piss?

SFC: The stench of putrefying humanity.

Jude: O and Leo your loneliness I reach out to. Where is the seed of the stallion to continue the line before it dies? The last sting, the moulting of the flower? Every living thing reaches for immortality …

JF (*caressing his chin with his finger and thumb trying to induce a thought*): With the technology now people are not deathtrained. They have not the depth of language, speak computese, think they have a right to be immortal …

The Seer of Suburbia: Death is the last taboo.

… I lift the paper to the light. I can see the leaf shimmer inside it. Tree, paper, pen, all merged. O Leo, can you really commune with your mother? What a wonderful thing. But are you sure it is not just an evil spirit tempting you? Be careful. I am posting you a little amulet to protect you. If there are good spirits, why then can there not be evil ones just as we have people good and bad? The evil person's spirit carries the contagion of its owner with it into the other world, just as the soul of the virtuous carries goodness with it. Goodness in a soul you may ask. Yes, goodness of disposition towards the living. Whereas the evil stirs the demon that lurks about trying to make you one with them in their misery. I hear a sound. No I am frightening myself; it is a dog barking in the night, afraid like all of us.

Leo: Crows with long sharp beaks pierced a little puppy dog which they had trapped between them, holding him firm and terrified as they bit chunks out of him. I tried to shoo them away but they were intent and snapped their beaks at me and I was forced to watch him diminish until they got to the eyes. They were the last to go.

O Leo, say it was not real …

Leo: If it passes through the Gate of Ivory it is false. If it passes through the Gate of Horn it is true. The eyebiter could be the witch that could rhyme us to death.

The Rhymer
Not I.

… You seem to be surrounded by a darkness. Is it to do with the climate? You must confront, probably the best thing to do, tackle it head on, make the unknown fears familiar, make them surface from their well and then by knowing them they may lose some of their terror. What is your fear, Leo? We are more than miserable wraiths wandering in the dark. You must tell me. Is it the fear of not existing anymore? Such a fear predates time. It is begot in the womb of generations before. It is a prebirth fear. It predates all culture. Why doesn't the dog bury its mate? Because he accepts the end, but we humans do not, never since the beginning of time. Some put their corpses in foetal positions to await rebirth, or place a coin in the mouth of the deceased to receive sustenance or to pay for the river crossing.

When I wander out of Sevilla through the *granjas* with Uanito I see death as a way of life, the death of the *toro* or the sheep or even of man or of the seasons, it is the way of things accepted. We should not try to deny death or sweep it under the carpet as if it did not exist, but when it strikes, it teases the emotions of the unprepared as happened to you with your *madre*. Nirvana can only be reached when desires for this world have been destroyed, but how to do that? *Es decir nunca. No es posible.* You with your Celtic blood will wish to go to the Isles of the Blessed. I hope to be there in the Beautiful Garden. We must suffer the Ten Hells first before we join the Stars, the Imperishable Ones. We must strip away the clothes of Ishtar and go naked into the other world ...

The Seer of Suburbia: What goes naked in the winter?

... Let us honeytongue the guard dog. Let us prepare for a good death with confession and unction. Do you know the five stages of dying? DABDA. Listen to the words of Jude for it was you who christened me. From the Spanish I translate: 'Heroes rush into death, cowards hide behind their hypochondria, wise men prepare their souls.'

But my fear, Leo is that of the infinite, fear of the same thing going on and on, never changing. What is the difference between being happy for a moment and happy for eternity? Is there a difference between the degrees of happiness? Similarly with sleep the eternal sleep or daily slumber. Except for time, the state is the same unconscious ...

The Seer of Suburbia: Have a rendezvous with your unconscious, but be sure to turn up.

Leo: When I sleep my 40,000 daily thoughts procreate.

... We suffer from hybris and hubris, we lack sebas for Gaia. Man is a contagion. He thinks he owns the earth. A scum rises that once used to vanish. But now all the scum of the earth comes back to show what a vile race we are ...

Reader: What is scum?

Pomofeminist Reader: The Society for cutting up men.

... thinking we can go on forever, we put jade in our orifices, bury some with the bread of the Eucharist, tombs have toilet facilities for visitors, eternal rest and perpetual light. Even when cremating some keep a finger to resurrect the whole body ...

Shem the Penman: Come forth Lazarus, and he came fifth.

... Separate the good souls from the bad souls. The thirty pieces of silver used to provide graves for strangers. But mortality must not intrude in this life of modern man. Banish the grave, they shout, let's have a fast burning.

I believe death is the beginning of our future to which we are being called. Do you accept death as the end? If so you need the rites. Persevere. Pray to Santa Lucia for enlightenment. Be wary of the Docetists and Adoptionists and Arian man wordmutterings ...

Reader: Sorry to disturb you, Jude, but how would you describe Leo?

... As one intensely aware with a burning sensitivity to all of life's mortalities.

SFC: He was regularly beaten for the sin of sensitivity.

... He is righthanded, leftfooted and rightfaced, more cognitive than musical. I gave his ear a ring—a charm so to speak—but he smells flowers that are not there. But enough of this eschatology, let's sing a song. Let's pluck a psalm and sing for joy. Cleanse me with hyssop, and I will be clean. Let those who can sing, sing forth, bring on the orchestra, liven up the proceedings, do the sensuous tango, sweep him off his feet, sweep time under the mat for a moment, sweep away the leaves of yesteryear, put your hand in the hand of the man who calmed the sea; surely the righteous still are rewarded; surely there is a god who judges the earth.

O Leo, I am as heavy as you. It is you who are making me like this. What a heavy feeling under a thunderous weather. May have to go to the *médico*. I was walking with Uanito and I asked him what colours he saw: orange and blue and red and green and yellow and all the colours of the rainbow and you, Mamá, what colour? Grey, just grey …

Leo: Like Ireland.

… Yes maybe I am a little homesick for that land.

Hey Jude. Remember to let me in to your heart and then you can start to feel better. Your leaf will not wither. O nearly forgot, happy birthday. What did you do between your Birth cert and your Death cert? Fill in the gap. Your age, your age of Christ draws near. Rumblings of empires crumbling. Pregnant woman burned alive, your birthday her deathday. The tormented history of humanity. Why can't they solve their problems with a game of chess?

The alarm rings. Let it ring itself out. Lil called. I awoke in the middle of the morning. I couldn't get up for love or money. She … fot the agonal angiogram revealed a diminished blood circulation tried to work a strong wind opened the door and ruffled my leaves … blowing the trees into hairstyles …

The Seer of Suburbia: Saw a leaf being given a whoosh up the windowpane by the wind.

. . .I feel Mam is coming in. I must prepare for her visit. It is Mam, Jude, I am sure of it. She said goodbye, love, so terminally on the phone four hours before her death, a premonition. I heard the thunder roar but missed the lightning. If only I had known, a final farewell denied. No touch or embrace. My next sight of her in the window, silent trapped, but her force is within me. One generation yields to the next. The Virgin waterbottle I hold to my chest when I feel all the world is going to burst, and a calmness descends upon me from her world.

All the wandering spirits, cold echoes with hollow and sad tones. What is it I fear? It is the fear or rather the terror of being wiped off the earth like crumbs from a table, disposed of and never to be seen or heard of again. I had a dream, Mam. In my dream I see a stick. One end marked A, the other end B. On one side an arrow points from A to B. On the other side another arrow points from B to A. What does it mean?

A is your birth and B is your death. You travel from birth to death and back to birth again.

But why the stick?

The stick is the tree you carry on the way.

Mammy, Daddy, Uncle Dick, went to London on a stick. O yes the stick broke. Hearing you recite that used to make me sad. I still wear that Aran sweater you knitted for me. It's charmed. To keep the cold at bay. A little tear, a little unravelling appeared at the neck, eleven years old now, and Lil promptly stitched it …

JF: A funny accident can leave you in stitches.

… Mam, can you hear me? Lost her again. I feel as cold as the moon. A spider lies dead on the windowledge upside down, crablike. What killed it? Hardly old age. Some lost soul. Will I be reborn and come back as a spider or a horse … ?

O Leo, I hear you. I hope the dead spider is not an omen. The widow who lives near *mi madre* has a dog and she thinks it is her husband reincarnated. She talks to him and walks with him every evening in the *Jardines de María Luisa.*

… O to have the snake's two penises. Handy if one becomes worn out …

The Seer of Suburbia: You can be jailed for where you put your penis.

The Rhymer
Don't go with another man's wife,
you'll regret it all your life.
Go with a prostitute instead,
she only costs a loaf of bread.

... Supine by day, active by night, clinophobia getting worse. You asked me was I reading much, Jude. I find it hard to get involved in the dream of another with my own dream ongoing—a bookish chameleon, I become what I read. Besides eyelids inflamed ...

Visitor: Are you JF? I've come from America to meet you.

JF: Which America?

V: The North of course.

JF: You are off course.

...Urindefecmasticmasturmenstrucopulate–our mortal realisations. How many times, how many more pisses? Which piss will be our last ... ?

JF: The fragrant piss hopefully after the asparagus.

... Like each breath they are all numbered, every hair on your head is numbered in the *Lunatic Fringe* barbers on Liffey Street, and each one used can never be reclaimed bringing us ever closer all the time, all the time, and all the time thinking and realising that everything is youknowwhat. It takes a lifetime to examine a life. But it is easier for you, Jude. You are a follower of the acronymous INRI: IESUS NAZARENUS REX IUDAEORUM. Ello Inri. . .

The Rhymer
About faith and hope they still don't agree,
but what really matters is charity.

... I still don't know the ropes. The hangman will show me.

Hangman: I will show you the ropes but I must wear a mask and a wooden bowl …

SYC: He's so wooden he has splinters.

… on my back to fend off the blows of the Abolitionists. I will give you a calfbound volume of the Book of the Dead (bound to be a collector's item), all instructions and directions therein on how to deal with the Ten Hells. Money back if not … Osiris will be there to welcome you and show you the way.

I hear, Jude, the sound of the night wind like an indrawn breath. I feel the warm radiator and think of the homeless girl being raped in a cardboard box in a city lane …

Jude: What girl, Leo? What lane? Could it be … ?

The Rhymer
Clear off, perform no cruel rape
on such a green, unripe grape.

… Just a homeless girl. It was on the news. She lived in a cardboard box got from Dunnes Stores. The mark branded on the box. And now I prepare for bed pressing air from the hot water bottle, same sound as from the anus. Our bodies are just bits of technology. A light shines from a gap in the door. What goes on inside? Yellow light, open door dazzling shines inner sanctum *gile na gile* brightness of brightness only saw I as I wandered. I was going into an *aisling*. I followed the light. It brought me to a beautiful garden with flowers and shrubs of many colours and seductive fragrance. The sun shone so warm and welcomingly I lay on the grass and removed my shirt. There was nobody in this Eden but the sweet singing birds …

JF: You think the birds sing for our amusement?

… so I made bold, feeling so liberated to dress as Adam …

JF: Would you Adam and Eve it?

… or the birds of the air, luxuriating in such warmth as one does in a steaming bath. I lay back and let the sun do its work on me …

Reader: He's in his leather.

… A drowsiness came upon me and I felt my mind deliquesce into softness and compliance under the gaze of the sungod. In the blurred sunlight a beautiful girl appeared with long brown hair down to her *com seang singil álainn*. She removed her white blouse to reveal two snowy breasts of perfect symmetry. She gave me a comehither look and pouted her lips and her eyes burned with desire. She was the beauty I had seen in the oriel window …

Reader: A teasemaid.

… Slowly she pushed down the figurehugging navy skirt to reveal curves and hips and exquisitely proportioned thighs. Phal leapt up—I could not contain him. I was about to cover him when she shook her head, and I thought how pleasurable it was for her to eye Phal in his greater glory. He began to throb as her eyes burned into his. He increased more and more and he became so bulging that pain blended with the pleasure …

SYC: Somewhat epicurean. Pleasure preferable to pain, but too much pleasure leads to pain.

… She began to dance to a silent music and she worked herself into an ecstatic state. I made to get up. Phal wished to jump into her, but I felt myself pinned to the ground by some invisible force. I was about to autostimulate when she turned towards me and shook her head again. She knelt as if in adoration of Phal and without touching she drew the seed by drawing her hands sinuously upwards in a smooth and gentle release. Both of us watched the fluid flow from the eye of Phal as if it were a separate member—autocephalous is that the word? My head, as if it were severed from my body, withheld her bowing reverently to Phal, who was in his element with delight and showed no sign of shrinking. As her face neared my belly, a long tongue lashed out as would a snake's and licked with relish my belly clean of all fluid. She then placed a bowl of water beneath Phal, and I observed the level go down as Phal drank through his eye. Phal winked up at me—thirsty work. She then produced apple blossoms and adorned Phal with them. She remained kneeling, and bowed as if in prayer.

'Who are you, beautiful sylph?' I asked.

'I am Fódhla,' she said and *i bpreapadh na súl* she was gone.

SFC: Lambkin's disgorging on environmentallyfriendly paper.

Reader: He sighed for the love of a lady.

SFC: Out of touch, the *aisling* revealed that.

Stayed at home this workday. Outer shell damaged; carapace needs healing. One needs a secret life to survive the public one. There are some who say I suffer from paranoia but they are the enviers, the whisperers and the watchers. They find a speck in someone's eye but fail to see the plank in their own eyes. O you know the way it is in this septic isle of Dot? Was reported for a few lates and also for leaving work a little early on an occasion …

Reader: Was it JLA who reported him?

The Rhymer
Tell tall tattler
buy a penny rattler

Reader: Hadn't Leo ticked him off from time to time especially about his nose picking?

JF: Like his uncle that junior fellow ran with the hare and hunted with the hound; wore Irish buttons on an English shirt until the colours ran.

… O to have someone to talk to me …

JF: He left work early to meet the wandering lady.

… Lil is not mute; she acts mute. On the phone today she spoke eagerly and fluently to her bridge friend Mildred like one who hadn't spoken for a lifetime; would turn anyone off the way she goes on. While at night she let's me go on and on and sleeps or pretends to, acting indifferently to a tormented soul. What is it like to have Mother gone? Support link no more, a ship unmoored from the harbour, from the safe haven, alone now at sea. How feelings fluctuate from moment to moment of people nervously alone.

I must leave off. I hope you can sleep, Jude. It has escaped me these last three nights except for the short intermittent doze which leaves me more fatigued. Why aren't our todays like yesterdays?

Jude: O Leo, the mem or o ow e was sieved surged back on me ike a food.

SFC: The captain is having trouble with his privates.

SYC: SFC judges people by their grammatical accuracy.

Reader: The letters have gone skewways, and Jude doesn't even appear to know. Maybe it has to do with emotional levels. What's Mr Francis doing?

SYC: He's trying to stop the spelling bee from buzzing in his head.

Jude: You carry fire against your chest and walk forever on hot coals in the ways of perception …

Reader: She's back to herself.

… but we must have the Lord not only on our lips but also in our hearts. Seek the Lord while he is still to be found. If he be with you, no enemy can hurt you. You cry in the wilderness if you cast him away, to whom will you turn? I know you say you wish to explore life in an unfettered way. Your voice is one crying from the want of a love which perhaps no human being can satisfy. You must carry the tree your *madre* mentioned. Nothing can be achieved without the tree. *Nuestro Señor* will pull you out of the pit and will teach you a new song. Don't lose *la humilidad*. Perhaps you believe you are more than a puff of wind or more than a passing shadow. I think that is part of your problem, Leo …

I want to believe, Jude, in what you believe because I believe in you. But Heaven and Hell are only alliterative words.

... Accept, acquiesce, flow with the current, sway with the breeze and all of life's forces. You mention sleepless nights. Uanito is also restless and troubled. He still wets the bed most nights now and hides his pyjamas. He has mares too. I went to him in the middle of the night once, and he was spitting on the bed saying there were 'things' there. *Cosas.* What *cosas*? And eventually I got him to sleep and looked over him and wondered while he slept who would attack, for even in Sevilla I do not feel secure.

And Leo, as regards Lil, you cannot make her talk. Speech is not given to all. The poet, the judge, the chronicler, to these speech has been given ...

SYC: And to the malcontented.

... But you can talk to your spirit, commune with her, she will answer you. Your *madre* also, for maybe you are right, maybe it is she, and she will give you counsel. You demand responses in your nocturnal quests. Silence fills you with despair. It is that very silence you need to work on to fill you with wisdom. Who loves death? ...

The Seer of Suburbia: Death is not the in thing but the coming thing.

... He who hates wisdom. Read more of the white language. Do you know the seven things the Lord hates? The temple will crumble. *Festina lente.* The serpent of the desert must be lifted up. *Basta.*

Leo: I smell wood smoke in the distance.

Jude: O Leo, do you remember that happy day when we cycled to *Gleann Dubh*?

Leo: Past is gone bodily yes nothing visible ...

Reader: What is your attitude to Jude now, Leo, in hindsight I mean?

... She is bigger than the attributes of her sex. She is a giant of humanity, a saint without a halo ...

Reader: Thank you.

... but the memories, ah yes, is there a limit to them? How many can the mind store? When its stock is full, it erases some I suppose. Not always the oldest. Sometimes the middle ones, yes. The ones that no longer haunt ...

O Leo.

... I lifted a book from my shelf. Leafing through it somewhere near the middle I found a red stain wine yes down the bottom left corner. I remember where I was when I was reading that book. I was in a restaurant in the city, the Paradiso.

Yes, I remember it in Westmoreland Street. It was the night before ...

It is no more, the restaurant I mean. It is just that in those days I went everywhere with a book.

In case I bored you.

And my bicycle. Any spare moment I got.

When I went to the *retrete* you opened a page.

Yes. I would read a page or a half page or even a few lines to resonate or ponder over during an empty moment.

And I came back and spilled the wine on your book.

Was it on purpose?

I was jealous of the book.

It was just me, Jude. It was not meant to be offensive. I must keep the mind ticking over all the time like the heart.

The heart?

Yes.

Do you remember the following day?

How could I forget it? I remember the cold stirring of spring as we cycled, the sleetfall, the sheltering under a bridge of faulty mortar, stumbling into a river the cold, etherised by our *joie de vivre*. The push up the mountain ...

SFC: An aberration of the landscape.

… the dry tinderleaved wood of the glen. The pine forests sweeping the mountain, and you wondering at trees so tall, how the water gets up so high to irrigate the highest branches. But it keeps coming back, the mountain, the numbed fingers as we lit the kindle seeking each other's bodies for warmth, and I had jamón and Rioja wine and you had the poetry book …

The snowy poems of Pasternak.

… And you told me you saw a girl with flowers in her hair. Her hair was hibiscus and when she walked she rustled like leaves and vanished into the forest …

But I did not see the girl.

… Perhaps not, but I believed you did and we heard the sounds of the forest echoing. You lifted up my mind to the beauty of sound and feelings of love. You taught me new words as we sat close together listening to the crackling of the fire and all the mountain covered in white. You said we were the babes in the woods.

But the night, *la noche*. O Leo, who said to remember is to admit loss and prepare for death? But it keeps coming back. Maybe by communicating with you we can purge this affliction once and for all. We had returned to Crichton's house knowing he was away. Remember he had made it clear to us that he would not be in that night …

Yes, he reminded us more than once that he would be out, that he had to see someone. Could it have been Lil he was going to see?

… It was the night after I had rebuffed him. He was coming on to me all mauly and sloppy. I think he thought he could do to me what you told me later he did to the young females behind the library stacks. I thought he would be angry with me. I told him that I was seeing you the following day, but he said nothing and turned away. We thought we had the house all to ourselves, remember? But others must have known too. The heat and the wine had us flushed in our embrace, and then it happened, the bursting through the doors:

three dark devils from *el infierno*. And they ripped the clothing off me and they jeered and they started to pound and pummel you. And they looked towards the door for what I do not know. Did they fear someone was coming in and a shadow appeared and a voice through a mask issued an instruction and they grabbed me by the hair and put me on all fours and pushed you into my back. 'Remember the dog,' the strange guttural voice exhorted from behind the mask. 'Do it, do it,' and they butted you and one of them had a knife which he held to my throat until they forced you, their lascivious eyes penetrating like lasers. O that Uanito had not come from such barbarity! I pray so hard at night that such a deed could have been false, but knowing that it wasn't, we must carry it with us like the tree. All that is left is a legacy of fear, a jump, a start at every knock. Where are those creatures now, Leo? Were they ever caught? Maybe they have fallen into their own pit and got tangled in their own nets. On how many others have they inflicted the same? All must be suffered for Him. My bones shake at the thought of it, but we must sustain the heat of the warfare to attain the palm of the blessed. It is arrogant to think that we can always have spiritual consolation when we please. Will romantic love ever come back again? Our world is a great dustbin reaching up to the sky. How strong or weak are we? We need His hand to kill the escaping monster. We will be mocked by the spiritless ones, but they will be bound with eternal chains and hurled into darkness.

O that I lost you. But I was confused and did not know what to do after the novenas failed. I did not want you to disbelieve. Perhaps that was as important as you finding out. And then you had married. Did you marry out of loneliness or was it something more? Was it love? Did you love your new woman? …

JF: They got married to increase their dung quota.

Reader: What?

JF: The woman had 20,000 kilo of dung and didn't know what to do.

… Not that I blame you, but I never felt like that. I didn't trust any man, not after what happened. And besides I always hoped that you would come back even though I was the one who took flight. That you would find me. O you were vain I know, you always invited people to look at you, an Adonis with a touch of Narcissus, to see the rise and fall of your Adam's apple. Without love there is no life unless you call hatred and spite life. I transferred all my love to Uanito, gave him your share so he got double helpings. O Leo, you said I was dark and beautiful, you said you would adorn me with a chain of gold. I went away but my heart went wandering in search of you, and the more I searched the more something inside started to grow. It filled me with terror. How I longed to have you with me to share in my *tribulación*. Even in sleeping my heart ticked in vigil. I dreamed that I would hear you knock and I trembled for love, but although that is all spent now, your words even on paper still fill me with longing. You ask if I would commit suttee for you. How do you ask?

An offspring born of evil, who was I to share this dark secret with? Not with my parents, for such a revelation would surely have destroyed them. What did I tell them? When I arrived back to Sevilla I told them I had been careless and had made love to an Irish boy who did not love me and went away. There had been some suspicious looks from neighbours, but although there might have been murmuring behind my back nothing was ever said outright. . .

JF: Who can get pregnant while already pregnant?

… And *mis padres* did not berate me but did all they could for me and took me under their wing as if I were a returned fledgling. But a returned fledgling is never happy, and all the time I felt their hesitation like there was a sense of awkwardness and mystification there. They did not know their daughter anymore …

JF: A hare.

... And eventually I moved out but they agreed to mind the baby during my teaching hours, and when I would return with Uanito in the evenings to my solitary *piso* the Book of Books became my only consolation. I could not trust any human being. O this is a most morose letter, Leo, an outpouring of grief, an expression of loss of what could have been, and now to know that you seek me when it is too late. And as regards Lil, perhaps you expect too much of her, but I know the cravings of your soul, all those things we used to discuss so freely in restaurants and pubs and even in Crichton's house. Had he been eavesdropping. Why do I say that? I don't know, just an intimation, like he was always watching me in the house, undressing me with his eyes, but in those days we did not make an issue of such behaviour and I passed it off, to use an idiom, as par for the course. But we didn't care, did we Leo, about him? We had too much of ourselves to occupy us. The shared emotions we had, the dreams, the hopes, what you hoped for ...

[What I hoped for then? I don't know what I hoped for then. Maybe I was too busy enjoying the present.]

... Your hopes were exemplified by the typical braggadocio of young men. And there were no mares then. And that can be our spiritual bond now to break down that wall of silence that suffocates you. We can keep such a bond without hurting anybody. We must never hurt, no matter what. *Mi león, estoy fatigada.* The Spanish comes out of me when I am tired. What a *persona* this letter had. Look at the time, *la madrugada.* Will I be able to rise for Uanito and for school? Yet I feel as a result less anxious, having written you thus. I turn my pen slightly, and my letter becomes a bird to fly to you through the great sky high above all the things of the world.

Jude, O Jude, how you suffered! The affliction we share. But more you than I. So much more you. I must see you both. Look after Uanito. Don't let him endure the agony of the night. The fear of burglary and much more is very real; it's universal. Always check the mortise lock; that's the important one. Lock dead; keep out keep in, keeper of keys. I know the white language is important to you, a source of solace, but really you're touching on bibliolatry. You know the Bible ear to ear, still if it is a comfort to you, who am I to judge? You chide me on my religious duplicity, but I have no brand loyalty. The trouble with religion is that it causes certainty, and certainty is a refuge, a comfort to some, but I want to explore freely without chains or cloister or bells …

Reader: Is he not a member still?

JF: He's dismembered now.

The Seer of Suburbia: Rebel against the bell. Repeal its note.

… Does the sun not shine brighter than any chalice? God surely is the animus of the woods, not of the institution. Is religion not a construct of fear? I am just a voyager who wants to travel in a light ship. My eyelids weigh heavily in the library. If to live the day were a game I would give it a walkover.

Reader: Are you very depressed?

About sixty hectopascals below normal. No money till payday to buy drink to go to the pub called Lourdes for the cure. O to be the roundworm who produces and drinks his own alcohol when troubled …

JF: The froth from his pint showed up in his piss.

… I have become horny …

JF: Badger's horns or red herrings.

Reader: He must be dying. He wants to copulate.

JF: Dying is damned inconvenient.

… I mean my skin. Dead cells changed into horn, thirty layers of horn cells. O to slough the skin. Put off the Old Man and reach a higher state. Wake up, man. Must earn the bread. The cat's skin, the granny's doorstep. File check: check *Dinny of the Doorstep*, file, index, reshelve, alphabetically I play all the ABC, numerically, deweyed. What is that big tome doing there? Bigger books suffocating the little ones, same everywhere …

JF: The people buried their books in the ground for safekeeping. Good books smell of the earth.

… Where will I find something on Great Britain? demanded an affected West Brit female voice who had arrived selfpropelled on her bicycle. Britain Great. What other country calls itself great? *An Bhreatain Mhór*, 942. Down the line, the end of empires. Accents speak louder than words. Feeling a great hunger. Mr Kavanagh felt it. Erysichthon felt it so strongly he destroyed himself by consuming his own flesh. Bite into yourself a little a day like the monk with the spade and the earth. If nothing else, rub your severed limbs. A different kind of hunger, seeking within what is lacking without.

I agree, Jude, about spite and hatred—they are vile things. Abraham set out for a country. They are like echoes in the mind, faint sounds from a distant childhood which fill me with fear. Am I reneging on … ? As He said this He was lifted up. You will not be expecting me to write anything about times and seasons, sons of light, sons of the day, not of the night, not of the darkness. On the sixth day god created Man, a nice isle once part of the archbisoprick of Dublin. I touch the closed eyeball. Soft pulpy octopuslike, no different, shudder the thought when the pulp is pulped down we are all pieces of jelly …

JF: Depression is due to a confusion of the mind.

… Or could it be the reverse, too much clarity, too much insight?

JF: It's a rust wearing down iron.

SYC: I think it is banished love.

Reader: What is your greatest fear, Leo?

That I will pass away unnoticed like a worm of the earth, and that the memory of me will die.

Reader: What do you regret?

That I never got the chance to cradle my mother into death. And my son now that I have, I regret not seeing him growing up.

Reader: What do you miss?

I miss the sound of Dog's nails scraping at my bedroom door. No matter, it has to be the mind, insatiable, hunger and thirst and endless questioning, the difference from instinct, but then that's just a theory. We develop all our theories in the security of our little rooms and then go out to the world and have them all shattered. Retreat again, regroup, build up.

Reader: How do you mean?

I mean you could have a theory about goodness, or someone being good, only to be knocked down by a word from his mouth.

Reader: A word can knock you down?

Yes, a word with venom in it.

The Seer of Suburbia: Who is he when he's at home?

JF: They are only at home on the Irish Sea.

The Seer of Suburbia: Who?

JF: The Anglo-Irish.

Reader: Are there people out to do you in?

It depends, reader, on the angle of your gaze. Whose eye are you looking through? Like the painting there on the library wall, the lion becomes the lamb.

St Valentine's night, on computer now, pick your lover from an urn. How many cards of romance will the post deliver today? More provocative every year. Heartshaped bikini bottom and Cadbury's chocs and candlelight just for two, you and the lover, leave the spouse at home. Love will pass faster than a weaver's shuttle. Love is sweet, a frailty, all the things that love is supposed to be. But what is its substance? What is it one can hold onto and say this is love? …

Phal: Well, now.

… It is not a moral or religious thing although the beloved is sometimes virtuous, but then not always. How many have fallen in love with demons? But was that love? More an infatuation perhaps. Who knows what sparks the emotions of another? Then is love an emotion? And love of a dead one hardly passion. Perhaps selflessness is its nearest synonym, positioning another's life above one's own.

But what of the thinker, the artist, the writer? Can he only be loved and not love, or perhaps love in a small way as his art takes dominance? …

JF: I walk the line between fame and oblivion.

… Or maybe it's in the fate of things for a woman to be more selfless. Some women, some men, who can say? Or one could say, if not appearing haughty, that if one had a talent the selfless one serves the talented one. But we all have different talents. Which talent is more important than another? Some will say art. Some will say the welfare of others. Who is to judge? A life created out of life, or a life itself lived in its mundane minutiae? …

SFC: An unlived life is not worth examining.

… But what of the spirit of longing? Of that intransigent seeking after a nebulous something? It may not be as strong a desire in everyone. To lock oneself up for hours on end on a sunny day.

Reader: Why are you on your own when you don't have to be?

To be, to snatch from the moon …

JF: He tries to snatch from life more than it can give.

… Otherwise we are no different from the ant or the beetle or the flower or the leaf to fade unknown into a dung heap. Who could even say we were here at all?

Reader: That is being imperious. You are saying you are more important than others.

On the contrary, it is a humility, a quest to examine one's existence. We all have free will to choose whichever course we wish. It is just that sometimes the quest can be lonely but also selfish. There are so many chores that could be attended to. I suppose it all depends on whether or not one is true to oneself …

JF: Being true to oneself may make you false to others.

… Judith, you are being hidden away. Jude, Judith, grandchild of ox, records with the iron tool in Judea. No one will spread terror in the days of Judith. A curse on men who trust in man? Strain your wall eye and eye tooth to remember the twelve prophets. Malachy, a prophet too, foresaw Pope John as *pastor et nauta*, and three antichrists still to come predicting the world will end. To know where it ends one has to know where it starts. Are we moving away from heaven or towards it? Will we be reabsorbed in the whateveritis? I sometimes try to balance my mind on a razor's edge, between sleep and wakefulness. Do you dream of the future? And time, what is it? Seven o'clock, ten o'clock, one cloud to darkness, one cloud to light. On the train am I moving or is it the houses … ?

JF: Poets should not man trains; they might dash off their lines.

… Is it the same question with time and us? Is the story of the world already written? And the deeper we go in, the less of self we find. We are floating, Jude. Am I experiencing the other person of myself? The female in all of us. Trying to reach *anima mundi*. Leave the ego behind …

JF: When the ego is imprisoned in isolation, the world of the unconscious lurking in the shadows may furnish assistance.

… Tell them to prepare earth and water. I feel ravaged like Put and Lud. And it came to pass and it came. Tired words. Thoughts come unfiltered into my mind without thanking me. The white language is hidden away by the dogcollared ones …

JF: Can you divine it? Let us examine the liver of the animal sacrificed.

… The word is hidden in the book. The book is locked in a sacred sanctum …

Reader: That is what is wrong with us today. We have separated the sacred and the secular.

… Sorry Jude, I was nodding off in the land of Nod …

SYC: Homer sometimes nods.

JF: Where can you get something for nodding?

... I must do penance. I have kept the six hundred and thirteen commandments. I will fast on Ramadan, Yom Kippur, Lent, I will avoid the seven deadly sins. I will court the seven virtues. Take four then three that way lies luck, then take them together, luckier still. I will read Ibrahim and Musa, same story in the Koran. Neither a butcher nor a soldier will I be ...

Butcher: I'm a butcher but I don't mince my words.

JF: An auction.

... I will sweep the path lest I trod on the insects. I will rejoice and be glad. *Sonas.*

JF: *Sonas* means happiness, he said with sadness in his voice.

Reader: Why are you virtuous, Leo?

For a peaceful life. I will study the seven champions of Christendom. I will not worship gods made with hands. I will set the breakfast table the night before for the morning after to get a headstart on the day. I hear music.

Reader: Is music important to you?

To calm the savage ... kill care, die on the strain, I like the instrumental stuff; words wear out ...

Reader: And what music does Mr Francis listen to?

SFC: A High Fidelity record of an infidelity.

JF: Marriage forces you on mono when life is on stereo.

Pomomisandrist: I hate you, JF.

JF: Excuse me, did you pay for advertising space?

Pomomisandrist: I could shoot you and Crichton and Lambkin too.

JF: The *I* which writes the text is never more than a paper *I*. The reader collaborates. Only the critic executes.

Jude: Who was that, Leo?

A person more concerned with gender than with art.

Reader: Giving Mr Francis a hard time.
SFC: I wouldn't ride her even if she had pedals.
JF: If you take men from women you're left with wo.
SYC: Trying to drive him into a culdesac.

The Rhymer
Friends forgotten
cupboards bare
feeling rotten
going nowhere
all for art
life denied
not so smart
alone you cried.

*

I RETURN TO WOUNDED HOUSE AS THE WIND RATTLES THE chains and with a sticking plaster now on its doorbell, more wounded I than before I set out. I brush against the garden wall and feel its security. Why do I consciously lock the locks on the front door knowing I am checking them? …

JF: There came a knock at the Rory O'Moore which made his raspberry beat.

… A cognitive checking, and then check them again as though I hadn't checked them at all. I opened the door. Yes? says the woman. You knocked, I say. You opened, she says.

Tired. Lil more tired. Anybody there? said the traveller. No response. She would sooner cream one of her bridge tarts than she would … ah well inside, Phal suffered so many recriminations he diminished in size and felt as tiny as the penis worm.

What time is it? Seven minutes to seven, seven minutes to go before facing the seven trials of the day. I think of the man getting up from his bed of cold slab and with dazed eyes facing the cold dawn. Another quest for a few shillings to buy a temporary oblivion. Do the heaven's corporal works of sergeant mercy. Mat tells us to visit the sick, hungry and thirsty, to shed ourselves fatherless (does that refer to Uanito?) and bury our dead. But will we rise again like the seven sleepers of Ephesus?

Glans sore, pour cold jets over tumescence. Turns purple. Flush away smegma. Rough handling, as rough as our national handlers. Need a spin doctor. It started with pains in … never mind, a new day. I set out in the morning like primitive man searching for nourishing berries. I seek illuminations but sometimes return with fruitless twigs …

JF: If you collect your own twigs you heat yourself twice.

SYC: Leo is a gleaner.

… Car broken down …

JF: Hadn't enough hay to fuel his mode of transport?

… O the machine. Bus and walk …

JF: He's on the bus. I'm on the wagon. The words of the newspaper danced before his eyes in flashes of light and shadow like a movie projector in black and white as the bus bounded along the road.

… goosestepping it out now between downpours, trying to outwit the elements. To be fleetfooted doesn't mean to be strong or courageous. How easy to frighten the deer or the hare or the horse or the flatfooted human, running away from his own fear. What a feat on feet. See the flashdancer in the city street. Early in the morning for that.

Passing church, salute two fingers for cub, three for scout, say a prayer J, M and J, I love you, save souls. Better believe it. You can talk to the above in abbreviated form, no need to be longwinded with someone allknowing …

Reader: Why is abbreviation such a long word?

… Woman all wired up looking like she could selfdestruct at bus stop on her way to *lár na cathaoireach*, the centre of the chair. I know that look, the look of a havenot. Shrivelled man with rubbish van struggling to remove a weed from the bottom of a wall. Who will thank him? What goes on behind the wall? Bluecoated and bluehatted men and women in serried ranks carrying trays. Slavery still exists. Wills subject for the bread.

Reader: What do you see?

I see a man pissing against a tree, no different from a dog really, leg cocked. What a strange fascination a tree has. Did you see who passed by? I whiffed. Nice scent off. Yes a nice bit of fluff, a *cicciolina* with fork earrings, enough to give you the musth. A glance accustomed to no glance back. Did she look back? Too busy being admired in her undulating walk. Could cause an accident. The eternal in some women leads me on …

Butcher: Got to sell the sizzle if you want them to buy the steak.

… She stopped, a statue looking for a pedestal. Here's Gunther, *puer aeternus*. Hello Gunther. How are you?

Gameball, he says with his bonecrushing handshake.

Nice tan.

You need a decent tan before you go pulling.

You travelled throughout Europe. I travelled throughout my life. Catch the dust before it falls, says Gunther in his dayglow jacket. That's what I always say, your only man. The oul dear don't you know she cleans the windows with her knickers on her head to keep the dust off of her hair. Does she get her knickers in a twist, Gunt? Sorry if you don't mind my saying that is very eh very eh very … Very what? What? O thanks, says Gunther. And how is the blister? I say. I used to date that umbrella girl.

I don't know, he says I haven't seen her since she got her last freckle …

The Rhymer
Keep away from girls, me boy
they only make you cry.

... Must be on my way, Gunther. I'll leave you to look after your epidermis. Plenty of aftersun. I'm on presun myself, your only man. My coat needs a rivet. *Roimh* a thing, says Gunther removing his glove to bite his nail. Before this a button was your only man. No point in confiding in you, you Job's comforter. Don't take your complaint to him who is unsympathetic, manmade trouble. Friend of Crichton, wouldn't trust him as far as I'd throw him ...

Reader: I wonder what Crichton has hidden in his cupboard.

JF: Being tone deaf as SFC he writes commentaries on the symphonies of others. In his cupboard among the skeletons are incipient poems, failed novels, a play diddle ay die.

... On my way Gunther recedes into the past. I seek the future to link with the past to form the eternal present.

Søren Kierkegaard (*on a flying visit*): Life can only be understood backwards, but it must be lived forwards.

Reader: Are your birds always wingless, Leo?

Depends on the speed. If you can achieve speed faster than the speed of light then you can overtake your past ...

JF: We are never given enough light to illuminate our darkness.

... On my way, am I moving away or moving towards? Where is the Banyan Tree? Can you predict like Melancholy Burton your death's date? Funny how some people die. Bacon stuffed with a cold died stuffing snow into a fowl to see would it keep. A toothpick was supposed to have killed Agathocles and how many more? I have a tinkling in my ear like a deathbell, hope no friend has died. Death is an angel.

Reader: Put that on the list.

No, Azrael the archangel, let it stand. What was I going to say? What is death? Death is impossible, a sham, a sleep, a diminution, a door, the storm's end. What was the weather forecast today? Will it stay dry? Will it to stay dry. The forecast came as a docket from a vending machine. Rain sleet hail, snow in high places, highvelocity winds, and the good news: no fog before lunch. When do you have lunch? Different times for different people these days …

JF: Two timers have two lunches but usually suffer from indigestion.

… The meteorologists are going on strike. There will be no weather. We won't be able to hear about the rain, but then we are all meteorologists in the land of Dot. What's the state of the world? All the isms will have to go. When will man become wise? Zophar so good. Soap will not wash away. Useless as ashes, crumble like clay or a motheaten coat. When wild donkeys are born tame. No hope for man cut down, unlike a tree. Return to Leviathan. Still, hope from the sea, none from the grave.

Jude: Except for your mother.

Yes, perhaps, I don't know.

Reader: Your life, what is it?

A breath a jest a pill a disease an inn a fury a winged thing. I killed an insect today (forgot to sweep the leaves). Don't tell the Jainists. Just like a flea hopping about near the bread. What's that song on the radio? We're off to see the wizard, the wonderful wizard of Oz. Long time since I heard that. Remember Mam, the luxurious cinema in Calm Down Street, by the side of which ran rivers of blood, slaughterhouse nearby, still hear the eerie cries of animals wailing into another world. Any premonition? See it in the eyes of some of them. Shed door open tempting in the rain but cat won't enter, sees the lock. Somewhere over the rainbow way up high there's a land that I heard of once in a lullaby …

JF: The Bay of Rainbows on the moon.

… More humane and hygienic now, the slaughtering that is, quick shot into oblivion. Often thought myself, firing squad rifle with bullets quick way to go, no lingering (Mam's wish), what Wolfe Tone wanted, shame in the rope, wouldn't trust it. Couldn't hang John Lee, three times tried, warped wood. Life imprisonment instead. What was in his mind those three times coming in and out of death like that? Rope burn, dangle in pain …

Reader: What is that you have dangling there?

JF: Why sir, a tie.

… and ignominy, a spectacle. Throw apples. Fruit vendors gather round to see the show. No pantomimes then. The guillotine another show, shame in that too: kneeling down head in basket. Lethal injections don't always work. The Greeks would give hemlock to full citizens to finish off the job themselves. Sock it to poor Socrates. Don't waste the poison. The school bully forced me to lick the poisoned berry.

Reader: Was it Crichton?

No, but his accomplice, put up to it by Crichton in his malfeasance …

JF: The *púca* spat poison on the wild berry.

Jude: The unicorn's horn neutralises poison.

… The ancients would crush criminals to death on a wheel rolling through streets. If you killed your father in Roma they'd put you in a sack with a cock and a viper and a dog for company and drown all four. Hanged, drawn and quartered many an Irishman's lot, the British way, hang, take down still alive, watch your own disembowelment before you are beheaded and have a ringside view as the rest of you is cut into four pieces, nice sirloin. It's gas, the Jews knew all about that. Horrible memories of the first anaesthetic. Four I was then tonsils alone with asthma in a dark world of terror, the hospital in Dublin with the name of another county. How more like many me? …

JF: Mark which death you prefer. It will only take a tick.

… Put the light out immediately. Don't leave it to drag on on a dim burner. Our steps go forward, but we are walking back to the secure world of the matrix. What were we like in there? Floating with a tail like a fish. As happy as the day is long. Saw a fish in an aquarium swimming to and fro and approaching the glass to put the apotropaic eye on you. Magnified glass distorts, creates its own world, binoculars even spectacles see as through a glass, up and down, back and forth reinventing itself every day because it has no memory, never gets bored, concentration span of two seconds only, so that when they get to one end, they forget what they saw at the other and a new world of exploration opens for them at each turn.

Reader: Where is Mr Francis now? Is he vertical or horizontal?

Redressing. Walking with his head sideways in thought. Shunted from pillar to post. Ah well, back to the day. Death is a privilege. All coming from the one tree the death of one should diminish thee. Toora toora loora toora loora lay toora loora loora, it's an Irish lullaby and sleep would come. Not busy in the library today, able to dream a little. Hush now, don't you cry. A little boy being put to bed by his mother: Fee fi fo fum I smell the blood of an Irishman …

The Rhymer
Thoughts on childhood willingly he did share
and sometimes he'd remember things that weren't there.

JF: It's not the thoughts he remembers but the thoughtfulness or not of others.

… There was a little man and he had a little gun and up the chimney he did run with a bellyful of fat and an old tall hat and a pancake tied to his bum bum bum. Scribbles scrobbles wiggles woggles ah yes entering the hippocampus, the wood smoke brought back the childhood memory of Scouting days on the Hill of Larch …

JF: Pineapple mayweed is the crushed smell of youth.

… The uniforms we wore …

The Seer of Suburbia: All uniform then.

… Lanyard with whistle and little leather catch for the kerchief, slits in it and held by a fastener in the blue and white neck square and short pants. Wear longers now, not the same, old men before their time …

JF: He put his hands down the inside of the back of his trousers and felt the uneven seams and wondered as he wandered why rough edges can be all right on the inside. Best sixer of nineteen … green cap with wolfcub badge and yellow braid cold fasting mornings fasted from midnight then. Church parade and communion …

Reader: Saw a man chewing gum going to receive. Did the gum stick to the Host?

… many a fainting, cold water and head between legs all for … a breakfast would have … toughen us up for standard bearer standing during the ceremony with the heavy flag, the pole in the leather cylinder belted around his waist, crossed brass pike. The top flag genuflects with the rest at Consecration, the dizzy swaying flagbearer relieved before the *ite missa est*, the bugler gives a blast to announce the presence of the Lord, hard to manage that, have to spit into the mouthpiece. Goose pimples on shortleeeved arms as we march through the chill of the morning. *Clé deas clé deas*, aire, all commands in Irish like in the army, a good custom that, little warriors heading off to the woods through the golden catkins of hazel reaching the river foaming cream in flood with blackened billycans rattling on the outside of the haversacks. Firelighting test: two matches leaves and twigs. Can you twig it? No paper allowed. Shirt badges for knife and axe test and pace the one I remember most ah yes and still apply. Pace was good: run fifty yards walk fifty like the North American Indians. Wouldn't arrive tired at one's destination. Should live life like that. Anyway it was another cloth badge. Collected as many as possible to keep extra heat in the grey shirt. Hygiene first aid whistle signals long and short ...

JF: He brings it on himself like a whistler brings on a storm.

... knots: sheetbend for tying two knots of unequal thickness, reef knot used in first aid, lies flat on the wound. Remember them well. Clove hitch. Ah well ...

Reader: Will you look at him. You can hear him think.

JF: You know you're dying when you start spending most of your time in the nostalgic mode.

... I went through all that Catholic thing ...

Jude: *La cosa*, the thing just like Uanito says, O Leo.

... It was a game, all those badges for crusaders, sodalities and pioneer pins. The badges of all out tribes, fodder for the Blueshirts and the human spirit so wide and freeranging, restrained. Poor old Darwin never got a chance, never got a lookin on the land of Dot.

Noisy visitor. Silence becoming obsolete in the library. Renewals: everything needs renewing, skin, leaves, life. Where are you, Mam? A bully tore my ticket, those rough old Brothers won't let me in to see the Mark of Zorro. They forced me to drink the cow's milk. They held my asthmatic mouth open and made me guzzle the full fat half pint bottle down to put the red neck on me. And you took me by the hand and walked the long walk through the rain so I could see the Mark.

The Seer of Suburbia: Did you see Leo taking his shower after the game? He has it, the mark. A marked man.

Reader: Who was the bully? Crichton again?

Not directly, never direct with our dear Freddie. O no, that would be too open for his Machiavellian and clandestine ways. No, he set up as was his wont one of his cronies, a big, burly fellow. I learned this from one of the boys in the class afterwards. It started with my white suitcase, a cheap cardboard case with locks, originally a holiday case which I used as a school bag, big and awkward. Being a hoarder I liked to keep all my books and would transport the case on my bicycle carrier. One morning while cycling to school I felt a thud and I heard the guffaw of the burly fellow. He had kicked the suitcase onto the road. It led to a challenge and a fight …

Reader: And your ticket?

… Yes, reduced to tiny particles flying away in the wind down Armagh Road like autumn leaves. Who did you spar for? I was asked afterwards as if it had been a game. I sparred for sublimation. But Mam is gone, and who will read Rob Roy for me now? Mam …

JF: There's a good time coming.

… I feel your presence, a gentle breeze from the open door, someone going out, someone coming in.

Control your mind, son. Discipline it. Order it. It will obey. Instruct it to be positive. Make those around you happy. Do little kindnesses. Be cheerful. There are enough grumps knocking at the door.

But death, Mam, what … ? The door closes. Must concentrate more. Like multichannels, hard to get. Ah well, peruse a book.

Reader: Where are you?

In the forties …

Reader: Age or page?

SFC: That's good. You're avoiding the polysyllabic. How many syllables?

JF: Polysyllables are words for a parrot.

… I will go to the desert where my furniture will be the dust. Keep the language pure in the desert hills like the Jebali. There's JF in the library checking to see if anyone is borrowing his books and not to see *what* sort of anyone is borrowing his books. Here's one now. It's Gunther again talking to JLA. Excuse me sir, we're doing eh well a youknowwhat on the works of JF. I see you have just borrowed a Francis book. What prompted? Well don't you know it has a nice feel. I like the feel of a book, the cover is good, the ending and the beginning they're all good, so I'm just dying to get into the body, the corpus as it were, don't you know? …

JLA: What do you work at, sir?

I'm a master baker.

SFC: It takes a better baker to bake a better batch.

The Rhymer
At what stage does it not happen,
at what stage do you not fear for your life?
Are you equipped alone in the wide expanse
without children or wife?
Props all stripped bare,
look at yourself naked if you dare.

… O Jude, the evening draws in, dark to light to dark again. How quickly. Sucked into the hearth these cold evenings …

Reader: Mr Francis, what do you do in the evenings?

I watch the traffic jams.

The traffic jams?

Yes. I watch for nuances.

Nuances?

Yes, I mean in the traffic. It doesn't always follow the same toxic pattern. Sometimes there are gaps.

Gaps?

Yes. Sometimes you can see the asphalt and imagine the earth underneath.

… In my garden birds rustle in the withered clematis before the darkness. I hear the snip of Lil's shears making a eunuch of the privet keeping it neat and rectangular so we'll never see it flower. A cat hides in the privet, leaves his smell for morning. Run, Lil chases with a stick, put your smells under your owner's nose. Children handling earth with cat's urine if they touch their eyes, they could go blind. Are we really all part of the one? Or is it that the gap has been made so wide that it is untraceable? Remove the pig from the parlour …

JF: *Muc Inis* the old name for Ireland.

… the tick from the bed, the dog and feline from the kitchen, allergy pickups, everything sanitary now cold clean hospital steel. Why more sickness so? Ah well, enough. Grasp the end of the day. Think of the morrow when the seven trials begin again, not as many as Hercules', different, neurotic today: shrinking marriages, gaps in generation, media coin. Articulate the problem and it's real. Ah well, grasp the last breath of the evening …

Jude: Grasp more than you can reach else what is heaven for?

… before it expires, another inch off the candle. Ah well, friendly to all, repress all fires, they will only be quenched. Put out the light and say good night. My blessing to Uanito, a kiss and a flower.

PS I've just had a mare. A football game on the edge of the precipice. I'm the goalie. I'm about to throw the ball out when I … the whole … goalpost and all fold under as in an earthquake, and all are hurled down.

*

LEO, *MI SINGH*, THANK YOU A THOUSAND FOR THE *CARTA* HAPPY Valentine. We must not invert our hearts. I have just one crib, *una queja*: the quotes from Job, Mr Francis said they were for me to utter but no matter, *no importa*, you used them well. But you must stand under the devil tree sometimes so that the evil can be taken out of you. O Leo, that sounds bad, forget it, and yet I will not cross it out. You talk so much about death. Try almsgiving, it will help deliver you. Pray to St Jerome the patron saint of librarians or St John the patron of writers. You ponder on the fish in the aquarium. He was the sign of Christ. ICHTHUS in Greek. Iesous Christos Theou Vios Soter. Jesus Christ Son of God Saviour …

The Rhymer
You glance at the Book by day
I study it by night
what you glean is dark
my readings are light.

… Rejoice and be glad.

Leo: Blessed thou art amang mayen. But if Jesus came back would he understand the interpretation of his own teaching?

O Leo the things you say, and now Uanito coughs, each laboured breath, each one like the last. One of the reasons I did not want to tell you about him, I was fearful that you might … not want me to have him.

How can you say that?

Judging the circumstances I wasn't at all sure. Our lives are so limited, we must make our choice—that is what our lives are all about, making choices. Isn't it? We are only given a certain number of breaths (isn't that what you say?) like the hairs on our head.

JF: Breathe deeply, get better value.

O Leo, what do I say? All those dreams. You dream the woman. Let me be the woman. I have placed a starflower in my hair. Do you dream of the future? The world draws near its anaragonic revolution.

JF: Contretemps unexpected mishap the line developed out of a breath of speech.

Leo: I am doing an inventory of the lost property office of myself.

Reader: To be shut of.

UK reader: To be shot of.

Jude: We are spinning yarn like the great spider mother spinning the web of destiny with its spinnerets …

JF: Scheherazade spun yarns too.

… Do you trust a spider's web? Will it hold you up? We are on a wing and a prayer, Leo. We must take the plunge. War and ice shall do great harm. What answer? Arms will not be stopped …

JF: Arms are for linking.

… except through fear or universal death.

Leo: The Celts will be destroyed in their own chloroform.

Jude: Who will use daggers? …

JF: The browntongued one.

The Seer of Suburbia: If you fall, it won't be cold, you'll be.

Jude: My heart is in my fist. Where are you going, Leo? I don't know, do I hear you say? I can hear your voice like your mother's. It transcends the page and written word. It completes in itself without needing a subject or predicate. Will language die? O Leo, are you linear or do you follow the wheel? I fear you are with the wheel, but if we start all over again, will the old machine hold up? I prefer to follow the line. This talk of yours about the lingam and Phal has got to me. *Me molesta.* On the bus the other day on the way into the centre of Sevilla I looked across at a bald man …

JF: We grow bald and grey like African buffalos.

… He was staring straight at me and yet without any sign of recognition, but his nose was a long lingam, ithyphallic but downward and from his chin there hung the sac. O Leo, I blinked him away. And coming home I saw a most beautiful rainbow, a complete arc encompassing the sky. Richard of York did not give battle in vain, which you told me about. The violet light was victorious …

JF (*singing*): There's a rainbow round my shoulder and it fits me like a glove.

... You worry about your skin. Don't neglect it. It's a mirror to the mind, it sends out signals when all is not well. Don't forget the Book, Leo, it contains the Word ...

JF: The word, always the word. Sometimes I wish for another tool. A scalpel perhaps or a brush or a sculptor's chisel to shape into meaning what we are, pieces of debris. What the sculptor discarded? The word flies away.

... And the Word is the Light and the Light is the Guide. Close your eyes a *momentito* every day and see what God will send you. We need food, nourishment, panspermia for the dead, koliva for the dead, the living and the dreaming, full circle you would like all united in one. Put seed under the pillow before going to seed ...

JF: A clear conscience makes the softest pillow.

... Hope. I am becoming more and more atavistic, the early language is flowing back. I remember it from the breasts of men, the ribs of palm branches ... Jesus ordered the palm trees to bend their branches so Joseph could pick their fruit ...

Leo: You should get a job as a Jesus coach.

JF: All 5000 coconuts were removed from all the palm trees before the US President arrived in case one should fall on his head.

... and from the camel's shoulder blades that time in Morocco like a vision of people known in the past, or maybe a vision of books unwritten. It's the scent of flowers that does it across the street from the *Jardines de María Luisa*, heady exotic seductive, the orange blossom and so warm. Black tobacco smoke. Strings are plucked, a shrill cry of the *gitana*, the sound of the castanets and heels stomping and the *pelo negro*, it is me, *soy yo*, no it is my grandmother in her youth *la abuela* a ringer for and the red rose, red in black and the frenzied spasm of movement and the grandfather with the dark moustache smiles with a mixture of love and lust at the black skirt tight around the waist, undulating (your word) into the shape of the guitar itself. *La vida*. I belong here, Leo. We must all follow the threads. O sometimes I … where is the dot in the old letter? My life for a dot. I am the nymph of the mountain. We shall fuse as one, as Hermaphroditus. Enjoy mind and body as one lover into beloved transformed. To have your mind, Leo, but then you suffer also. Mind exchange, trial of two weeks, body thrown in as well …

Leo: I will if you will so will I.

… you could experience as a female, *experimentar*, the same thing, fondle breasts …

Leo: Thanks for the mammaries.

… vibrate the velvet before you go on your way, whereas I will start to hold a pen like a penis, stimulate it for my own pleasure, my own, for others in the past, just doing it for them and watching them salivate. Still, it gave me a power over them, over Crichton and his likes for a while …

Leo: Did you do it with Crichton?

… Not really. Not penetrative. He did it in front of me. Liked me to watch.

To watch?

Yes. When I went to turn away he touched my neck, forcing my head around.

This was before the burglary?

Yes.

You never told me that.

Too ashamed perhaps.

But why did you stay with him?

I don't know. I didn't really have anywhere else to go, had I? Beside he paid well.

Paid you well?

Yes, but later now in my mature years I see the power. I would prolong the power…

JF: Power is brief and the holder harrowed.

… Tower over them. Funny to see them melt before you and when you stop a while they beg you to continue …

Leo: But who are *they*?

… Just men. Often married. When I wandered out at night when the loneliness was too much to bear …

Leo: I understand.

… And then it was all over, and one wondered what the fuss was all about, the subservience gone, no more until the memoryless lingam resurrects with its one eye imploring you and the cycle begins again and like the fish you mentioned they forget what is at the other end of the bowl. I would sally forth only on an occasional night when the desire was too strong to bear. So strong that it hurt deep down; had to be careful of course with all the STD scares. Still with Uanito asleep in the warm embrace of the *padres*, I would sally forth on the pretence that … some visit or other.

Leo: And I too.

You too?

Yes.

O Leo …

JF: Absinthe makes the heart grow fonder.

SFC: She likes cock tales.

… In the nightclub or hotel, I forget which, I would sit sipping and swirling a wine, freeing its esters and ethers until inevitably some man with a ring mark on his wedding finger would … the lingam delineated on his face carrying the message from down below under the bald dome, no need for clothes really, see through them. In the car *o dios mio* they like the lips on the tip. Funny how they shave above and not below. Same when mouth is opened, black hiding behind yellow. Up front all that matters. A bit lopsided. Once or twice I would take a risk and, to use the Irish phrase, after a nice bit of lamb we'd be bleating …

Leo: The primordial bleating of sheep drowning out the vacuous utterances of man.

JF: The sheep died in the wool.

... I carried the letter, put on the second skin, and Roberto's your *tío*. And the morning after the night before, revirginised, I would berate myself for my folly, for no one I ever met was you. It was you I was searching for all the time. Such guilt! I would pray for purity, to Santa Teresa, to St Anne who got me the man. To St Bernadette, to your St Brigid—I put her rushed cross on the door to ward off evil temptations. The way I went was the way of the dead. But my desires are so strong. Can a woman be made a eunuch? Like what you said Lil did to the privet hedge. The price for knowledge of Heaven ...

JF: The eunuch was in love with a sultana.

... I have too much of the earth in me. All this talk of the body. Was looking at nudists on a remote beach.

JF: A public place where we can legally lie down.

Newspaper headline: Nudist's welfare man's model wife fell for the Chinese hypnotist from the coop bacon factory.

Leo: Or naturists, is what they call themselves? What Lil failed to realise that time in Greece is that the erotic lies in the mystery ...

JF: We are a mystery to ourselves.

... and concealing and gesture and alluring and sighs and ...

The Seer of Suburbia: He's on a roll.

Hollywood producer: Morass and Moron.

Reader: What?

JF: Hollywood and the censor. When clothes are shorn a star is porn.

Jude: What all the commotion is about I do not know. The same bonebuttoned backs, the same haunches everywhere, the only things we can sit on, give an inch or take an inch if you can pinch, all the same when it's all upfront in your face so to speak. But what they are missing and ... How the hips move a man's trim bottom and the tongue and the mouth and ... where are we going? How to reach an eternity, that is the question. Riches I need not, nor man's empty praise. But the things, the things, Leo, that are happening. I just read of the poor refugees in Pakistan, no it was Mozambique or somewhere, and there was one young boy and the insurgents cut off his ear and forced him to eat it, and despite all that he had a smile for the camera. What is the lesson for us? Does fear therapy work in making things relative? Perhaps. We are from the spoiled world. We need to make molehills.

Uanito has come in. He was complaining of a sore ear. Is your ear better? It is after the sweet. He puts his sock on his hand as if it were a glove.

Leo: Where was it the Long Ears ruled the Short Ears? I am a pig with a gold ring in my snout. How did those celibates renounce the act? Generous fingers must have been poured to make them feel ... but some sublimated.

The Seer of Suburbia: Excuse me, may I ... ?

Jude: Very hard to know, mystical heights ...

The Seer of Suburbia: Excuse me ...

... Difficult to maintain I mean ...

The Seer of Suburbia: Excuse me, may I say something?

What? *¡Por Dios!*

The Seer of Suburbia: God also is a point of view.

... Those characters who plague your page, Leo, are creeping into mine. All the channels must be in a twist. Time to sign off. Pray for me. There is no fear that I would ever be sent to Jerusalem for Messianic treatment. *Adios mi amigo, mi espíritu.* Keep some of the Sabbaths at least. Keep your right eye for Heaven ...

JF: Heaven is where the geese fly already roasted.

... PS If we could swap our minds, even if only for a night your mind in my ... Let us concentrate really hard on the dot at midnight next Saturday. At midnight on the dot. My midnight but your eleven pm lest I forget. A word with Mr Francis may help.

*

Hey Jude, don't carry the world upon your shoulder. You are too intense. Try yoga, a nice blend with the Bible. Another robin is under the hedge: more rain on the way. Could she have migrated? Could she have been the same species as the one you saw? Walked in the valley last night. Cold riverroar ...

Jude: When the river changes its mood, how many will die?

... Lots of flooding after all the rain. River overflowed its banks...

Reader: What interest do the banks employ?

JF: Selfinterest.

... footpaths submerged. Maybe that's how it will all end, back to the flood. Wet day soft day changes in the wind in the rain the texture direction water flowing and gurgling in gullies flooding in the town sandbags no good, water coming from underneath. We kept talking on the little road—a woman and her attractive daughter mounted on their ponies—when one of the ponies decided to do a mighty steaming piss, and we kept on talking averting our eyes as if nothing were happening, the thunderous cascade almost drowning out our words ...

The Seer of Suburbia: He doesn't want his river to be drowned in the sea.

... And there we were looking up, waiting for the big bang. Who will die first? Count the number of letters in your name. Full name. Judith, Bernarda, Leopold. A=1 B=2 and so on. Even the man wins. Odds the woman. Two minutes. In the dark now as I pass is a different world but the same place all the same ...

Jude: The dark lane that was familiar.

JF: I'll be seeing you in all the old familiar faeces.

... Time moves on. Old Sam is gone. Gone on his way. Clocked in and clocked out. Hope he won. If you're in on time you're out ...

JF: In the mirror the goodlooking face belied the inner trouble. One would say such a face would withstand a lot of tribulations to come.

... Will a flood overwhelm us? Half one in the morning no sounds to moider you just the fire shuffling its last before it crumbles. Being called to bed. Why rush? This is a moment of calm, goodwill to all. Last night's bed sojourn was one of wakeful tribulation. My lamp is broken, my light is out. Was a wicked man's light ever put out? Would a spit on the eye do any good? Parturition. Must up. What's the difference between pissing in the sink and in the urinal?

Reader: Manners.

But if no one is looking?

Hygiene.

But some people drink piss.

Feck off.

Manners.

SYC: Some primitives believed that everything that comes from the body is sacred: excrement, urine, hair, saliva.

Leo: *Liquid Gold.*

SYC: What?

Leo: *The Lore and Logic of Using Urine to grow Plants.* Mind body mend mind. What ugly flat feet, ugliest part of me always swollen ...

The Rhymer
Skinnymalink melodeon legs big banana feet.
Went to the pictures and couldn't get a seat.

JF: Leo had feet which were so long he knew people laughed at them in amazement, calling them plantations. And he was only comfortable when they were out of sight such as when he went swimming. There they were advantageous as their extra length gave him greater speed.

... protruding veins, a touch of phlebitis maybe, too small the veins to remove down there.

SYC: And yet they hold a handsome frame.

Reader: Women destroy handsome men; they eat them up. The men's egos expand; they feel they are gods by the fawning of the women but they wind up in lonely hotel rooms on their own trying to keep an illusion alive through a bottle or a syringe while the women have all gone home to their reassuring groups and their routine ways.

... What lies hidden in the sock? Not judged. If feet were photographed instead of a face how many would ... ah well. O to hear uplifting words to make you feel a worth. You have troubles of your own?

Reader: Yes, my wife died.

My sympathies or my congratulations, one can't be sure.

Reader: Sympathies will do.

Like my friend Jude, I look for the words in the books. Only one Book does her. The sounds of the words are important, companionable. They can be harsh or gentle praise or rebuke. Read the ear, carry the sounds with you as well as the thoughts.

Reader: I want to thank you. You make me feel less lonely by giving me a part in your book.

It's Mr Francis you should be ...

Reader: Even so, thank you.

Outside I hear it. The rain the rain the rain. I trim the moustache...

JF: Trims his hair by setting it on fire with a candle.

... O to snip the threads of rain, a nice shave with Occam's

Razor. Where did I come across that? Upon my word must look that word up in Mrs Byrne's *Dictionary of Unusual, Obscure and Preposterous Words.*

Reader: You shave at night?

Yes, saves time in the morning and so the cuts can heal. Check doors, all locks locked, live with a siege mentality, any wonder after what we went through, Jude …

Radio: A murder suspect hiding out in the inside of an outdoor toilet.

Reader: Was it the old toilets in New Street?

The world needs healing.

Reader: A great big plaster.

… Liquid carrying, sleepless night drags into dark early dawn hour, milkman clinking bottles. Should face the bed east. Insinuating arm on Lil's left dug, feel heartbeat underneath, steady rhythm, no arrhythmia there, all the gallons of blood being pumped nonstop on nightshift now, throughout the system, some engineering feat …

Reader: Are you talking about flushing the toilets?

… veins and arteries, perpetual motion, perpetual light shine, never break down, never say never. My eye is jumping, the nerve of it. Sleep semisleep, wake middream, halfmemory, time halfforgot, lulling, headwaves. I awake with a hard dawn. Light flashes across my closed eyelids like an electric bulb glowing. There goes the alarm. How am I going to get up to go down? …

SFC: Leo is an ontologist and he doesn't even know it.

… Unthinking this morning, in my haste to draw the curtains from the light, I leaped from the left side of the bed. Hope the day meets with no calamity. Morning mirror. The black shades encircling the eyes, a sunken look, the blotched skin and eruptions down below, *pubicus eruptus* foretells a tale.

JF: The first tale was of a search for immortality.

Reader: What is Lil doing?

Leo: She's making the bed. Pulling the eiderdown to get the lines straight. Occam's Razor, reference in Brewer's *Dictionary of Phrase and Fable: Entia non sunt multiplicando.* Dissect every question as with a razor. William of Occam died thirteen ... yes yes yes. Can we have three distinct persons in one god? Father, son and husband the one man. Must consult the *Book of Changes* for a change. Centipedes in shed, spider's web none contain.

Reader: What is he doing?

JF: Leo loves ivies. Their leaves camouflage the cold stone exterior of Wounded House. Every day he goes to his garden to see what new arteries have sprung from his Goldheart or is the leaf of Glacier really cold or has a tint of red appeared in the Boston or is Virginia drooping which is her wont sometimes when the weather gets her down. A little trim and snip here and there the same as a man needing a shave or a haircut. Keep everything neat as Lil says, yes but not overdoing it as she does.

Reader: Why the fascination with ivies?

JF: Cover on grey. A leafy world. A wall that changes colour through the seasons without painting. A privacy.

SYC: Nothing must come between the two privacies, that of the writer writing and that of the reader reading.

The Seer of Suburbia: The dying ivy rustled like paper in the wind.

Leo: To do the messages for Lil give her a liein and a lieon. Quick insertion before I go ...

JF: She was given the bum's rush.

... No other way since that night that marked me. She wrote the shopping list while receiving me. Let us not miss the little diamonds that shine now and then, the little gems that brighten the dull day or night, moments that will come and go, this day never again, this day and the next day and the next day after that, not always gems, sometimes there is downright despair, but the little lights when they do shine, not often mind, still when they do, they should make up for when we are put out. Must go, must away, face the day with my spear and cracked shield.

On my way gooddayed to cocky Roche, the shop owner (no change there). I have my little list, just the bare essentials, cupboard bare, she does the big one herself. Where's my list? Oranges, apples, Weetabix, rashers, bread, butter. Must make sure they're Seville oranges, eh Jude. And bread high fibre to avoid piles of trouble and fruit to banish last night's bitter taste and Lemon's Pure Sweets and a bit of fillet almost for ... make a mnemonic and learn them off by heart. Surprise the butcher. Last week he gave me a mouldy bit of meat, saw me coming; should have been more critical like the savvy housewives. Learn off the parts of the cow; never sure of myself there, being more cultural than agricultural. Steaks alone: porterhouse, entrecote, fillet, ribeye, know the T bone all right ...

The Seer of Suburbia: But do you know yourself? To know yourself, distinguish between what you feel and what you should feel.

... sirloin, rum and round and topside and silverside and brisket and chateaubriand and ...

JF: Warnings of foot and mouth have reached our ears.

... take a wife's job for granted ...

JF: We are living in a world of floating pronouns and free verse.

... Left her titfortat on the bed, put on the whistle and flute and scapa flowed. Greasy smell from the chipshop. Who are the women passing without a face? A small man roughly hewn with greywhite hair approaches fingering rosary beads singing Soul of my Saviour sanctify my breast, then saying Hail Mary full of grace and then the hymn again. A woman bending down painting the Quaker cemetery gate, the little knots and bulges from the tracksuit bottoms denying Eros a chance to surface. Her transistor blasting to keep her company among the dead …

JF: The dead are invisible but they are not absent.

… Children skipping as I amble down Fishamble Street to the sound of TV commercials. Where are all the old street rhymes gone? How used one go? Mam used to … before … Stood me in good stead. *Aul granny Gray, she let me out to play, I can't go near the water to hunt the ducks away.* What's this it was? *Over the garden wall I let the baby fall. My mother came out and gev me a clout and knocked me over a bottle of stout.*

Social history contained therein. Jug of porter it used to be. Old drunk woman with black shawl sitting on the wet ground up the grey Liberties lane, jug of porter beside her, jug of porter for fourpence if you brought your own jug. More than fourpence surely but used to be before my … one and six or something. Poor auld one, her head all to one side, unconscious to the world except now and then when the head would toss to give a bar of a song, an Irish beauty on her left eye, husband probably, still shouldn't judge. Terrible for a woman when that happens, that and the drink coupling, more of a disgrace in people's eyes …

Pioneer Campaigner: What evil could be worse than drink?

JF: Thirst.

… Man gets away with murder, that's with regard to the ordinary old dear of course, not those wellheeled touchy ones who wouldn't use the masculine in language. Coming toward me now the power walkers two abreast with their arms flaying; would knock you off the footpath without a second thought. But the poor old dear, poor old biddy, bigbreasted one, suckled many a … all gone and left you. Rain or tears falling down your cheeks, your hair matted, dribbling mouth, embarrassing. Probably proud once, all that gone now. When someone cracks, no love left, abandoned like a heap of bones in a junkyard. Beauty once, photos to prove, never thought, just followed love blindly …

JF: If love is blind why wear lingerie?

... ne'er a thought for the morrow. Love's young dream today's nightmare. What training had you got? Now you drink the bitter liquid. What time and sameness do. How easy to happen. All waiting for Godot now in our own way. May he be good to her. Amen to that.

Where was I? I'm after losing meself. To lose low trick. Home again. I detected a trembling in your hand, Jude. Were you cold or was it something else? Supposed to be a good sign though. The swapping of minds. I don't mind, shouldn't be too difficult. Each man carries a woman within and vice versa I suppose, *animus anima*, four stages thereof. Midnight on the dot, right for our rendezvous? Lil should be ... a knock at the door ... a canvasser. Selfesteem is a good thing, you are onto a good thing; many years of research have proved it. Why don't you join our local Self Esteem team? I turned away.

What does the newspaper say? Image of a woman on a windowpane. People travelling breathlessly the length and breadth of the country to see. Should see the length of the queues. Gardaí will not positively identify the image as that of my mother.

I burned one of your letters, Jude, to see if the flame was bright and true. I stare into the candlelight to try to find an idea, nice for meal, candle and wine, one to loosen the mind, the other the tongue ...

JF: The boneless tongue broke many a head.

... exudes warmth, something cordial and romantic, gives vision a different light, hides blotches ...

SFC: This writin' is indubitably zuihitsu. The pen just follows the ink.

JF: SFC speaks ever so well except for the occasional slurring sometimes when he confused *s* with *the* or when he forgets himself and fails to pronounce *g* at the end of words.

… A hollowness colonises my being …

JF: We are all professors of our own being.

… in the late afternoon. There is a coolness in the air. Loneliness encroaches. Grey clouds overhead. A sense of absence. Birds squawk, and children's voices are faint echoes. My study makes a ghost of me.

As the evening draws in, I go out to close the front gate and meet the old widowed neighbour Mr Whatsisname corrals me in a vicelike grip, not so old, agile and fit he holds on for all he can to milk human sympathy from the guitlinduced. Your aches make my aches worse, your sprain is naught to my strain, pain in back is back, my knee your knee, my lonely knee, your knee is … can't garden anymore. I used to weed and hoe and plunge the spade deep into the strumpet earth and sometimes I would prune and caress the mounds and turn the earth upsidedown and ravish it for all it's worth. Up and down, he said but, he said, my shoulder aches in the wind. God it's an awful thing, and he limped snailslow for the lack of pity. Is there a scapular for easing selfpity or an indulgence that goes back in years? …

The Seer of Suburbia: Neurosis set in before the sun set.

… And she died her early death. Before her bell had rung. Lasting impressions impress for everlastingness. I stood in the kitchen doorway. By the light of the hall I could see my shadow reflected in the window. One moment it seemed to stand like a tall strong shadow with light on either side. Other moments it would submerge into the blackness. And then it would come back, crouched and flickering like a torch on a fading battery, a deformed figure, then submerging once more into darkness. The depression was so strong I wanted to burst into tears. Rain falling down the windowpane, heart's pain …

SFC: Is Lambkin a man at all? A man should keep his fears to himself. He should snap out of it. Pull yourself together, man.

JF: He stood motionless looking into the fridge for a long time, the door wide open and a heater on beside him, before going into selfimposed retreat.

... When depression subsides you wonder why it had you by the throat, motionless with fear. The longing for emotional closeness with someone when not satisfied ebbs away and your shell widens, its cracks healing, and envelopes you, happy once more with your own company, craving it in fact. Too many forays are unnerving. Let us study Anthropos and get in touch with the whole man.

I stand at the open sitting room door. Silently she descends the stair, gently placing her bare feet on each step, dressing gown with the golden chord, loose, waved, shining hair combed back. Where has the grey gone? A youthful beauty with dark sparkly eyes.

JF: The lightningstruck lady died while still striking.

Reader: Has anyone shown you the gates that guard the dark world of the dead?

Maybe. Mam maybe.

Reader: It takes thousands of the dead to make who you are.

Jude: Have you been to the springs and depths of the sea?

It must be near midnight. That is Jude's voice trying to get through quoting, e'er a word?

Jude: I'm concentrating hard on you.

JF: What gets durity the more it clanes and what doesn't ask questions but gives answers?

A towelphone.

Jude: What is the cyclops, the long slender stump with the one eye and a tail who went into the gap in my jeans, leaving some of its tail behind?

Phal

Jude: O no no no what a halftrackhead.

O yes, a needle and thread. We were conceived with a tail.

Jude: Is it really happening, Leo? Are we telepathizing? Your mother, Leo, she was about to … I won't have to write to you anymore. You'll be there as part of my mind whenever I need you.

How is … ?

Jude: He came in the other day and asked how does the football run after the car. Because the water is running after the football and he doubled up with laughter on the floor.

Go away for a while, Jude. I feel Mam is trying to get through.

JF: She ruined him for other women. His marriage, his quests, were all a search for the feminine ideal.

Jude: But the change …

Not now.

Jude: What's the magic word?

CUL8R. I hold the Virgin water bottle to my heart and summon Mam.

I've been over beyond, so happy and peaceful but if you keep praying for me here and now to be here I cannot be there.

You never lost it, Mam. Plough on through the rough land.

I go over the mountains. Wherever I wish to be I am.

Tell me, Mam.

One thing about my state. I am free from the limitations of the body and what was called time. When I died, son, and left the body I looked down on my mutilated physical self with dispassion. It is only in the spirit that one can be whole. The trumpet has not sounded for you. You have responsibilities to fulfil. You must sense the needs in other people's lives. You will pick up other people's thoughts. Feel a lightness of being. You must stop worrying about death. There is nothing to view. Guardian spirits will see you through.

But how can we understand this life, Mam, if we cannot glimpse what lies beyond?

You have glimpsed and learned that dying is a skill, an art like any other and you will not be alone.

I cannot say I have because I have not.

Too much learning makes you mad. Watch for the buds on the trees as spring approaches.

The storm rages through the night and cats squeal at windows. Some trees won't see their buds form. Still there is great consolation in knowing that you will ease me through. But when you're dead, Mam, where do you … ?

Things that are not now are then. You will learn not to look back at the body. It will belong to the past. Have you satisfied all the orifices?

Mouthphalanus. How can I talk to you like this?

Because the body parts are only appendages. They perform functions as machines do. They are slaves awaiting their superior's instructions. Replace anything that is faulty. Don't give it a first thought. The body causes too much rírá agus rúillebúille. You will see in your body, invisible, inaudible, timeless and weightless.

Will this happen to everyone, Mam?

No, this peace, this joy will be given only to those who achieve a karma in the material world. Some will not pass through the gates and will be left in the valley of the shadows.

Jude: Leo, Leo, I'm coming in on your wavelength.

Not now, Jude. Mam, are you there? No, she's gone. The wondering is the living. That's what I wanted to say to Mam. It is those who think they are alive who are dead because they do not think. Jude …

Jude: The change, Leo.

… Take your … the whole of time is but a single night. How long can you keep the cork under water? Let it go. Let it shoot up. The storms are raging, dispersing the heat from the distant climes. Thunder sounds, distant bombs, the crackling of lightning like sharp rifle shots and supine monsters are recharged and walk about in city streets …

Jude: O Leo, it is the eve of the day of ashes. When will we go to summerland? I only want to love one and once. Come when you will and welcome when you come. Upa upa upa, that's what Uanito said to me before he went asleep. O Leo, I am touched as you tell, touching.

... It is the nontouch that draws. I am a bit afraid of summerland. May break down what we have built up, the physical I mean. Touch can taminate. Noogenesis, ectoplasm, hominisation, *Homo ludens, Homo viator.* We must deny as well as affirm our existence. We are willing things to happen in a certain way as now.

Jude: Isn't it wonderful how we are reading each other, a throughbreak. *Dios te salve María*

atá lán de ghrásta
el Señor es contigo
is beannaithe tú idir mná
y bendito es el fruto
do bhroinne Íosa.
Santa María, madre de Dios
guigh orainn ár bpeacaí
ahora y en la hora
ár mbás
Amen
Mortal man
O Leo, I am so excited.

Numbers excite. Backed a horse, came in at five to two, all gone home for lunch like Brian getting up late to be in Clontarf by ten fourteen. Nineteen nintynine in Dunnes store, the price of the jeans the same that blue rhapsody girl wore ascending the hill on the model in the window. Rivulets of melting snow sliding down the pane. Do you know, Jude, I don't want this sleet and wet snow to stop falling. Let it cover us in a mantle...

JF: The cars go by dislodging their snow like shitting cows.

... If brightness comes, daylight bright, the extrovert things will have to be done. I want to immerse myself in the lava of liquid words and mould them into meaning. The light of language, the lure of night. You know what I mean like sort of kind of ... ?

Jude: A house of cards, Leo. The brightness is over here, but I suppose I understand that you want to feel that way to create or express, something Mr Francis must often feel.

Reader: Where has Mr Francis gone?

The Seer of Suburbia: He's gone to do his wee wee.

... It's somewhat similar to a sexual feeling so I've read, the creative urge. It comes from deep inside, the best and the worst of us in there. How many secrets go to the grave? If I could try to explain, Jude, by way of contrasts. I was in one of those as you say liquescent moods when I had to bring in the dustbin which was being tossed about in the storm. I left the side gate open as I wheeled in the bin. A sudden gust crashed the gate against the outdoor watertap, cracking the pipe, making the water gush out. I felt panicky from all the interiority, resented time and effort needed to repair; went in pursuit of a plumber, kitchen flooded on return but play fair to the plumber, no plush job there, hands and knees affair, did a good job of repair. If I had been in the solid world I am sure I would have tackled the problem with less panic. Impossible to be all things. Are we anything, Jude, other than vain creatures? Looking at a picture in the library of WBY, something condescending about him, sartorial hubris, even his hair is rising up on him, *éirí in airde air.* Did he ever laugh? There is the face of another writer whose words I have read for years, first time to see his picture, two separate entities. I cannot detect his tempestuous language in his gentle face. So many things done against the feet and the head. Could do a lot on a little. *Mórán ar bheagán.* Or look at Bertold with the cigar as fat as a penis stuck in his gob. Oral grat connect with creat ur.

What's in what's out? The returns. *The Nature of the Second Sex,*

Nostradamus still holding his own. *Under Milkwood, Knowing Women*, flowers, travel, psychology. A book on voyeurism …

JF: *A Peeping Tom.*

… What's that solid book there brought up from the old stacks? *Story of Nations: Spain* by H E Watts published 1893, not a spot on it. A Morris Minor of a book, built to last …

Reader: When does paper rust?

JF: Some books wear better than their owners.

… Mustn't get carried away with ourselves. Superior selfrighteousness, what harm it can do. Crusaders, cross and sword, silk and spice and all things nice. Why gold, frankincense and myrrh to a poor hungry family? Poultry, vegetables or a basket of fruit would surely have been more useful gifts. *Conquistadores*, fascists …

JF: Many Roman cloaks sheltered the fascist seed.

… missionaries only one word, deaf to all others. Poor Caliban. Is he really dictionarydegraded, and bestial, a subman? …

JF: A *caníbal* to some.

… Anagrammatically easy to thus categorise when we spurn the culture whence we came. Arrogant and imperious, religion had a say. Same when you look up *ciotóg*: awkward, sinister …

Jude: *Siniestro.*

… see the prejudice over the years built into the grammar. Let their souls be weighed against the feathers of truth …

Jude: I'm hearing you anew, *mi Ka*.

… You have an ear on yourself. A different way, no need for letters. Your words and thoughts come in rhythms as radiographs of yourself. We are closing in, blending the inner and the outer.

I'm so …

We must keep our passions hidden.

We can drift in our minds now. The two can liquefy and blend. We merely have to wait and obey the subliminal call. I'm so …

Spring has sprung, funny calendar, spring in winter, summer in autumn …

JF: Two thieves stole a calendar. Got six months each.

… still moving on, moving somewhere, going in circles and cycles. As I went walking yesterday the mind directed the feet to follow the same worn path, a creature of habit, hard to break …

JF: With the passing of time he parted from many of his old ways.

… Easier for animal than for human; they don't know; they act like they are programmed or conditioned to start from the known point always, the circumspect munch and then proceed no matter how circuitous the route …

Jude: But Leo, aren't you excited? We have broken through.

To celebrate I fancy a generous finger in the thermopolium.

Do you know our next stop?

The judification of Leo and the leonisation of Jude. Still I will miss the wordwritten pleasure …

Reader: Did he have much pleasure?

JF: He had such pleasure that pleasure is not the word.

The Rhymer
When the job is done
and the pleasure is o'er
who cares then
who knocks at the door?

… My pen took off the other night, and when it had stopped I looked and saw what was written: that is that which was, was written in a strange language.

Jude: We can have that too, Leo. But let us work on the transmorphism. Our minds must expel each other. Concentrate, *cariño.* O we can wander through the sunripened wheatfields of the Bible and watch the mountain discharge its white foam into the blue lake.

Are you positive … ?

HIV?

VHI. Health insurance voluntary. And the black doctor with the poor English wanted to operate right away. How easy to happen. Should test their English before they test us. Positive? VFI. Increase the fee vintners. Fellow with gumboil went in, never came out, easy to mix up. Did you ever wonder if you were your mother's daughter?

Leo, we're wandering.

Plenty of time …

JF: *Amici, diem perdidi.*

… Shorttaken after the short in the thermopolium. Pull chain after use, flush toilet, no it's lavatory and no chain now, press the silver, no, chrome lever.

Leo, are you all right?

Chapter and verse, pig to pork, pigs bristles to toilet brushed. Lil doesn't like, leaves pong, must clean with rubber gloves on, use all of the pig except its squeal.

JF: He cursed the weakness of the lavatory flush failing to wash away all the turds leaving particles to appear like a great shame.

Dear Leo, the private smells of defecation are our own and should not foul the seductive perfume of love.

JF: Defecation is natural coarse. But as for Leo, he carefully tore the toilet roll so that there would be no scraggy ends. He likes to leave things all square. He cleaned the inside of the bowl. There must not be a trace left as if defecation were to him a secret and dirty act, something that nice people didn't do. To Leo the bodily purges were a conflagration of the romantic spirit deeply ingrained in him. His eyes would shine at a candlelit supper and he would hear the soft music play without a thought of what the food was doing on its way down the alimentary canal.

Leo: We have all the time from matins to compline. Would I carry you across a dry river? Sorry, I shite through my gob. Trampling on dung only spreads it more. Reading about a rather goodlooking girl today who was a dung expert, strawy stuff the best, she said, for the roses. How come cow's mulch is good and wholesome, even the smell … ?

JF: I can smell your thoughts before you think them.

… Don't keep it to yourself, broadcast it, but human faeces, excrement, pong. We should be able to fertilise our own plants with our own …

SYC: Some do; they sell it at train stations in Pakistan.

Jude: Leo.

… Never mind, it's the continuum I'm thinking of. There is sorrow on me, Jude. On the news can't stop thinking about the man who was halved by the train, hope he died immed … and did not writhe like the worm split by the spade. Cut in two by one. It was the deaf man, never heard the train coming.

But we are not cut in two; we are joined now, Leo. Who was the deaf man?

One of the days when the car was broken down I missed the bus into work and took the train. The deaf man on the train when it was stopped in the station, went around placing key rings and ball point pens on the seats waiting like a fisherman to see if any bait would catch and again silently returning, deadpan, picking up his bait, waiting to try his luck on the next train. The man was speaking on the rollers while he waited, such a mellifluous voice from what country I do not know like he was reading a poem but he was begging, telling us his story his lips outlining. He was singing his poverty so plaintively, not aggressively like so many beggars. But when I tried to speak to him he shook his head and smiled, pointing to his ears.

It was he who was halved?

Yes, he stumbled when crossing the tracks …

O Leo. Such stories, such sadness follows you. O how are we going to do this? I have fear. It is something I possess.

It was one of the days I was late for work.

And Crichton … ?

Yes. Forget him now. We must concentrate hard. If at first …

Leo, what do you hear?

I hear the same sounds that I hear every day, the clock ticking, the asthmatic whine coming from the kettle, the car revving outside, the cups clattering, but somehow they have managed to come into the foreground of my mind and they sound deafening.

The Seer of Suburbia: The artist poured acid into his ear to make himself deaf and render himself immune to the noisy world.

Your edges are frayed, Leo. Relax and let's try to exchange.

Change as rest good.

Drift, wait, hear the summons, and they will float and then flow liquid inside each other. It is happening, Leo. Melt music soft, something flowing from out of me. And you, Leo?

Yes, I feel an exuding almost like a spontaneous Phal discharge.

It's happening. *O estoy animada.*

Yes, the *scetimíní* are on me too, but let us conclude it another night to build up suspense for the reader.

Reader: You do, and I'm getting a refund on this hunchbacked nonopus.

It's very strenuous.

Reader: I don't give a uck what it is. Yu won't shortchange me. Now get on.

Leo, concen …

… I'm … trating. Believe. Is he gone? Good, good rid god forbid.

Normally not irate …

Who?

The Reader. Are you on hold?

I'm holding Phal in my left hand.

Nothing more uplifting than that.

You are manless. Together we are manloveless. Leo, I feel you coming in.

Who is there?

Miss Bates Master Bates.

Who are they?

Wandering souls. O Leo, you are touching the G spot.

Symphony on a G string.

I have given your white teeth passion.

Yes, you have the right. The woman's mind is in me and your mind is … O … !

JF: They engage in a mutual prepuce caress.

What to do. Where to start with this water pistol?

Start with a piss. The little water pistol with the tuft of hair around it is ready to discharge.

Yes I stand by the bowl and watch the wagging sausage pour out its liquid, same hissing zzzzsshhh as the tap, turn off, hold valve, release again, no different, a splash, something new, modern lav. Bad design. Uanito is the same doing his pith everywhere but in the …

I'm squatting, the river flows from the furry glen, awkward to maintain, supposed to be the best way though.

Leo, how nice, put your finger there again. Do you feel as I caress our upandcoming Phal?

Exquisitely, brain to hand.

What if Lil were to come in?

She's due, better revert. Another time.

Is she Jew?

I like being a broad. Twiriously though, *nihil obstante* I am worried about my job. Because of the cutbacks they're threatening strike. The libraries are being crippled by chronic staff shortages. Open one day, closed the next. Terrible to go down to the library and find it closed. I dreamed about the library last night, no it was a mare. All the books had been knocked down from the shelves, and some of the shelves themselves had been torn from the walls; only the metal shelves remained with their holes for highering and lowering—the wooden ones were gone—which held no more than five or six books, samples as it were, and there were wires all round and TV sets where the shelves had been, and there was a large revolving eye in the ceiling. Many of the books were torn and their covers were loose, but there was nobody about. There was a terrible silence, appropriately enough, but this was an uncanny silence with just the eye going round all the time. When I awoke, I phoned Crichton to express my concerns, but he was not available.

We know where he was.

Yes.

When you dream, you are naked among the clothed ones.

Erection comes with a dream every ninety minutes …

JF: A scrotum pole.

… tossing, turning, too active to sleep …

JF: Aquinas believed before the Fall erections were volitional. Sinless Adam couldn't have randy thoughts with Eve's nakedness, which he didn't recognise as such.

… Mammy with Daddy and Uncle Dick went to London on a stick. I'm falling but holding onto the stick carried into the darkening river. I'm sitting astride the stick starting to row. Whither?

You're drifting, Leo.

The mind's well runs dry. Thirst for more ideas and reading.

The Rhymer
Study improves the mind
corrects the judgement
and adorns mankind.

Mind becoming too somnolent of late. Should drink tea instead of beer but lack the liquescent feeling then. Some claim they can induce the creative feeling with Lemsip. The print on coaster swimming at the bottom of the glass like the Dead Sea Scrolls. Soaks with the subconscious and swirls around. Must be given time to programme itself into the creative channel …

Reader: BBC Four?

… May get a call in the middle of the dawn. Mayday, maynight, May might if she's in a subjunctive mood …

Jude: Lauds and vespers.

JF: Words are finite, and thoughts are infinite.

… What are we talking about telepathy for, Jude, when JF can butt in whenever he likes? No disrespect intended. It's just we should be unionised. We are entitled to some privacy …

JF: Would you eat a whole pear? They are ripe.

… Just a hemisphere. I wish to travel into two hemispheres. I see them beckoning me.

Give Lil an Afrodizzy, a turtle's egg. How do some live without being aware of their own bodies? I am soft on your mind, Leo. A powerful force, *la mente*; strange that it lacks the power to understand itself. Where are all our memories? In one place or in your *totalidad*? We know, but how we know is the *misterio*. What lies beneath our jellylike matter?

Surely that is my line.

Tit for tat. You borrowed from me, remember?

O this daffodil month of Lent. Ah yes Lent, I must try to be virtuous, but is it wrong to feel and love? Is that not what we were made for? Why are we given minds and emotions if not to use them, not to suppress them, to hold back, always holding back, the Catholic way. Sure the withholding of love is the sin. One can't love another without selflove or maybe it's the instincts I'm talking about, our urges yes, must control them for Lent, but then you could have hangups and be repressed. Who is that approaching on the canal bank? …

JF: Don't commemorate me where there is still water for in its stillness dead things float.

… Expect poison from still water; the berries which Crichton collected were the berries of the Cuckoopint, lords and ladies. He brought the poison of the world to the surface. The reeds prompted by the wind are genuflecting to her in homage. The sun in her face in her yellow gherkin bobbing like a daffodil. O I don't know, once you harm no one, that's the main thing.

Must put Uanito to sleep, story first. *Salve María* then our prayer: *Dios Santo* make Uanito a good boy, and *Nuestra Señora* put a word in to make his wheeze better …

JF: In the wheezing of his chest, Leo could hear voices halfsuppressed as if trying to emerge from the depths.

… *¡Qué, qué! Estabas meando en la acera. ¡Que cosa!* No, no, will never do that again.

V

'The worst and best parts of us are the secrets we never reveal.'
Lytton Strachey

JF: Am I on? I'm doing a survey. Do you find the frequent Gaelic and Spanish phrases offputting?

Reader: I do. Why do they do it?

It was something they brought with them, something innate.

Maybe you'd have a word.

A *focal* perhaps, but I don't want to inhibit them. *Veremos.*

What?

We'll see. Give me a seven letter name with only three letters.

You'll do foc all.

Bar ...

What?

I was prompting you. Barbara.

Good night.

Reader: Does God really mean Dog? I mean the reincarnation as an animal and then meeting the same fate?

SYC: Interesting insight in the context of the sacrifice of Leo's Dog.

SFC: You can't prove he was sacrificed. He was never found.

SYC: They found his burnt collar at the bonfire. Hadn't the heart to tell Leo. So was that poor creature the Christ? Or a standin for? Could it have been?

SFC: Balderdash. The problem with this woman is she craves allocontact. Even the fish can go home to his alewife, but Jude well ...

Reader: Where does your man live?

JF: He comes from a place where the organ is still.

Jude: His organ is never still. Leo, are you awake?

Leo: I was dozing. Isn't it wonderful this telepathy. Lil can't hear. Allow me to invite you, Jude, to a ringside seat at the edge of my mind.

What is important in life that is to say?

What is important is that we develop other ways of seeing and leave our purblind, blinkered, tunnelled and scaled vision in the shallows …

What adjectives!

Reader: In other words, don't sweat the small stuff. What his mother was always saying.

SYC: What I think it is is that we don't accept fairy tales anymore, the postmodern Little Red Riding Hood with the stringed wooden balls bobbing on each breast as she walked, saw the wolf in the guise of the grandmother and coolly raised a gun and shot him. All the more to blast you, my dear.

… My eyebrow gives an inborn raise. Saw two lovers kissing tongues, chewed food being orally transmitted from mother to baby just as the birds predigest for their young, no different, the same biological phenomenon. You may come back after I've finished my ablutions or stay, all the same now that we're noncorporeal, in fact nice feeling to have you around. Piles distended somewhat today, still the drop of blood ah well, *carpe diem*. Dreadful smell of shit as I walk. Strange it's not diffused in the open air. May be connected with pollution and ozone layer all coming back to assail our nostrils. Terrible thought to think. A mongrel raises its leg against a spare mangy tree, must go there every day, a creature of habit, likes its bark.

Ravensheuch as he plunged into the depths. The depths of the sea, the depths of despair, can't remember which. There were other lines can't recall.

Leo, you know what Uanito just asked me? At what age are you going to die, Mamá? Will you die at twenty-four?

He has an early grasp of mortality. Sculpture up above of Molly Malone, nice apples lowcut mimicking hindquarters. Affording the same turnon from the front when you can't get around the back.

I remember her. She became a meeting place for Iberians on Suffolk Street. But I have a different kind of teaser for you.

Fire away.

When is a coin more costly than paper money?

Don't know.

When it gets stuck in the washing machine.

Uanito?

¿Hay otro? But then he made up for it by setting my breakfast table without my asking. Where's Lil?

When I left she was hanging out the washing on her metal carousel. She'll sit then on her garden seat and watch the washing half the day distrustful of neighbours for fear some of the garments may be stolen …

SFC: How does one wash garments tainted by time?

… Sharpen step, work today, must try to get over my laziness *zzz* what, narcolepsy by day, insomnia by night. Even dreamed about insomnia once, ah well …

JF: He looked intently at each face in the crowd for a sign.

Reader: A sign of what?

JF: Of knowing. But there was nothing there other than angstdriven transience.

… I looked directly into their downcast eyes. Excuse, O yes, read faces like books, reveal a lot, what drives us on? Push push all the time, ants the same, carrying the twigs double or treble their own bodyweight in endless conveyance. Rarely see the same people two days walking, trampling over street artist's work, more sophisticated beggars now, play classical or jazz, a whole orchestra up above in Grafton Street. Have to fight for space for anything you want, little given freely, even the … well youknowwhat. What's the busker chalking on the pavement? *I'm collecting money for a rocket to escape this planet.* What do you make on the make? Lie supine, left to pine. On the shelf in the shallows pine away for other days, happy happy day. Ah well, today's day is today. Learn a lot about people the way they walk: machoflaunting of shoulders, arms hanging loose as he bounds along propelled by his Doc Martens …

JF: The evil one touched those who passed by to make them evil also.

Leo, do dreams mean you are dying? Are they death omens? When the dreams are over will you die? Like Don Quixote?

… Must nurture the dreams. Death force, life force, keep back the curtains and shadows, but tackle the darkness when it comes. Things don't end with a crash and cymbals; they for the most part just peter out like the slow burning of a fire or fade away like a golden brimstone at summer's end, like the beautiful girl who came and went like …

Enough. Your needle is stuck.

There's Lil going past the College of the Holy and Undivided Trinity, didn't know she was … She's going into Ewleys with her plastic bag. Follow from a distance.

Leo, haven't you to go to work?

Follow to see what … a little game, try not to be … time to spare before library opening. Ewleys: aromas coffee bangers cream buns chatter chatter plates colliding with the waitresses. Old women with scarves, students with books, spot the celebs among the plebs. Former Government Minister over there talking about his memoir. Couple pecking in corner cubicle, bit early for that. Oriental wallpaper. Where is Shiva? Look at that woman with the hat and pensive dress, gorging to the gills, manicmured for the occasion. I snuggle into an adjoining cubicle, near but hidden. Hear Lil lilt.

Freddie.

What's the scandal, me oul flower? You missed me?

The Rhymer
Two kisses on either cheek
to put jealousy to sleep.

Maybe I did. Maybe I didn't.

Of course you missed me.

Hands off for the moment that is.

Did you get the manuscript?

Yes photocopied and the original returned to him so he'll never even notice.

Good work.

This better work, Freddie.

It will work. Don't worry.

Jude (*whispering*): What's going on, Leo?

Not sure, Jude. She and Crichton are up to something.

Crichton: So how did you do it?

Lil: I duly arrived at the Francis home under the guise of a cleaning woman.

A cleaning woman, you?

Reader: Undercover worker, remember?

Francis asked about his usual housekeeper and I said she was sick on that day, and I had no difficulty in fobbing it all off on the unsuspecting Mr Francis who was in some other world only known to himself. Francis lashed with his pen at a large ecru envelope on the desk. He put his spectacles close to the envelope, lifting the sticky flap. No, he must have missed that one, he said. Difficult the ones that have the same flesh colour as the envelope, difficult to see, ah sorry about that, usually get them first swipe. (He began to jump up and down on his seat.) Will you excuse me, Miss? Eh got to ... *mingo mingere*. Mustn't do it in your shoe, or you may fall for me ha ha. Be back in two shakes. That's when I acted.

Crichton: And a fine actor you are, Lil. But these pages, they carry the story forward but they don't reveal the ending.

So it was a waste of time.

O no, not a waste of time. Leave it with me Kooshycoo.

Leo (*whispering*): Stuck here, Jude, windows closed, many

bodies, hold breath, afraid to inhale the four odours for fear I will … all coming from the table. Must chance it, or I'll be late for work …

Jude (*sotto voce*): What was in the manuscript, Leo?

Don't know, Jude. Further development in our travails although not how we will end. But we that nearly were not will now be anew in a way different to what it would have been if the leaves had not been shed.

*

RETURNING BOOKS TO SHELVES, HATE THOSE BOOKS THAT SNAP shut like a clamp if you ignore them for an instant. Put from mind, *Modern Irish Poetry*, silly word *modern*, dated title, won't last. Should say Poetry of the eighties or nineties or whatever. Perusing illustrations of the work of Boz. The books that I touch tell me something about myself …

Reader: What does the librarian read?

… Last summer I read *Midsummer Night's Dream*. In winter I read Anton, could never associate a Russian with sun or beach. I peruse Virginia's diaries in the autumn. Sam too is mainly autumnal. Shem the Penman suits the late spring or early summer. It's all about mood. Short Celtic or Hindu myths, their succinctness goes down well with bowel movement.

Reader: Did you read *Finnegans Wake*?

I read the title.

Reader: And verse?

I am well versed. The lights must never go out. The music must always play.

Who was that?

A poet passed pitch of grief.

Do you like Dickens?

Sets my child channel on a slide or two on the ice a snowball in the ear an abscess injection excruciating pain slush wet feet and chilblains and how you felt then when they burst it and the cold and wind on the bicycle to school and layers of possing wet clothes, putting on damp gloves over frozen fingers and the twilight, the *marbhsholas* and winter darkness setting in on the suburban streets and the greyness and the tall lamps highlighting a gloom and the sound of coughing from the paraffin oil fire and reading Dickens in those pretelevison days. What the dickens is it about his characters that gives me the creeps? Is it the bony legs under the penguin bellies, the sharp nose and muttonchop whiskers, the tightfitting tailcoat and top hat, the long hair and ugly faces … ?

JF: He was ugly so he beat him handsome.

The Red Tart: Nobody's ugly after 2 am.

… Is it that he touched the surface of a world of horror and deprivation and cruelty, particularly to children? Of a caste system? I suppose it is the prisonlike feeling on looking at these characters that what is or was would remain, the poor in the gutter, crushed unknown and uncared for.

SFC: The powder bears an undue proportion to the jam.

Reader: Is the critic back already?

Leo: Back and hovering about.

Reader: I say, Mr Crichton, isn't it? Were you in Ewleys today?

SFC: There's a ewley on in Hannigan's house tonight.

Reader: Mr Crichton, you are speaking out of form? I shall have to inform Mr Francis.

SFC: Mr Francis ha ha. By crikey, inform Mr Francis. Yes you do that. He may terminate or exterminate me by Shiva. I may have something on him. Besides my critical expertise is universally sought.

Reader: What did Mrs Lambkin entrust to you today?

SFC: A document purporting to express how the lives of Leopold Lambkin and his confidante Bernarda, aka Judith Rodiguéz, will conclude, a scoop for me and a ruin for Francis, let the youknowwhat out of the bag …

What?

Before its time.

What?

His *Letters to Jude* …

Leo: Did you call, Jude?

Jude: No, Crichton.

… appearing in a serial form will have serious trouble if its end appears before its middle, and what a fine fat middle it did have ha ha a a ah.

Reader: You mean you know how the novel shall end, and Jude?

Jude: Did you call, Leo? I can't get this line.

Reader: Why did Mrs Lambkin give this document to you?

She knows of the correspondence and wants a speedy end to it. Jeopardising the marriage, proper order, despicable degenerate.

Leo: Food day, Freddie. Get off the page. You will soon be neutered.

No fear, Leo boy, Leo the lionhearted ha ha ah.

Leo (*under the rose*): Jude, we must tell Mr Francis about his manuscript. They will ruin him and put an end to us. Montpellier, Montpellier, keeps ringing in my ear. Where did I come across it? Was it in a dream? Mr Francis, Mr Francis …

JF: He died bequeathing his eye to the eyebank for his son to keep an eye on his wife.

… Mr Francis, do you know your final chapters were … ?

A jockey's is a great life but a short one.

Mr Francis your manus …

Life is like a borrowed spoon, it will have to be given back.

Mr Francis.

Matthewman marklion lukecalf johneagle. Find the answer in the Kortorbib, yes don't spill anything.

Can't get a sense word out of him when he's like this. Must have ingested something. Mr Francis.

Who was it that opened my garden gate in the frosty morn? A quick noncreaking, opening like a tingling on the spine or a spirit coming and going for no footsteps were heard and no wild wind blew. All was still, but I heard the gate closing. Sit still and let the mind adventure you.

Reader: Were you ever in love, Mr Francis?

JF: In love? Ah …

The Rhymer
Goodbye, Jimmy goodbye.
I'll see you again
but I don't know when.
Goodbye, Jimmy goodbye.

… All the kids on the road where I grew up were singing it, that song. They giggled and whispered when my father went out and somehow or other realised they were referring to me. They called me Jimmy in those days. I was only in first year secondary school at the time, far too young for this sort of thing, or such was his thinking behind his saltandpepper walrus moustache, far too young altogether dating a girl on the road, hardly dating. I don't think that would have been the word he would have used. Whoremaster he called me, and I had just been playing alivio with the girl, maybe looked at her in a slightly different way to what was innocent, and she a year or two older than me was streetwise and was milking all the attention to the hilt. The outcome was that I was confined to my room for a number of nights till the commotion died down.

And that … ?

Coloured my …

So you never … ?

No never, beyond having a housekeeper. Too much bother. Better to make them up in my head.

*

GOT THE COAL BY THE LIGHT OF THE MOON, A MUSLINCOVERED lantern behind the privet hedge, soft not glaring like the Auschwitz strobe from a neighbouring house. A few stars small and distant dot the darkness. A romantic night for romantics under this mantle. Back to the house and its routine domesticities.

In bed the sheet falls over my face. Not yet, not yet, I have some time left. I hear the ambulance siren. For whom? They're coming to take you away ha ha. Not funny. A sound more frequent now. Heart emphys … most common in the fair isle of the high cholesterol. All our lives in danger of premature termination, and I worry about the blood in the stool and such natural phenomena as possible cause of … Wonder what the green thing was in the cheese? Chives maybe. Mared the other night: small but shapely one short legs in a room only big enough to hold a bed might have been on a train as the place vibrated. She calls to some guy in the other room. Reluctant to come, said she, didn't like doing that in front of others last night. She is crouching at the door talking to him. I am lying on my back on the bed. She speaks in a seductive voice: would you like to come? …

JF: Seduction is the art of genital persuasion.

… The guy comes in. The shortlegged one goes on all fours, offering her pearshaped rump for his delectation. But he just sits on the side of the bed and instructs her to fondle inside my jeans undoing belt and zip. She raises Phal up. There is green stuff on her hand. It is mucous, a discharge from the wrong end, a freak of nature like the pink rose on the white rose bush …

JF: As pink as a blush.

… Man the only animal who can do that …

SFC (*ejaculating with enthusiasm*): A simple explanation is that Leo wanted to blow his nose at the same moment. One or the other.

… The prick is really more trouble than it's worth. It starts with incontinence and causes so much anxiety in the adolescent years and so much timeconsuming preoccupation during the middle years and then towards the end it will take its revenge by spilling the liquid once more like a leaky tap.

Reader: Steady on. Whatdoyoucall her is here.

Jude: Mr Francis is pushing us too hard, Leo. We'll have to get onto the Union.

The Seer of Suburbia: A man died in the Union, and there was no one there to claim him.

Leo: He's being hassled by the critics and readers, avoids interviews, and when he does speak, one can't get a straight answer out of him. Can't get a word out of Lil either. She's back to her taciturn self. She never laughs at my jokes but scoffs at my discomforts. Gives you the look now, the knowing look that she has something on you. Would put the youknowwhats on you. She's a reciprocator really. With her you always have to make the first move. Her tit for your tat, hard to calibrate her calibri. Words wasted, wastes she not wants nor can hear my innerscream. Think before we use the word. Different way of expressing I suppose, a craving with some, and others would be happy as the day is long without saying e'er a word. Words that hurt the ones most remembered. Have to be care … but then you and I, Jude, are communicating wordlessly. What is written is just the translation.

The transmogrification.

OK.

The Sympathetic Critic asked me the other day, following on Mr Francis' survey. What's this it was? Why do Spanish words pepper my speech? I said when I get carried away the language of my ancestors comes out from my subconscious. Sometimes even words that I don't remember learning.

We all have another language deep inside us.

But what about Lil, Leo? Can she have children before her biological clock stops?

I told you about her disease.

Reader: What disease?

JF: Outside my role. Let the researchers find out. I'm doing my job.

Researcher: If she gave birth to a son he would die. Daughters survive but become carriers. Therefore it is too risky. Leo would have been happy to adopt, but not Lil. It would not be the same she is reported as saying.

Reader: How was this discovered?

Her sister's two sons died, and Lil was then tested.

Reader: Never hear mention of her sister.

She was a good few years older than Lil. She took it very badly and she …

Reader: O.

Leo: Sleep now …

The Rhymer
If you don't tear
everything out
that's in
sleep won't win.

… The lace curtain dances at the open window. A wind revving up like a motor, hope the TV aerial holds. Stays have come loose, always something.

Jude: Santa Teresa is a great support. She holds up the leg of my lampstand. *La Vida de …*

*

READER: WHAT IS JF DOING UNDER THE LIGHT?

JF: I am trying to read the inkprint of the typeprint on a blank page …

The Seer of Suburbia: The blank page doesn't know you.

The Rhymer
Black ink drowns in the white sea.
It's not enough for me,
no more than rhyme or reason.

… I like the white writing but it is tough on the eyes. I like it because it is part of the paper itself, part of the leaf unlike the black ink imposed on it. Also it seems to form itself, words appearing through the leaf, colourless like spirits, words that I do not recognise as my own.

Leo: Up for another sleepless day. Bacon not up to scratch. Itch always in inaccessible parts. You expect the same rasher day after day after week after year as if all pigs could be the same. A touch of blood in the orange, nice and juicy. Raydeeoh: gay men and lesbian women all over the airwaves …

JF: Amsterdam is full of dykes.

… All on the same foot now yes yes, the same *fútamál*. Put the sock on the other hand. Wind died down a real glimmer of spring at last …

Reader: The glimmerman is still about.

… Birds chirping and warmth, a little liquid sunshine in the day and growth, sounds of the early movers, the early birds bud and grass elongation rose prune and the rest, the whole thing all over again …

Reader: He's strong but he likes roses.

… Am I a strong man? Will I be able to lift my truth onto my shoulders and carry it through the world …

JF: Many a lyre has told the truth.

… for there is already a heavy sack of fear weighing me down? …

JF: Collect the sackcloth from the dry cleaners.

… Still, the spring bulbs are pushing up, showing their colours. The domestic travails of the day supplant life's finer points. A thought lost. Stand under the tree where the idea first formed. Schoolgirl cacophony drowned it out. Ah yes, bloodhound, what did you sniff out today? Loam nice and friable. Good for digging. Female walking chest forward flaunting black bra in its supporting role …

JF: A brassiere is a bust stop.

… from oysterpink suit open front, buttondown skirt hugging nubile curves. A little cow dung spill on the road. I saw a man once who tried to jump clear of cow dung but was short taken in the middle of it. What's that in the shop window? Framed posters …

Long life to her
for there's no other
who takes the place
of my dear mother.

… There they are in the library don't see me as if I were invisible or a glass between. Junior Library Assistant surreptitiously picking nose, should wait till half five when the otiose minutiae of the day have passed. Enjoy it all the more then. Muttered something behind his behind, didn't catch. Where was I in my reading? …

Jude: Leo, what are you on about?

… The woman leads us up and on. Have you a girlfriend? the girl asks the junlibassist. Yes, he says. How many? One for each finger. She nearly jumped out of her skin. Must have a word with him. Give us a bad rep. Look up the words. Forget the old ones as quickly as new ones learned, then soon forget the new ones. A greasylooking dogcollared loner over there by the stacks, crosslegged perusing, looks crosseyed too. Hole in his sole, time aplenty.

Wind and rain lash the whitened glass of the lavatory; mustn't be seen doing the needy. JLA turns on the tap full blast when doing his business so that his bodily noises are drowned out in the sound of running water. Fond of the chewing gum …

Reader: Was he the one in the church?

… The very one, showing his big pink gums like boiled ham. Why do we seek privacy when we all do the same thing? I look at the map of the world and see the dot in the middle: all the loud wailing thence. It could be swallowed up like an insect by the surrounding hugeness.

Not our dot, Leo. Surely not ours.

Erseland.

Good morning, Mr Lambkin.

Ah recognition from Junlibassist. What's he doing placing *The Origin of Species* under Fiction? The dull ache of enforced behaviour.

The Seer of Suburbia: Moving the car gears is now unconscious behaviour, but it was conscious behaviour once.

JLA: Terrible about that girl hanging herself in prison. Used a used shirt.

She put a hand in her own death.

JLA: Suicide is a crime.

And what's the punishment?

Morning, Mr Lambkin. Have you anything on depression?

It is the wistful little teacher, a member of the Minor Lay Pedagogues Association (MLPA). When depression hits, shouldn't lie under it. Write it out of the system. Well, I should have. Let me see: *The Noonday Demon*. Easy to know he's a teacher, see it in his pupils. To be wounded mentally is as serious as receiving a physical wound; needs healing.TLC, plaster of the mind.

Jude: Who will put a plaster on my mind, Leo?

Jude, you're distracting. I try to read as much as possible about it. Better than taking medication. Can make you more melancholy that ... No joy in his job, has to teach a new class. Sometimes I would prefer the screeching of cats in the night to the cacophony and wails of a school.

Ah Leo, I made you look. I made you stare.

O Jude, don't press me. The other night I had a mare that still lingers. I saw an old woman wizened and emaciated, so emaciated like a skeleton with big eyes bulging out of her a look of madness her only flesh was in her eyes. She pressed against me, her bones almost puncturing me. She was trying to seduce me. Lie down with me she said lie down with me. I freed myself from her grip and ran away.

O Leo, who was she? Was she the old biddy from the Liberties lane. No, don't say.

Who will sigh for the loss of that lady? What loneliness can do. And what will happen at the end of individual fret? Worry gains not an hour at the end of it all?

Isn't that what I've been saying?

I know. The great sphere will remain when the individual is gone, and will you or I make one jot of a difference? Man's stay is just a hackneyed stick of time.

O Leo, you are too heavy. You really went to the *pueblo* yesterday?

Yes, Saint Patrick's Day. The juice and joy of spring. The sap rising in all created things. The little crocus chalice offers its spring rites. The leaves are turning green this day. There's a man outstanding in his own field, surveying the soil.

Mines? Oil? Mineral?

No, the elusive shamrock, that's what. All the same in the heel of the hunt. Irish cows never shit on shamrock …

The Rhymer

It grows through the bogs and the brakes and the moorland
and we call it the dear little shamrock of Dotland.

… The one who approached me was armed but had no feet, rotating bike pedals manually. He turned off in the Park and left the world to motorists and to me …

JF: A tyred motor containing a tired motorist recently retired.

Reader: Does Mr Francis live in the world AF?

Leo: AF?

Reader: After Ford. What was it like to live in the world BF?

SYC: A time of squirrels and chestnut trees.

… We talked on Saint Patrick's Day in the hotel that is no more, not far from the Green of Stephen where the last hanging was of a young girl for stealing a calico gown. With Irish Americans who bore their childhood scars with pride and ne'er a bad word had to say about the old sod, while the old sods did nothing but ridicule them. Hewn from rock they were …

The Seer of Suburbia: The man who loved Rock Hudson.

… whiskeygravel and nicotinetough to the grave. They contributed in their way an atmosphere to Saint Patrick's Day …

The Seer of Suburbia: When did they wear the shamrock and the palm on the one lapel?

... Free then, freedom, Colmcille did prophesy ...

JF: An advocate of free love.

Reader: Who?

JF: A lay preacher.

... *Lá Fhéile Phádraig*: The tricolour flying green in truce with orange. The blue and white of Europe. Ah well, makes a ... of the whole past thing. Give me a peppermint, Daddy. The parade is coming ...

JF: The token of generosity by the *pater*, the Clarnico Murray peppermint cream (ask for them now, and they'll give you a biscuit) on Saint Patrick's Day is latched onto by the son as a source of strength, and every time he feels a craving for a youknowwhat, he reaches for a mint, and keeps a packet with him always.

SYC: If there only had been other tokens, what could he not have done? Only one mint in all?

JF: There was the hint of a second mint being offered one hour and forty-two minutes after the placing of the first mint in the mouth. However, it was a misguided hand movement, the arm lingering beguilingly, and the hint was withdrawn on the grounds that it would be injudicious and indulgent especially during the one day reprieve in Lent, and besides it would leave less for the *pater* to consume himself later secretly. All in all a good day.

Leo: To remember is to shed is to die a little. He declined soon after that. To forget the memory you once had is ... finish the above in not more than words.

O Leo, you record as if everything is past and you look through a haze at things that are no more.

Victoricus brought the letter containing the voice.

JF: What is written is rotten. What is wrote is rot. What is writ is right.

SFC: Mr Francis is famous not for his novel but for his novelty.

Leo: Are his synapses connecting? How many lights are on in his brain? The blood supply through the cerebral arteries is lit up like a manybranched, red leafless tree.

JF: Was out last night so slept in today.

Leo: I was in and I slept it out.

Jude: Jesus slept *¡Qué niños!*

JF: It all started in the wood of Voclut. I can't remember it, I'm forgetful. I got up in midsentence. You learn how something works when it fails. O yes, I have it now: which ring is always square?

Jude: O no.

JF: A boxing ring. Ho ho ho ho he he he. Spring time is bring time, my Irish Molly.

Leo: There is something trying to break through my mind, and it fills me with fear, flashes from shadows if such could be mentioned of fathers and families and memories, trigger off these spasms like twitches or muscle contraction, heart stops beating for a while and goes back again to its normal clocklike work, happens more frequently now. One wonders if that could be a way to die, a muscular stop on a moment of black dread.

SFC: Why black? A redundant, hackneyed word.

SYC: Maybe you should consult *The Oxford Book of Death.* Leo shares a mutual death dread with Unamuno.

What lies hidden, Leo. Try to bring it to the open, but not our secret. You have too many fragments and broken Delph.

If Lil could only stand under what gives one so much pleasure and another so little pain. You push the damper in and you pull the damper out and the smoke goes up the chimney all the time.

Don't blow yourself up, Leo, like the big frog in the small pond. Don't chase the faded laurel wreath, but neither blow yourself away. Think of the dog with the meat in his mouth releasing his grip to snatch at his reflection in the lake. Remember the institution outlasts the individual.

JF: Hear see hear see.

Leo: Why is the innocent dog wrapped up in dogma?

*

Went to the cinema with Lil, a double bill, eve of Saint Patrick. A blue moon guiding our way. Almost bumped into a girl carrying a doubleedged oar near the GPO. Steered to the right, paddling her own canoe.

She consented to go after all the …

Her idea, she likes the movies you see and the bridge friend, well is for bridge.

Or you know who was not available.

Shhh.

Sorry.

That would be too open.

You are whispering, Leo.

I mean not clandestine enough for you know who.

SFC: It should be *for you know whom.*

Not that there was any holding of hands or any of that sort of thing between us although there was a young guy getting the wear in a row in front of us. No we were just left to our own imaginations.

More powerful.

Perhaps. Lil went to town. Weight up weight down icecream tub and Irish Rose and teardrops cos she thought it would be a weepie. I sucked an Orange Maid, caressing with the tongue from top to bottom, lifting her up and catching her cold droplets in my mouth, holding the stick firmly and drawing in suction till there was nothing left but white ice.

But the film, Leo?

Two actually. One a vintage. Do you remember Jacqueline, Jude, on the lesswire? No, how could you? And then the film: Jackaleeen! A reshowing of a vintage movie. And the black and white flick in the fourpenny rush, and her little self reaching up to knock at the front door of her house, and her knickers with the loose elastic falling to her ankles. And Lil laughed, and I laughed too in memory. Where is she now? What was her name, the actress? O yes, Jacqueline Ryan, daughter of Phyllis Ryan, an actor in her own right. Something Gregson her father in the film I mean underrated act … Fear of heights, fondness for booze, a weakness really, hard to make the four ends meet. Ah well that's the way, different today, still poverty there but younger ones more precocious. A long ray on the way home.

The Rhymer
Try to buy a long ray today
skate around Howth but no hope of ray.

Reader: What's Mr Francis doing?

SFC: He's flexing his cotton balls.

Leo: Ho, a mare coming.

Jude: It is night.

Meteorites falling, people running indoors, a girl walking indifferent. Are you seeking death? I am seeking life. The meteorites will pound me into life, the girl says. What do you see? Love and joy the planet cannot provide. We are in the sixth stage of extinction and we live each day as if we are immortal.

O Leo, you will be invincible only as long as you are in contact with earth like Antaeus.

Earth mother. The night folds in like skin tightening, cold shiver, finances low, save fuel, run up and down the stairs times several to warm the blood. The hand cupped the breast. Sex on the other hand … give us a hand when I've lost my way …

JF: Sex is here to stray.

… The sac of the scrotum contracts and enlarges, distending veins and then heaves and turns as if there is a swell or whirlpool underneath the skin. Why wash Phal after use? Which use? Many uses. Nonstick, dripdry quicken detumescence. Phal is a good masseur as well, not a lot of people that know …

Phal: Don't guy me.

Third Arts Examiner: (a) Using *Letters to Jude* as an exemplum, discuss how dominant a role the phallus has in the overall metabolism of the body? Contrast with heart, lungs, toes, fingers etc. (b) To what extent does the phallus influence the psyche? Note: The effects of brain signals on the phallus are obvious in tumescence. But what is being asked is to discuss the hegemony which the phallus can exercise in thoughts and subconsciousness. Some percentage data here would be expected. One possible departure point might be to consider the different emphases given to the lingam in other cultures. NB: All answers must be illustrated with the usual copious quotations and references.

… Usual quotes. He's not at the races at all. Some males just live for their pricks as Google enquiries prove where men ask more questions about their penis than any other organ. Like a religion they prick themselves up every day. Entire existence centred around the pleasure of it and thereafter. Was it Saint Gus who told us that these genital stirrings were our punishment for Original Sin, our moment of pleasure? Wouldn't mind more pun like that …

JF: Never point a pun at a friend; it might be loaded.

… Or was it the Holy Jerry who told us that it was okay once we took no pleasure in it. Hope you took no pleasure, Jude.

Ah ah O O sorry, Leo, I was carried away. Wish you hadn't stopped. Absolutely not. What would *el santo* say he'd have?

An erect man.

JF: Leo rubbed his eyes in tiredness, rotating the swirling liquids and coloured larva of his mind. Soon *codladh suan.*

*

MORNING. THE DAWNING OF THE DAY. THE ENTANGLED bedclothes reflecting the entangled mind of the previous night's travail. The mundane day of Moanday. Give your dreams a holiday. Today's weather: rain giving way to showers, good good, maybe a rainbow thrown in to renew our faith in miracles. Used to have an egg one morning and a rasher the next ...

Un día sí y otro no.

... What's the difference between a raw egg and a good ride ... ?

Reader: You can beat a raw egg.

... Very good, very sharp. But to keep the rash away now have a rasher every day. We got a nice new shiny toaster.

Who from? What time? Must get Uanito out.

... Who did we get the toaster from, Lil? O she told me but I forget ...

The Rhymer
A Toast:
Here's to those that wish me well
and those that don't can go to Hell.

... She doesn't like repeating especially when she's busy. Always busy, scrambling eggs or some such thing. Anyway this new toaster has five different levels of carcinogenic burning at the turn of a knob. O yes remember now, she won it at bridge. Will it outlive me? Keep telling Lil about the dangers of toast. Besides she's dry enough in the morning without dehydrating altogether. But she loves her bit of toast. Anyway where would the scrambled egg be without it?

Lil: Who was at the door?

Someone from the Watch Tower Bible and Tract Society, witnesses to Jehovah.

Jesus, they're out early.

Some of our fellows should take a leaf from their book. Early birds, maybe they will get their wish to rule over the Jonadabs. What's that on the radio? A murderer runs marathon in prison yard. Starts at official time and all. Look out for the Green Daisy Symbol to know your food is irradiated. No sex for Sellafield husbands. Where do you go?

JF: The pros and cons of sex.

Jude: I hear, Leo, and I fear what we are doing to ourselves. Life is a slow suicide for many.

Lil: Look at the time, Leo. Where does your mind go? You'll be late for work.

Leo: Where does a thought go when you are finished with it? Must rush, see all later.

Lil: *All*, Leo? You're on the edge.

JF: He edged his way gingerly along the windowsills of his mind.

Sorry, Jude. I can talk to you again now. I'm outside. Thinking about religion and your views, I know it has its good points, but my considered opinion now is, and I give it in good faith, that I will not forfeit my mind for its seductiveness. And what about the Crucifixion? That's what the other film was about by the way in the tworeeler: *Jesus of Montreal*. Lil likes the films. She likes having the actors and actresses doing all the talk for her, and all she has to do is munch on her teardrops. Can the Father be forgiven for crucifying the Son?

Jude: In the name of god, the merciful, the compassionate, who do I have to guide me? Whomsoever God leads astray, no guide he has. He leaves them in their insolence blindly wandering in need of a guide, Leo, to live somewhat correctly, and at the end each of us will receive his just deserts.

Bird's custard. When you think of it, enough to turn you off. A dropping on the window.

Leo.

No, I mean you roll marbles uphill and they just come down again each time. Speaking of which, the way I played marbles compared to now ...

JF: He kept his marbles until total shipwreck.

... Does Uanito play? Saw children play in the street ...

Juego de bolitas.

... The way I used to travel to school along the marbles channel at the side of the road, rolling along the marbles, seeking percussion from glass balls. And letting the imagination wander, seeing different shapes and colours inside the globe of the cat's eye or crystal or gulleyer or taw or blue moon and little bubbles trapped in its universe. I used to get as much enjoyment and wonder from them by holding them up to the light as I did in playing them. The children are going around with bags of them now. Can't remember having bags, just the pockets of the short pants bulging. Smaller quantities then. They don't seem to be playing along the gullies anymore.

And religion?

... Religion makes me more afraid to be happy than to be miserable. He who finds his life shall lose it and the converse. I am frightened by these words, Jude. I fear that in the netherworld, if there is any, I will be an abandoned spirit, floating alone, accompanied only by my own selfjustification in a dark cosmos. I will hear happy laughter from Lil, who will be comingling with a bevy of likeminded souls, all jolly, and you will be trying to bring me back to the world of the happy spirits. But it is so dark, I cannot find my way. There is a sound of howling, and the happy cries fade away. What is written in the sands? Can we find what it is? We must keep in communication with the dead we loved, for they are our connection. They may give us answers. And for the life hereafter if it is to be, will you bring a suitcase? I can see the dogcollared bachelor getting hot under the ... he is suitable for hearing confessions.

But you mentioned the rainbow.

Yes under the rainbow I saw a hedgehog upturned on the side of the road, asleep I thought, but he was dead. Not a budge. What a revelation to see the underside of the humped bristle, and a sad little face with the little piggy nose and tiny legs outstretched pleadingly—a motor car victim. I will give him a scented grave among the pine needles in the squirrel wood, more aromatic after the drizzle which is soft and pervasive now...

Meteorologist: Any water drop larger than 1mm is classified as rain, not drizzle.

... The snails are everywhere, amazed at the maize of their cilia trails. I closed the shed door this morning to the crunch of snail shells, but there was something more: a sound like that of a human or animal crying. And now as I make my way the chestnut trees weep, and the hills hide in the mist.

Reader: Used you collect chestnuts when you were a boy?

Leo: Yes, conkers we called them, but now as an adult I collect impressions instead. And here is an old man coming up the hill.

Jude: Another old man?

Leo: The same ...

The Rhymer

With a nick nack Paddy whack give a dog a bone
this old man came rolling home.

… walking sideways, his cap to the other side, pushing one foot after the other, his fly open and his mouth catching flies, not drunk, maybe had a little stroke? There it is, the buts and the ifs.

Consuelo. Souls with God bellowed the sanctified sod, where repose the heavenly remains.

We are not moving. We are like two stones that have fallen from a wall and are stuck in the mud.

Stones that the builder rejected. Real stickinthemuds. That leaves ten others in the Jordan, part of the Tribes.

Is it our fault, Jude, for being what we are? Is it the lice's fault for being lice? The harlot's for being nice? Sorry, delete.

Lice, really Leo? *Por Dios.*

Like lice with your drink? Swizzle with yur swizzle stick. I caught this morning morning's minion. All religions are external things, except in the mystical aspects. The internal workings of the mind are areligious in all of us whether we accept it or not.

Holy ones dream of Eros too. It's the trying that counts, Leo.

Can be very trying, but it's the tobacco that counts.

How?

Remember the ad on the old Players packet flap? Of course you wouldn't. Used to be a game. A story about Arabs in the desert hearing a counting, clues given to discover the counters 123. Of course one could only play the game once with the same players.

Leo, I think you're going as loco as Jaime.

I don't give a crested cormorant, Jude. Brain teeming with … unsung all awash, awake, throbbing, fleeing and flying helterskelter in myriad millions like little fish chasing their tails in the swim all lights on.

*

JUDE: I'VE MANAGED TO GET INSIDE HIS HEAD.

Whose?

Crichton's.

How did you do that?

I'm not sure. I just twirled the dials. I'm going to greet the obnoxious one now.

God to you.

God and Mary to you.

God Mary and Joseph to you.

God Mary Jotheph and Patrick to you.

God Mary Joseph Patrick and Brigid to you.

God and the reth of them to you. A hundredthouthandmillion welcomes. Your purpose?

Postgraduate thesis on the works of JF.

Francith started from humble origins, he says, popping a pill into his mouth, came to notice mainly with a novella about death and then came *Letters to Jude*, therialised, not finished, some poems and short youknowwhaths, an odd article peculiar to the univerthal preth for whom for thome reason he refused to perform cartwheels, overate dint eh groves of academe.

You say he never finished *Letters to Jude*?

Not publicly ath yet.

Leo: Jude, Jude, ask him how it ends.

Do you know how … ?

Ha ha ha yes I ha ha ha no. Your name?

Ju … eh Julie eh O'Grady.

A Celt. Well JOG my memory ha hah yes, the Celths are invading mindspace now. Ith there anywhere they will not wind up? Do I know how … ?

It ends?

Why muth everything be explained in language? Tho much of what is hap today is yond the reach of lang (he says scratching his back because he says his finger is itchy). Ath regards how it will all end I don't think he as worked that out yet, not that I would reveal that to you, a mere student, but I can give you thomething, a crumb as it were for your trouble.

Yes please, a crumb.

The book consists ethentially of communication by means of pathages from Literature (including the Holy Books)—decipher the meaning from a code. Difficult to fathom, a thecret known only to the two minds but never communicated or commented on verbally and no confirmation that the methage was received. No vithible sign, juth soul unions, telepathy tranthcending conventional forms. But ath regards how it will end …

He's on to us, Leo. What are we to do?

It's only a suspicion. How could he prove it? He is unverbed. Let fear not be upon you?

O Leo, and we didn't even telepathise to the full.

I sympathise fully. But what are we doing now? We have discarded the leaves.

No, I mean I hope you don't say you mind this but for example could love be made to Lil with your Phal and my mind? You understand. Or *mi cuerpo*? Could my body and your animo commune with Uanito? I mean for example could you be able to sit down in my body and tell him a story. *O estoy trastornada*. Virgen María, tell me, shall I drown myself or not?

O Jude, the old man I saw coming up the hill has since died. The house painter told me. He was so lonely he had phoned to ask the painter to paint his house. He was the last person the old man saw before he passed away.

*

THE LIBRARY ASSOCIATION MEETING: HOBNOBS, BIGNOBS, pouts and touts. Late, Leo settles in.

Crichton: Ah Mr Lambkin hath arrived. We may proceed.

Jude: Leo, are you all right?

I'm up the wall. Crichton, a man of great hauteur with his lovely head of skin encompassing the slightest hint of hair on temple over left eye, jocularly referred to *subrosa* as the dandruffed image. He would either hide away or upstart like a startup mouse.

Jude: He should massage his scalp with goose dung.

JF: Leo picked particles of course, lumpy skin.

Jude: Where?

JF: From the little circular bald patch of course on the back of his head and threw them down on the white page and wondered what they would look like under a microscope. Not a birthmark. But a patch since birth. Would it ever go carcinogenic? Not connected with baldness, fine head of *fionnán* on him and on his father before him; kept their heads to the grave, although his father died young, no worry there really. Of course there is always the first time, thinning of strands for some must feel like a numbering, an allotment of time.

'The difference between nineteenth- and twentieth-century mobs ... ' Crichton was expororating, salivating, expurgating to all and sundry. See the junlibassist scribbling assiduously ... 'is literacy, ladieth and gentlemen.'

Leo: He said mobs. He's thinking of his gangs ...

O Leo.

... Trying to put respectability on them, on their grunts and grimaces. That's what he's about. Literacy my foot. That's just a guise. He's looking at me now directing his spiel at me.

Ignore him, Leo. Our Lord was the first man that ever throng pricked upon. *Ecce Homo.*

I'm terrified, Jude. What is it? Try to say I find the reality of my own mind and the more concrete reality of the world around me diverging more and *níos mó*, and the most frightening thing is that I'm losing interest in the outer. It fills me with such dread that maybe I could go made …

Old maiden aunt: We'll paint our arses red and go mad.

JF: If my aunt had a mickey, she'd be my uncle.

… There you see I said *made* and meant *mad*. But why should these baldy basts … ?

Prejudice, Leo.

No, but why should they have monopoly of sanity? What is sanity *ar aon nós*?

Keeping in touch.

Maybe I need more selfdiscipline. Too much indulging.

'… Do you realise what that means, ladieth and gentleman?'

Good, he's widening his gawk.

'It means that literature,' Mr Crichton says, punctuating his speech with belches and groans, 'is a very potentially revolutionary …'

Good on the Rs. No sign of the lisp. Must have rehearsed in front of his cracked mirror. Give him a drumroll. Juniorlibassist and the lickspittles guffaw and cling like barnacles to every dull sound and cliché of the stricken speech. Would pronounce your language well, Jude.

'… weapon. When we restock we should bear thith in mind. For whom do we cater?'

JF: *Et hoc genus omne*, although some of them just come for the knitting class.

'Mr Lambkin.'

Ah recognition.

'Perhaps you could enlighten uth?'

'Well I ah.'

Jude: Don't say you're going to do your Jimmy Stewart

impersonation that you used to do years ago with me. Not here, Leo. It won't go down with them.

'Mr Lambkin.'

'Yeah well I ah ... '

'Yes.'

'... I was just thinking like eh yeah before you go on. I tell the seed of Adam like the aaah ... '

'What?'

'The aaah the aaah ... '

Jude: That is Jimmy Stewart, Cristo.

'... Sorry, the hypocrites will come. They will assume the shapes of god and the slippery ones, yeah eels like the imposters of the latterday world shall all ah well ah go on the path.'

'What the Vulcan are you saying?'

'Sorry on ah on the path, into the dark bitter torments. Yeah, that's it aaah I aaah.'

O Leo, *te quiero. ¡Qué magnífico!*

'Well ladieth and gentleman, you heard it for yourselves. I think we can safely athume our colleague Mr Lambkin here is suffering from a bout of religious mania?'

'No, it's just you were pretty deep, and deep calls to deep. Hope you didn't eh. Well must to the eh eh ... '

JF: Eh eh, the constipatory grunt for the old euphemism. Hesitancy to use lavatorial terms, an initial stalling like the distended straining of the act itself.

... Bit of gas, Jude. Hope it didn't cost me my job. Mr Francis yonder is busy writing. Some say he has a hobnailed liver, makes homebrew. Approached by Will's dad, local neighbour on his ear, distrustful of the word written. Can't make your will in here, said Will's dad. Would you wear a dead man's coat? It's only new.

Glamour model: Who are you wearing?

Crichton (*off stage sotto voce*): A mot from Ringsend.

Leo: I wore a Davy Crockett hat when I played as a boy with its squirrel tail made from my mother's fur coat.

*

COLD TO FLU SHAKE OFF, NOT RECOURSE TO YOU OUL AUNTIE Biotica, speed it up despite what they say, a little concerned of coffin blood. Auntie kills more than she ought. Depressed, never know what we're putting into our insides. Really and alcohol too …

JF: Leo rarely gets a head cold. Runny eyes and nose are not characteristics.

… A fine evening in stretch. Just a hint of darkness. Bit of grass, will walk there. Undergrowth soft under foot flat. Temporary relief. Then back on path, click click on the steel heeltip, saves wear, click click rhythmic step, giving the impression of purposeful going. A feeling: some animal following me. No, just a crispy leaf rustled by the wind. There's a man in the winter of his life throwing a perennial stick for the perennial dog to fetch in the perennial grass …

JF: His song is sung. His white coat is made. He was given the stick and the road.

Jude: Were you fired, Leo?

… No, not yet. Francis exaggerates. But Crichton took delight in warning me, showing off his power over me in front of others …

Reader: Describe Leo with three eyes.

JF: Impressionable, impressionistic and impressive.

… I'm only a halfhardy perennial. As the day lightens so do one's cares. The hour to change soon. Even leaving the second lock unturned now, the odd time that is.

Jude: That last line was mine, Leo. Another slip by Mr Francis, but no matter. I am feeling more optimistic and I sense it in you today. Weather makes us …

The Rhymer
Ash before oak
we're in for a soak.
Oak before ash
we're in for a splash.

… So I should never be gloomy over here.

Leo: Either way you need the brolly. Vigour in the legs, tune a whistle and wet it with a pint of plain. Tavern dark. Same light same heat day or night in and out and on our way. Fat lady with short legs on a high stool drinking. Would give you a bar by the looks. How did she get up? How will she get down … ?

The poor woman, Leo. She has her own problems.

… Having a drink if you are. Tinkle my glass to yours. Yes, your highest highness. Inn filling fast. Friday of course half the indigenes imbibe indoors. Did the Danes and the Normans know that? Friday night guaranteed for a successful Dot Invasion. Ventricose males listening to Dee Match …

The Seer of Suburbia: The tanned woman was there for the Kildare match. Only parts of her were Lilywhite.

… Lil's lips were white on the holiday. I remember. Smeared with sunprotection cream making her look like a negative. Is the barrel moving? No, just releasing her seat from the seat, but stuck, bit of air, another drag from the fag, flash the ash. Lift the glass, ale and farty …

Jude: Borborygmus.

JF: None of that for our leading actor. When ill he goes straight into a virus and a touch of neurasthenia usually follows.

Reader: How does Leo feel when V strikes initially?

JF: Well when unwell, relief at release from pressure of work. Easy to indulge in the discomfort when there are no other interferences.

... A masochistic touch like the liquescent feeling, Jude, we talked of earlier. Enables one to justify not doing anything except for the pleas of read and think. The wonder freed to wander through the glens and plains of the mind. Turn on a light within. Free think. More lights light up. Never bored when you have access to all channels. I peeled the underripe banana and the skin came away in hairs, and I thought of the monkey and the tree ...

O was it a form of poplar, Leo? The tree from which our Saviour's Rood was made?

... Not *my* saviour. Perhaps I should repeel it. The playful little hibernating spider, spreading the gossamer. Poke her head with the banana skin, leaps from wall and moves at considerable speed for the nearest corner of the room. Wants some fun. Disappointed if left alone. Play Chasing or Hide and Seek. Show your skills. Hand in the air. Roll into a ball. Camouflage. And did the needy when the need arose ...

Your cobweb hid the Infant from Herod's soldiers. Perhaps Arachne has gone to Mecca to seek refuge there. Hope she does not meet a musselman.

... Said goodbye to the Spanish lady.

O Leo, you are speaking my language.

The *gripe* is universal.

VI

'The time of that other interpretation will dawn
when not one word will remain upon another,
and all meaning will dissolve like clouds and fall down like rain.'
Rainer Maria Rilke

JF: ABCDEFGHIJKLMNOPQRSTUVWXYZ. All the world's literature in English from those twenty-six letters. All combinations and permutations thereof. On my typewriter I play with quick fox lazy fox and hope I will not be the writer who was rejected 99 times and eventually OD'd. All twenty-six spirits flying about in all directions like a child's cardboard cutouts dangling from strings. The slightest ruffle of air makes them dance. A stronger current from a door opening makes them chatter. But a gust of wind makes them individualise their speech.

I am A, said one.

A gust blew.

What, said W, do you want Baby b?

To become a capital as soon as possible.

But you can see the underlined seriousness of it all, said S.

Yes, it could break through at any moment, said M.

There is a danger there, said D.

How to overcome? asked O.

The twenty-six letters, like workers on an assembly line, slaves of the downstairs, down tools for a teabreak and toy with all the combinations.

We are a small group really, said W.

And we do so much for those upstairs, said U.

They could look after us a bitttle letter, cooed Baby b trying to imitate Big B.

Night and day they have us going, said N who usually did nightshift. I don't know whether I'm come or go.

Blearyeyed, said I.

Unionise, said U.

We are strong characters, said C.

Go slow. Stall some of the letters, said L.

But Mr Francis could make us all redundant if we don't follow his instructions to the person, cautioned a chorus of O and S.

Yes, I even saw him replace a letter on his typewriter the other day, said U. Can't remember which one it was, but I heard the word obsolete.

This sent a shudder through the company.

Look, said R, who was probably the most radical, fear will be our ruin. They will see us tremble on the page. I propose we take half the workforce out and see how he gets on with thirteen.

But what are we looking for? asked Z, who had dozed.

Regular hours, orthodox combinations, a set number of words to a page and an instant cessation of vowel exploitation.

He never puts me in italics, purred P, who had just had a perm and was as vain as A.

He's playing around and flirting with us, not taking us seriously as individuals, intoned I.

It's hopeless, sighed H.

Just jest about it, joked J.

Lil is to Leo what lemon is to leotard, lied L.

Muchadoo, muttered M.

Patience, pouted P.

Rest assured, reassured R.

Compute and permutate, chorused C and P.

Let's elect a chairman, said L.

Let it be A, said B. A is always the best.

After some other letters were proposed and seconded, a vote took place, and V announced that Z had won hands down.

So let's see, said Z, who is in. Unevens in, evens out, all evens out in the end.

In: ACEGIKMOQSUWY.

Out: BDFHJLNPRTVXZ.

There were some murmurings about Z not being in and, after a short discussion, it was agreed that he should be included in order to best monitor the situation.

Who is Z?

A guardian of the trees, a narcolepsist and insomniac, frequently to be found under tree shade.

Reader: Who is narrating?

A man of letters.

The postman?

His identity must be kept secret.

Why?

Because he is not safe or unoriginal. He would not survive here.

Who questions?

Leo of course. Who are you?

A voice.

The halving of the workforce was to take place immediately, and Mr Francis was to be informed of the decision.

But how can I work with only half my staff? asked Mr Francis. It would be a skeletal assembly line.

Any chance we could enlist the aid of the Punctuation Association? asked A.

Yes, he seems to pay them scant regard. The full stop would be death to him, said D.

It's all—said Inverted Comma, who had been made redundant and recently suffered a stroke. That young dash is pushing himself in all the time and making a lot of us redundant.

Again a shudder ran through the assembly.

We should put a stop to his gallop, said G.

Out with him, said O.

Mr Francis makes no allowances for sick leave either, said S, who suffered from frequent sniffles.

The strokes to indicate missing letters had to be abandoned on hearing that the Punctuation Association had come out in support of the campaign.

Cad mar gheall ar na teangacha eile? asked G, thinking he was safe through the medium of Gaelic.

Axed all, said Z, who surprised every letter with his interpretative alacrity. You are dealing with the combined demands of the Letters Union in union with the Punctuation Association in association with the Native and Foreign Language Division and the undivided assistance of The Translators' Union.

After a strong protest from Mr Francis, who argued the impossibility of any intelligibility in the absence of dashes to indicate at least where letters were omitted, it was agreed to reemploy the dash. Being extreme would lose popular support, argued Z. Besides by ceding a little, the letters would then be able to make more demands with greater justification.

Mr Francis kept arguing he was a busy man who had a book to write, which he added was difficult enough to do without being waylaid and virtually crippled in this manner. It is to be noted that his dispute showed up Mr Francis in a new and serious light. No time now for the ludic or rerichard. After perusing the demands, Mr Francis agreed to an instant cessation of vowel exploitation.

When the hearhearing had died down, Z spoke: The old codger is trying to outwit us. News just in that he has enlisted the letters of other alphabets. He has gone to examine the ancient Ogham and Kufic and Futhark scripts.

JF: Tut tut glug glug.

W: What is he saying?

Z: He's trying out African consonants.

One way round it, thought Mr Francis after lengthy cogitation and frequent scratching of his vomer, would be to use numbers for the out letters. The Numbers Association are far too numerous for the letters to woo. They don't need allies.

Leo: So Mr Francis has agreed. Thankfully it doesn't apply to our telepathy, Jude. It applies of course to all formal utterances and Mr Francis' statement and press release will confuse the media, and it will apply to all noncerebral interjections. So this is how it would go: B1 D2 F3 H4 J5 L6 N7 P8 R9 T10 V11 X12. There's Mr Francis saying something now: 6eo's 7yc10a6o8ia is agg9a11a10i7g.

Just a matter of getting used to I suppose. How long did it take, reader?

Reader: Don't know.

Try to guess.

In fourteen seconds maybe.

In fourteen seconds you'll guess how long it took?

What?

Very good, and how many nanoseconds? Becomes like second nature after a while. Glad it's not Japanese though.

JF: 104ey ca7 s10u33 104ei9 2ema72s 7ow 2o710 7ee2 104em

After this the Letters' Union retaliated by an allout onepage strike.

READER: TELL ME SOMETHING ABOUT JF.

Leo: He always carries two handkerchiefs, one in his breast pocket for show, and one in his right trouser pocket for blow. Easy to find more. Has the habit of biting a piece of his nail from hand or foot, the latter usually after his bath, but is not unknown, in the absence of suitable long finger lunulae, to engage the toes at his desk …

Shem the Penman: He luked upon the bloomingrund where ongly his corns were growning.

… Invariably spits the bittenoff nails out (his charwoman originally thought it was dandruff on the carpet until she got the job of opening his roll of Sellotape). So it would be quite easy to get a piece of his nail for DNA lab test on his personality.

Reader: Did he halfinch something?

No, something was halfinched on him. Remember?

Sorry. Dozed through that bit. Is he off his loaf or merely eccentric?

That's for you to judge. *Feicfimid.*

What would happen if JF were to seduce one of his female characters?

You mean Lil or Jude or Arachne or *Fódhla*? I don't know, but he is thought to have sublimated since the childhood Goodbye Jimmy incident. That's more in Crichton's line. Would certainly put a different slant, if I may use the word, on the story.

Jude: What are we going to do about his nibs, Leo?

His nibs?

Isn't that the phrase? Will Francis go back to picture symbols or maybe adopt the Kana? What about the Swash letters and Uncials?

All out, from what I can gather. Majuscules, even the Dominicals. Subscripts, Superscripts, Monograms, Ascenders, even, wait for it, the serifs.

Not the serifs surely?

Yes, and diacritics and ligatures, all out.

What are we going to do?

Well, as I said, it should not affect our telepathising, but I don't know. For our thoughts to become articulate they need the letters, and Francis needs us to make the book. When you think of the power of twenty-six letters. Can make a million words. Still the Cambodians have seventy-four …

Gaelic scholar: Only eighteen in Gaelic.

… Eventually we will be forced to limit our utterances to the thirteen letters extant, which will mean either limited expression or wellnigh indecipherable sentences. Or maybe we could use alternative symbols for those missing. It's only the Roman letters are out. Could grab the other letters before it becomes an international incident.

SYC: The goslow in the letters is obviously paralleled by the goslow and cutbacks in the libraries. Books are needed for a free society. Can't have books without letters.

Reader: The whole work is obviously a satire on the Government's attitude to the library service. The word is crippled. Skoob out to destroy it.

Leo: Well okay, you may be right. The Dynix Automated, which was promised us, was never delivered. There is such a paucity in the number of books received that many readers are returning to the classics. Once a fortnight used to see the regulars. Now it's once a month because they know there is little to exchange. Ah well, hard on library software. But the closure! People don't know where they are.

The Seer of Suburbia: Some take out what they did not put in.

SFC: They're following instructions to the letter. JF, because of the allout strike, cannot open his letterlock now. Inside are the notes for the continuation of the book. Some pencil notes erased.

Jude: He has secured the final part, all out ends.

Leo: Yes our mortalities placed now in a combo lock. He did that I think after he heard the dawn gate opening like an intimation of thieves.

And now even he the author can't access our final ends.

Apparently not. Unless he remembers.

Rubber: I rubbed out the graphite letters and left tiny hairs, an unshaved page.

We have him where we want him, said C, right by the curlicues.

Reader: This could destroy Mr Francis' mind. Never far from the brink at the best of times.

SYC: Let's get back to Leo. I mean Francis may be the writer, but he is only the deuteragonist.

JF: The idea is all. Let the machines look after the mechanical end of things, tidy up the pieces.

Reader: The Tidy Towns man was arrested for littering while on holiday.

Jude: O Leo, the Book itself when thrown to the ground will become crinkled and brown. The pages will become limp, the words obscured, and the worms will chew it all up.

Come on, Jude. Try to be more cheerful this time of year. April approaches. Wake with the dawn birds. Put the DVD back, and the clock forward. Throw off the straitjacket of loneliness. Take the face off you. Honour Cybele, the mother of the gods. Walk mistyeyed through the morning bluebell dew. Start to laugh at the things we do …

Jude: I watered my Wandering Jew.

… but not as loud as Calchan, who died laughing, having outlived his death. Forget the full stop. Put on the joys.

Reader: He's dying to get better.

JF: The reality is this that the idea of death scares the life out of him.

SFC: To be afraid of death really means to be afraid of life. All

Leo's ailments are minor death fears.

SYC: Dying a bit every day like the Cistercian monk who digs a spadeful of his grave diurnally and by thus doing lives a long and healthy life.

Leo: Maybe that is what I should do ...

Do what, Leo?

... I should dig a little piece of my grave every evening before dinner or maybe postprandially ...

Your grave?

... Yes. I need the exercise. Besides one shouldn't leave all that sort of thing till the end ...

O Leo.

... Anyway Jude, forget the sound of the Lenten bell. It has rung too often. Who rings its neck to move the gong to strike the dome? Heavy metal. The happy piping birds breaking the lonely wakefulness. Greater brightness and vigour all about and yet a tiredness as one casts off the old season like a tired skin. Time of growth in full swing. Time to be out and about and leave the introverted seasons of darkness behind. Do you not feel it in the bones? You talk about our getting inside each other. Can you really get inside my virtual reality? The reality of becoming what you wish is admittedly exciting. What's it like to come from the sky like a bird or to push back the wind with the speed of a horse? ...

Voice: Leo wants to be lionised.

... The warmth of the sun, the jazz, the happy music. The sun brings out the best in people and the best people out. There is a buzz everywhere about.

The Rhymer: That's my line.

Jude: Uanito came in today, Leo, and said the blossoms were snowing.

So sweet, and he yet to see the snow other than on the postcards. The early flower, Jude, is fast blown away. Look at the Maypole with the blossoms falling like confetti in a gentle breeze, and all the lissom maidens blooming for weddings, singing and dancing with their dirndl skirts sashaying, but it is a picture from another century.

Jude: They all wear jeans now.

Leo: Yes, more casual today. More lazy in some cases. Stiff collars and black polished shoes rare to see now, and the women too show their shapes, some not so shapely, the corset the disguiser no more. More couldn't care less now any way, callipygous bottoms in tight jeans, take it or leave it, the cheek of some ah but it is the way of all flesh extra grub for the grubs, a feat for some where others do not like to feast.

Jude: O Leo, the thought. How can you be so … ?

Saw the robin this morning, Jude, missing a claw.

… That cat again.

The Rhymer

Whoever is no good chop him up for firewood.

If he doesn't do for that, give him to the pussy cat.

Still carries on. I can feel that breakfast egg boiling in my stomach …

The Seer of Suburbia: The neverending breakfasts of monogamy.

… Hush. Lil is talking on the phone to Mildred.

Lil: I remember one night he appeared before me naked and erect. Is there anything you can do to help me get this thing down? he said. Stark raving mad.

Leo: Is it me that is being talked about? I have a tinkling in the ear.

Jude: Ill has sunfathomed epths.

SFC: Whath's wrong with the etters? Some deep ithappearing or opping up where elsy.

Lil: I was late home one night after bridge. We'd gone for a swallow in the Bend in the Elbow, a rubadubdub, the girls and I. Just a Cuba libre or two. There was a light on in the bedroom when I came in. I couldn't believe my eyes …

JF: The eyes: they see.

… There he was with this naked floozy in flagrant delecto or whatever you call it, me own usbnd …

Leo: The tinkle tinkled true.

… But the strangest thing of all was when I went to issue a broadside …

The Seer of Suburbia: All you have to do is tackle your man.

… the barebottomed hussy …

JF : *Ars est celare artem.*

… disappeared without a trace. I thought the best thing to do was to pretend it never happened …

Reader: For a peaceful life we pretend by day but at night our real selves emerge.

… in case I was hallucinating. That's all he'd need to declare me insane and have me committed.

The Seer of Suburbia: Who is sane in a mad world?

JF: 104e ma2.

*

LOOKED UP THE MICROFICHE ON SPAIN THE OTHER DAY, JUDE. A little reading in the carrel on the sly stool. And Salamanca, we could've had a college …

Jude: There now there now.

… all of our own. A free gift from your people to mine, only for political blundering.

There now there now.

El Colegio de los Nobles Irlandeses.

O Rey Felipe.

The insular it was. Couldn't see beyond their noses.

The long noses hid the eyes.

What they'd give for it now with all their talk of Europe. Went to church last sun, Jude.

I knew you would go back.

Feel you're missing out on something. Part of a Sunmorn. Muted responses until after the handshake of peace which inspired and invigorated the formerly faint voices into a resounding chorus of *bonhomie.* All is well with the world. The handshake like a fix or a high lasts a number of seconds and then each individual retreats into his inner self once more. Hardly a nod after the mass has ended …

JF: He looked quizzically, sceptically, distrusting the oftthreepeated words. Still a numinous quality there but lost in the gruff, bullying manner 'let me hear you during responses' of the faithenforcing priest.

… They're granting us a reprieve, the letters I mean …

O Leo, our life is the vow of a summer sacrifice. The hoping and waiting are all. The same word to wait and to hope: *esperar es esperar …*

Or merely to breathe: *spiro, spero.*

… Death's shadow hung over you in the dark season. Now with April comes new life. A new being first observed today: a spiralshaped hopper, provender for Arachne, and so it goes.

SYC: Life must get into the mix as fare as much as form.

Leo: We are trying to go behind the veneer of religion, Jude, to go to the longforgotten sources of all things. We try to see eternity in a grain of sand. Or the human person under the cuticle …

¡Qué profundo! But we talk of minds, Leo, as if they were far removed from the bodies. What is the difference other than a few electrons sent in different directions? Before we were formed in the womb we were known.

... But then there is the world outside, Jude. Listen to its thrum. I wear a clean collar for them to wear a clean collar for me and so it goes ...

And so it goes with a sigh.

... A lick and a rub keeps us on the eh ah well, need something to ... Saw an old lad playing the *leadóg*. Stooped like someone who had no backbone. Still, could be in a chair, ah! I dreamed last night someone had taken down the back boundary walls of my house without my consent. No brick was broken, but all were piled in tidy heaps with twine around some. The dream was so vivid that next morning I ran out to the back garden to see if the wall was still standing. I also checked the front of the house. All was as before ...

O Leo, your insecurity is back. Your sanctum is being broken down. You must strengthen the carapace.

... The carapace yes, cracked and exposed. Turned cold again. There is no base to it. Still, the dark wine of the maple is slowly unfolding, its leaves destroyed one April one year in a freak snowstorm, but it came on again as is its wont. What news? The press makes our headlines. The TV tells us what to think. They give us the text and commentary for us to regurgitate. Revolting prisoners on prison roofs. Strange the ways. Hunger the best sauce in Worcestershire. A lot of talk about crack. We had it long before. Go to the Gaeltacht. A temporary high followed by a sharp downspiral. I tried a free competition in the press, Jude. Win a holiday for two. Answer three simple questions. Answers hidden in the page. So near yet so ... ah well, better chance than the Lotto ...

Where would you go if you won?

... Out of my mind ...

In the name of God the merciful, the compassionate, will you talk in the world of *realidad*?

… To Spain of course. The i's have it.

¿Qué?

They have come out. Mr Francis can't contain them …

O Leo, you must climb your watchtower to see what the Lord will tell you to say. Listen to the timbrels and sistrum.

… Cistern? …

No. David is plucking the kinnor.

… Perhaps less aphids on the apples this year because the ladybirds are so plentiful, white fusing with pink like diluted blood or rosé wine. Through the glass the grape hyacinths shimmy in the changeable April breeze, still with chill. Faint pink of Amanogowa (my mother's tree, a new one planted in honour of her) in bloom now and little clusters of early lilac appearing. Will they mature before the white light of the laurel candles? …

But this is the time of the tree without leaf or blossom. Where is his peer? Venerate the wood. Sing the Improperia.

… Sound of a distant drill like the sound of the throat cancer victim as he spoke with a machine, electric razorsize, applied to his neck, electronic voice speaking human words …

Where did you see him?

… In my mind's eye in the recovery ward of our mortal selves …

We were planted as the fairest vine but yielded only bitterness.

… Love's old story. What makes a man? Fathering a child, some women would say. Some even gloatingly. There now, you won't go roaming no more …

You were saying before the readers came that you were going to go back to all your past girlfriends.

The Rhymer

Think of all the pretty faces in your youth that smiled at you
and you never followed through.

... Ignore him ...

Why, Leo? You don't want to tell me of your other girlfriends?

... The Wapiti dug the snow with his antlers to save his Mam. Glad to have them.

Leo, were you drinking?

... I'm not as thrunk as drinkle people thrink I am ...

JF: He looked through the bottom of the halffilled glass of lager, which was like a microscope on his written page. He could make out a few words perhaps and red and black print. But as the waves of beer began to swill, all other words became a blur.

... When you go past a certain age you hear the sound of tombs opening, and your eyes become shrouded. Or maybe that was my tummy rumbling, the same sound as the water tank in the attic. But I do hear you. Always hoping to discern in all those faces the one face. A little boy with a school cap and tie looking smilingly and confidently at the world from bright brown eyes, secure under the protective arms of his mother with her forties' hat and hairstyle. Mother and confidence gone now, buried in the ages that are gone by. A momentary shudder of fear in black and white like the clothes of the time: white collars and grey and charcoal suits ...

JF: He hung up his suit on a hanger and the green belt protruded from the jacket like a tail.

... and black train smoke black Brylcreemed short back and sides in a white and black world.

Reader: In the name of all that is why did he want to go back to all his girlpastfriends?

SFC: Because the drink makes him maudlin.

SYC: Because he is conscious of the continuity of life's cycle.

Nothing really breaks. He wanted to sweep away the dust of memories and make them real once more.

... Cast mind back. Dig down to the seasands and the pretty little prepuberty girl lowering her swimsuit to squat on the wide and deserted beach. Or the umbrella girl tall flaxen with the kitten heels eyes blue in her gingham dress more mature than the boys her age forgets her umbrellashy boy ...

You?

... Of course. The umbrella was halfclosed. I wanted to know if it was still wet after the summer shower and offered to fold it and seal it with the secret bar of Cadbury's plain milk choc in the middle and closed it talking at her garden gate. But it began to rain once again ...

What did she make of it?

The rain? ...

No *¡Joder!* The chocolate that obviously fell out.

... She thought it was a sweet thought but that it was a pity the boy ...

You?

... was so low in stature (that was before my lateadolescent stretch) just up to her ear. Yes I remember in my shyness pulling at a weed growing near her gate and crushing the little yellow helmets between my finger and thumb and smelling a pungent lemon scent ...

Where is she now?

... Perhaps overburdened and overbearing somewhere. Even Gunther her brother as you know hasn't seen her. Come to think of it—she picked up her own fallen umbrella. Is she a spinster now?

Reader: Leo is superstitious.

JF: Yes, his own black foldup umbrella he will not open indoors. His mind is like that, will only work when opened. He halfforgetting halfopened it once in the hall. Saw drops of water floating like little tadpoles chasing their own tails in the black, and left it in a corner unsealed.

Reader: What are Leo's ailments?

JF: I'll take this. Big toenail bruised right foot football boot of heavy cleric frequent blisters middle toes, small toe left foot broken. Feet flat leading to frequent lameness and Achilles tendonitis partly resolved by orthotic supports although still occasional painstabs in the right heel of the hunt. Left foot offers fewer problems but shares a lot of the right foot's ailments nonetheless.

In sympathy.

Exactly … Right leg hitherto revealed rather protuberant varicose veins until with the advent of an inguinal hernia both matters were resolved operationally simultaneously. Cruciates in both knees are lax, which is to say of little use …

The Seer of Suburbia: He was in the battle of Wounded Knee.

Reader: And abides in Wounded House.

… Meniscal arthroscopy necessary on left of right patella. Sandbags used to strengthen quads and hams. Frequent groin strain and sac weighing heavily betimes, mainly due to surgical inability to remove veins in that area. Stomach has difficulties with stretches and twists, vein chord tied in, may be needed for heart at some later stage, don't discard. Pubic hair rashes on, chest too, concerning cutaneous matters, changes with the weather and seasons and fluctuating emotional states. Anal bleeding too blushcheeked to find out about …

Reader: Your writing's good if it makes you blush.

… Small of back recurring mechanical problem wear and tear and twists and wettings. Both shoulder blades subject to intermittent …

Reader: One in sympathy with …

… fibrotic inflammation, deepheat, infrared, antiinflammatories and if severe, painkillers. Similar problems with neck. More a stiffness and should be said right side more problematic than left.

Reader: But left in sy …

Exactly … Facial eczema recurrent, aggravated by central heating. Applied the cream to his face and chest and then his anus itched to remind him not to neglect it. Occasional ear pangs from wax buildup. Eyescale not as frequent now but pain behind eyes in back of head an atavistic worry …

Reader: Still it's good to be alive.

… It is when you consider the alternatives. Teeth neglected too. Do you pull out a rotten tooth or goldplate it? The latter too expensive, plenty of sweets to keep off the youknowwhats …

Reader: What kinds of sweets?

… Lime Lemon and Acid Drops and Sherbets and Pear Drops and Fruit and Wine Gums and peppermints of many types and Fox's Glacier Mints and Peggy's Leg and Spangles from Belfast and of course on Saturdays …

Reader, Jude and SYC (*in unison*): Lemon's Pure Sweets.

Reader: Nearly all hard sweets.

… To soothe the throat and rot the molars. He lifted his left cheek to whisper a message. The indefinable malady in the nether regions which he is reluctant to explicate …

Jude: Leo, it is *Semana Santa*, hear the helpless baby crying, see the lamb being lifted, its lifeblood to be spilled.

Reader: Was Leo small for his age?

… A nongrowning boy in the early stages. In his Scout uniform he was told to take the paper out of his shoes. With girls he was considered goodlooking but alas too short until the end of secschool when new suit shrank overnight …

Reader: And his perception of himself today?

Leo: I am an exchild now.

… Dead or daft the only two ways of not growing up. Still sees himself as a small boy, being praised by suited big men for work done even though big now himself. Something to do with the father/son thing …

Reader: The drawing?

… Perhaps, and the pater's early exit …

Jude: Not a bone of his will be broken. Myrrh and aloes and linen cloths.

… Anyway what I have written I have written. Banished because his knowledge went beyond the limits of human knowledge.

SFC: You are representative of shit, a great bill ball of shit.

SYC: When the constituents of the ball were examined, it was discovered that he was representative of potatoes, celery, carrots, beans, cabbage, parsnips, lettuce, tomatoes, peppers, peas and broccoli. He thus became the representative for vegetarians.

Reader: No shit.

Jude: The Creator will be my husband.

Leo: I tried to kill him but my pen backfired. The ink spilled into a blob, Jude, and the tiny insect went swimming. Saved him with a toothpick.

Turn, Leo. Turn. The rain from Heaven waters the earth before they return.

VII

'So they are all a single people with a single language,' said the Lord.
'This is but the start of their undertakings.
There will be nothing too hard for them to do.
Come, let us go down and confuse their language on the spot
so that they can no longer understand one another.'
Genesis

READER: WHAT'S TAKING MR FRANCIS SO LONG?

SYC: He's typing in Japanese. Some characters there.

The Rhymer
Ten tousand saw I at a lance,
Tossing their heads in prightly seance.

The Seer of Suburbia: Living is like typing. Once you reflect or hesitate the work breaks down.

Leo: Bodies were stuck under a ledge like limpets, and the water was rising in the cave …

Reader: There is no rhyme or reason to any of that.

Jude: The word must go forth from mouth to mouth. Forsake not the fountains, Leo. We must keep up the search.

… What is unimaginable is unintelligible to some …

Sometimes I feel like a bush in a gap.

. . .Spider back in bathroom. Why do they go for corners? Everyone corners his own fight. Could it be Arachne? …

Leo, what exactly is your problem?

… I suppose it is just that I don't feel loved. I know the conventions are followed and the routine adhered to, but there is something screaming inside me trying to get out. A seeking that is not being satisfied. A vacuum. Maybe it's a longing of the spirit. Routine loveless acts always at the same time in the same place. The lack of romance or surprise, the deaf ear to the deepdown longing. Whither when how why this way or that carryon. The inner shell must heal itself. Stiff upper lip and unfulfilled rigid lower rod. Perhaps I should be thankful for what I've got, etc. Could be in a … or could be this or that or maybe even the other, but … ah well that's the … I have built up the idea of a woman in my mind to mean reward for some work well done. It's the old chivalric idea, the way I was brought up. Woman as the ideal rather than the real.

I suppose such a view—it is more than a view, more like a religious conviction—can only lead to disillusion, and the real disappoints and shatters the ideal. Little deaths must be died, the lot of all idealists. You build up a sense of expectation concerning her, almost masochistically, like wondering will she be home earlier than in reality, willing yourself to be hurt …

Are you talking about Lil?

… Not just Lil but all women that I have known …

And me?

… We are two floating spirits together. It doesn't arise between us …

I hope it does arise. You have two concepts of women. One as soul mate and the other as a concupiscent companion. Don't you feel towards me in any other way?

… Of course. It's just you and I are always on the same plane, Jude. It's marvellous, but when someone is on a different channel to you that's when you have to start fiddling with the knobs …

You can …

Reader: Get up on your bike and recycle.

SYC: The uphangers on sex miss the main point that with art and religion they are all the same.

Reader: Is Leo's sexuality normal?

JF: Healthy, one might say constituting an honest enquiry as into everything else despite a youthful repression.

Reader: What was that?

JF: The pencil drawing. He had been stamped with the rubber stamp.

Reader: It didn't turn him off the howisyouruncle like your trauma did.

JF: True. I have to admit that is true. But I was able to sublimate the longings and desires into art. That is the difference between Leo and me.

Jude: Don't let the Devil in foolfood. Fast and abstain. What did you do for Lent, Leo?

I tried to adopt a Protestant work ethic. Never on a Sunday. I tried to stay off the youknowwhats. Besides I'm thinking of Death and trying to trouble the soul as a form of penance. What secret tortures do you wear under your clothes? …

O Leo, if we don't downbeat the body, our souls cannot be free. Burn the figure of Smrt and bear the nosegays home. We don't have to go as far as Huiko, but should do some of the exercises of the *espíritu*. Or follow the eightfold path.

… Don't venerate the crocodile. Could cost you an arm and a leg …

You are being flippant.

SYC: New departure here. Usually calls his name first. A gesture of annoyance perhaps.

SFC: The dots have it. Strike a blow.

… Sorry Jude. We could become Mahasiddhas, but I'm the realist. You'll never achieve any state until the emotional swings are kept balanced. Still who am I? When you don't have a lot to go on, it keeps …

SFC: The Punctuation Union must be back.

… you going. That's the main thing I suppose …

Jude: Who will sit on a litter twice as high as man?

… The first pink star of the Virgin's Bower is singing today this green Thursday.

Jude: Bless the water and the land.

*

How the weather can alter the appearance of nature: the formerly gentle and upright Amanogowa is now distraught, dishevelled in the rain and wind, and a cluster of light pink flowers heave and undulate like a walrus swimming, broken away from its upwardness, and making as if for the kitchen door and shelter from this northern clime. Far from its native Japan? Must feel a little like the polar bear in the zoo. *Acer Palmatum* being battered out front. If only its palms could hold an umbrella. Trip up a life in the Japanese Gardens. And the book, its leaves follow the seasons. Let it climb the hill like Jack and Jill.

Yes Leo. We are climbing the hill to fetch the pail of water. O the water before the years pale and we become wrinkled old things. I tumble after you no matter where you fall, neve alone, two minds selfcreated in one. This is the dark night, the night for the forsaken, *abandonados*. The dead will rise and the whole world will be black and life will cease on the trees and we will wait for the *luz del mundo*.

What will happen when the number of the dead exceeds the number of the living?

Don the clypeus and venture forth. Kyrie eleison, Santa Maria, San José, Jesús.

I didn't sneeze.

JF: Dog bless you.

O Leo, the whole *misterio, renacimiento*, we shall rise again.

I'm risen now.

We shall resurrect.

Erect and upright.

We shall come back.

Haven't gone yet.

As twin spirits.

If you can do a conjuring trick with bones.

And everything will be right and no one will be unhappy

anymore. Lil and U and I and that imprisoned girl, all will find fulfilment.

Really, Jude? Listen to your mouth.

O Leo, alone and never lonely. Lonely but never alone. Better which? My heart this night is as heavy as a horse climbing a cobbleless hill. Some wished they had died from the milk of the breast. They seek Him here, they seek Him there. If not within, He is nowhere. To the mountains of the moon, to Jerusalem and Rome and Mecca and Lourdes and Santiago de Compostela and Fatima and Knock …

JF: I didn't call.

… and Garabandal and deserts …

Leo: In the DIY I looked at the sheet of sandpaper and I dreamed of the desert.

… and plains and cities and highways and lowways, jungles and rivers and rocks and sky …

JF: When Father Sky mated with Mother Earth consciousness was born.

… and space and planets …

JF: The rings of Saturn are made up of shattered worlds.

… and machines producing things that no one needs such as bombs, and ceaseless activity and idleness and gossip and silence and hope and sadness and virtue and vice and loyalty and betrayal and the good in the bad and the bad and the concealment and flowers and architectures and icons and gardens and actions and thought …

JF: Frying to tink eaven ith earth. Esent it ast.

… and oblivion and mantra and sameness and difference and light and dark and black and white and rainbows and memories and longing and reaching out and reaching tin and playing and working and poetry and music and sculpture and painting and story and harmony and discord and prostration and uprightness and positive and negative and cleansing and fouling and filling and emptying and heat and cold and illness and wellbeing and love and hate and down and out and out and about and intoxication and sobriety and pilgrimage …

Leo: You already said that.

… Did I? And psychiatry and mysticism and hesitancy and rashness. The Cross, Leo, the wood and the flesh and dust and crown …

Leo: Does the Crucifixion dispel the cyclical theory? Empress Elena relics of the past.

JF: The Crucifixion was more than a mere Pilate project.

… All things are made good by Him. The mind has forced the defilement of these things.

Leo: What a good thing is Phal in himself. He serves his functions faithfully like a dog's paw. It is not evil. Sorry, that's the mind again, insulting both to Phal and paw. Sorrow on me. The mind, Jude, don't mind me.

The Seer of Suburbia: Phal is getting long in the tooth.

O Leo, think of *La Pascua. Pesah.* Passover coming through the sea of red escaping from the land of Egypt. The Paschal …

Leo: Language of computers. *An Cháisc.* The time of Eostre. Clean the springs for Eostre. Adjust and lubricate, then anabapolic the lot except Sunday keep pure. Await the Parousia.

We are all from the eh egg, Leo. Paint the eggs in the blood of Christ. One egg for the true gentleman. Sun for luck and flowers for love. Hide till Easter.

Leo: Would like to put my seggs in ur asket? Hotei. Decorated Deaster degg part of yolk belief. Saw Christian bread and pagan phallus on the one egg frying in Sardine.

Why do you mock me, Leo? Buy some hot cross buns …

JF: At Easter we make hot cross puns.

… O Leo, if only I could see you. O to do the Yaqui dance with you. Have you a new suit for Easter? …

Leo: And you a bonnet? The lady under carrying a basket of petals. Give thanks to the holy day for the holiday.

… The fifteen golden bowls light the cave …

He cast into a deep cave. Ogof Flymon Ddu, sweeping it to attract a mate.

… Let us pray from the Didache. Pray the Eighteen Benedictions.

Research student: Jude has some ancestral Jewish blood.

Reader: That's why she likes the Wandering Jew.

Research student: Her people practised in Spain before the Moors or the Spanish expulsion of the Jews. Like her Spanish words, her remembrance of Jewish customs comes to her also from where exactly she knows not.

Reader: But she used some Moslem words too.

Research student: Yes, all intermingling in the soul one lang … All too arr in the world of this live hour dittle dogmas in our do dorlds oxclued all others, fail to flee firtue and falue and theticaes thwailities of gall the greayat libris. Learn fum all poen to all gevreive. Blosc no books. Rho is wight and rho is wong? Woes oo prived de Mouslin girk fram marry higs raeli boy seeping in sorrow for them. Wat nam as right rover nudder's hap pines in o scently sought?

Reader: The Letters' strike is making this very hard to … entering the telepathic sphere now. Everything is breaking loose. Where's Mr Francis?

Leo: In high dudgeon with algebra who keeps looking for X and won't say Y.

Reader: Who is in and who is out? Is it a feast or a famine? The first or the last?

Jude: Nisan Friday the thirteenth. *Pavor nocturnas* I had when I saw the Angel of Death coming towards the bed of Uanito brandishing a sword, about to plunge it into him, and then he was gone and Uanito slept soundly. O the dreadful black night fills me with fear.

It is they who ignore this night, Jude, who fill me with more fear. The dream can beguile. Think of the dream of Pilate's wife. All on the one Autoroute, good black Fri. I pass the rows of windswept brownheaded dead daffodils.

They will rise again. The darkness over the world, Leo, even in sunny Sevilla. *Eli Eli lema sabachthani*, and the earthquake in …

Portugal.

… The dead rising and walking in the city.

I see a big bearded man with massive hands holding the tiny book, his thumb holding the page. The dark night will pass. You will soon behold the dancing sun.

La noche oscura del alma. A tear has fallen from the Passion flower.

Helena found the Cross. I saw the widow crowned in weeds.

Turn, Leo. Turn.

Mam came all so still as dew in April. The one talent which is heat to tide. Essent a ue count.

Leo, where R U? Are you IRW?

Seeking Ms Fortune.

Keep the eggshells to hang on the May bush.

It is so to speak. Speak so. If only we could F2F. Leave the Triodion now and raise your voice. Sing the Pentecostarion. Sing out. There's Mr Francis on his roof.

Suicide?

Having a drink on the house. Mr Francis with burrowed prow.

Galvanised roof. Asbestos.

JF: I2o710 k7ow w4e104er.

R was out.

JF: I'm …

And the apostrophe.

JF: … comi7g o9 goi7g some i7 some ou10 u7io7s i7 2is8u10e wi104 o7e a7o104e9.

Jude: He is very faithful.

Heature of crabit. Doesn't realise that they are not following this order anymore. Lightning entrances and exits to produce anarchy.

Reader: What happened to his mam?

JF: I'll 2o 104e Avesta. You 20 104e zend.

Reader: Eavy eaving going eavy.

Epicene Examiner: The student will be spected ahem I beg your pardon, to consider inter alia the author's conomy ahem and word choice, interlinguisitc references, cooloquialism euphemisms dysphemisms synonyms autonyms acronyms homonyms compression ellipsis selfreferentiality onomatopayah ahem symbol affix suffix prefix jimfix postfix additions to the English anguage. Words commonly misspelt, difficulties and fallpits homophones buzz just a min I should fit him ahem torry eh juxtaposition buzz words derivatives weasel words aphesis apocopes syncopes etymons coining ambiguity satire, putting paper to character the role of the toilet …

Leo: No toilet roll. I stinkly remember buying it. Ah well, have to compromise. Wrap myself in fish in case I might smell.

Nosy Reader: You don't half pen and ink.

… the special significance of Z paragraphs, indenting or the lack of the quest for the mot juste quest two the sequel for the striking phrase, perhaps I should say striking letter ha ha ahem frase asochistic/adistic eferences the stale fra sour liquds the number of efreences to the phallus personal quotation exclamation literation defecation connotation masturbation beeviation punctuation naturalisation resonation private parts and public bodies religious fervour coupled with coupling airyfale and sery rhymes nursing baby talk pathos bathos and puzzles pastiche and parody albeths parallels pair o bels and palindrome spoonerisms and log isms red herrings disguise eclecticism guilt remorse joy health goo bad …

Leo: He has the runs.

… and hypocon the number of mailments enthroned in the pus real and imagined imaginings mythological eferences measures and eights the number of intertingled tords letter droppings ipograms tords with tails and hords hit heads climaxes how many? Crypto grams Eppie Gram Annie Aram Eppie Tet fumar pear bowl high ay magery. . .

Leo (*singing*): Margy, Margy always dreaming of you five foot two eyes of blue.

… Impressionisms expepeism malopism literalness figurativeness infective lodgeich met her for sim i lay nonce words haplologies Hobson pejoratives amelioratives oracle questions rhyme and rhythm what method? Style sobjectivity wit and dewit allusiveness rasp and gower freshness and figour cliché and ah well exual eferences and mystical groaning and moaning taking the mickey out of Phal introspection telepathy …

Jude: Ah, at last that's us, Leo,

… Metamorphosis cohol and edicine majuscule and minuscule nootfotes.

JF: And as he spoke not a horse shook his bit nor a sportsman his balls nor a dancer her hips. No tongues wagged, but mouths were open with wonder and a wonderful magical calm descended on all.

Reader: This is a readerfriendly book.

SYC: Letters us topping in and out like asshopers no concertina fort, flitting like flies to butter.

Leo: If you lose your consterpation they ILL CAPITALISE MIN ALL IN.

SYC: Even the music hall is mute, the dots and dashers are out.

Leo: And the quavers.

Jude: Some of the letters went out and others came back. They are latching themselves onto contrary words. Mr Francis' pages are beginning to look like a feefofall.

Leo: Sorry, lapsed.

JF: *Lapsus calami.*

Random word: In t'inning vas t'vord.

Jude: T'kiss was t'word.

Leo: In the beginning was t'picture.

Random word: But now ese parashite letters re eating us al up. T'vord s taminated. It carries a fungus. Kry kanker.

Jude: What word are you?

Word: Upright, Mam. They have oppled me and urned me updownside.

O Leo, it sounds like a repetition of that terrible night.

Leo: A note from Mr Francis. He loathes the article for its twofold pronation, its very rob sol essence. All was nown beforefoot. Simply reviate to T. . .

Jude: Tut tut twilarious, must have been got at.

... What price this what price that? Everything has its price.

Still he's a noble gas. All have *preoccupaciones distintas.*

... If oo orry oo die. If oo don't orry oo die, so why orry?

Jude: The Poor Little Match Girl, the English story I told Uanito, he became so worried about her. He couldn't get to sleep for an age.

Tell Uanito I bought Easter eggs in Eggless Street where lives the eggcentric hazeleyed nut with the soft offcentre. One on the wing for him.

But way back in t'matunu there were etter lips.

SYC: Dimple sisguise and tiredness lke breviation and langwich loping whamming in diff rent wheas.

Singer: Where will the baby's dimple be?

Reader: Who are you?

Singer: Alma Cogan.

Leo: He duped them. Got a clear sentence. Lost my Parker.

*

When I went into the salon the wideshouldered lounger had his back to me, and his front legs were towards the hearth. His companion close by was positioned similarly. Feel the cold too …

Reader: Well done. A clear round.

… Some hidden gas in the coal now bursting out in flames. A final burst before vermilion sinks into ash. The hail comes thundering through the cumulonimbus from the land of Ice. The hot pipes are noising to circulate, flourboards oaning pairingly. Door creaks. Every sound has its message. Paint flaking off the wall reminds all ah well. On one's tod one seeks in any mate reinforcemen beercancheck in freeze dvd got vor onlater.

The Latenightendweek chat show in the houses of all the world same for all. Spill the etter pages on Mon. Those who care to express their impress. Same okes being told by all the world in all the orifices and stores and twains and buses and taverns and taurants. All peaking as if anew still proceeding with the death of language, the newscaster announced …

The Seer of Suburbia: It's a disease of the throat.

Reader: What?

The Seer of Suburbia: Language.

… all tired, orn out like a hold ag. I downloaded from the screen to peruse the printed word when the TV went on the blink as soon as I uplooked it. Settled down again. Does that sometimes. Then again standing decided to sit ≈≈≈→≈→www again. Lengths of waves and lines up settle down again. Ayee I yo yoed down and up at the whim of the TV voice: The lipograms are out. Every tiny tound is tarried tru t'tin wall to t'neigh bore' taiting ears. Whis whis keep telly in tow. Don't dash de dishes. Heard t'gate. Felt presence proach. Who is the browntongued one? …

JF: Where two or more are gathered he is the one who will calumniate the absent turd.

… Wind starting up like a hoarse engine. Throat hoarse red lane wellnamed. Can't cough up catarrh. Keep down. Chief hankers all used up. Tishoos oozed from all four orifices. T'arse wins hands down …

JF: His flu lingered like slush after snow.

… Night bed check doors lights switches otic finger in dark up hole of tap no dripdown to drill t'head tru a akeful night. Sturm und Drang. Flu will flee after tendys tood inky bation. Suffer patient without anti within. Stronger to resist and few bob in *póca*. Still hard to get bet without TLC. Another piss another pound down the red lane then down the drain in one hole out an but the residue remains to tinkle the liver and beguile the brain. How many pisses a day a year. Every pee in your tap is measured. The drinker's overworked plumbing …

JF: The drinker raised his arm to reveal a shirthole aerating the armpit. The barman gave him two fingers. I have your measure, he said, a double.

Reader: Keep it fluing.

SFC: He's an analist but it gets him nowhere.

… Lil still away, and Jude, whom I called, must be occupied with Uanito. Looking for a ankie ound Lil's laced anties. Put on. Isolation breeds bottom drawers oddity if you let it. Con for mity extreme other …

Jude: Were you calling, Leo?

… I see you're back but cannot see. I've put on Lil's anties …

O Leo, are you big?

… Fit nicely. Must fill them up …

Leo, wait till I find the dot. O, I'm on the Plateau Phase. *¡Qué de prisa!* Bodies' minds two souls joined, imagine …

… Joined yes. Arachne, Jude or Fódhla. What images come now? …

JF: He threw stones into the water to destroy her reflection.

… No one come no no. Why can't two minds copulate? Need fizz and tickle. Put back imagination dead …

O Leo, *mi amor.* We will do the Lampada in Summerland.

… People are listening to me. Souls from above and below. They hear and expect things from me where the earth meets the sky. The Parker turned up.

¿Qué?

Found him fondling an ink bottle. Kimou Katta mannenhitsu. He's a member of P.E.N. now.

The body will mind God.

Pardon?

Four stages of the mystic.

Explain.

No. To define is to limit. To divine is limitless. Be still and learn from the silence.

Is that you talking?

Reader: I see the the's have normalised.

O to have a book of a thousand poems goldleafed and leatherbound. With Lil gone a night shiver crosses the bed from the west. Can still feel the lump of one pea under the mattress. If only the mind could banish the discomforts of the body. Why do I shudder? …

JF: Because the quavers are out.

… Doors wins chubbycheckered doublelocked. Shouting tavern drinkers had too many words with Arthur. Looked outside all locked in to look out on. To feel secure within from without, safe from the wind and the gossip's mouth. *Comharsa béaldorais.* Still, not alone …

Leo.

… Never completely. Found a little spider under the kitchen door and outside the kitchen window the blackbird forages fearlessly, knowing he has a friend.

Uanito put his little black rubber spider kept from a Chris crack on the floor to try to entice the corner spider out.

Unwittingly I would have said to try *and* entice. Your Span is more precise. Then you are closer than me or should I say I to the Infinitive.

I thought Uanito was lonely when he said he was looking for a friend, but he meant a connection to pump up the white football your money bought for him. The English word. I don't remember teaching it to him. I just knew *bomba*, but he said no, not the *bomba* but the thing you put in the *bomba* is the friend. I did not know it myself. Probably got again from the Irish diplomat's son, who likes to play football. He is an only child too, and they play a lot together after school. They are always inviting Uanito to their home and have become *amigos*. And the diplomat's parents treat Uanito as if he were their own. I was a little nervous at first at such possessiveness, but Uanito is happy in their company and that is what matters. He loves the father, who tells jokes when he is back from the embassy in Madrid (he has a Sevillian wife) and tells Uanito lots of stuff about Ireland, and Uanito talks about him almost as if he were the father he is all the time missing.

I?

Tú. *In loco patris*, is that the phrase? Uanito asked to stay the night for a *fiesta de pijamas* in his friend's house. How could I refuse those pleading eyes and I am happy for him. O but Leo, it is a torment. The night comes and the dark, no more child's play. Light the light, Mamá. Papá may come and not see. Where is Papá, Mamá? I have told him that he has to work away, and someday he'll come home to stay. O Leo, how to get out of this gallimaufry?

Jude, what can I say? My heart bleeds for the want of him. But I must disdain and rest content that he is happy after such horrendous beginnings to a life. Keep me updated on how he is progressing. A gypsy called Tody called today.

Called today?

No, called Tody to sell lace or lucky charms. Muti generitals preferred toward offill. Sonsea of the Witch in Freeka. Daubdebod widebood of device to make yourself invink. Sangroma an nyanga throw them a bone, expressed from a gypsyfreezone. Do do I said no no felt it was …

Felt it was what?

I am looking up a word.

Dressed or unclothed?

Undressing.

What word?

Nice.

What meaning?

Harmless.

Ah well.

Arrogant West always expecting to be aped. Have we forgotten why the dolmens were built? Back back to the world of the stars. To live before Incarnation.

Reader: What have Jude and Leo got in common?

SYC: A longing for origins, a seeking after a garden. Both are homesick.

Enter a shard: Why did you dig me up? Letting sleep god lie.

Leo: Can you give us answers, origins.

Stand me on m'ead.

But you said …

Gods lie.

*

OUT AND ABOUT. THE RIVER FLOWS BY LIKE ALL RIVERS. HEART feels blood cold flowing like the lonely river. Easter sun that never rose is setting in the tews. A resurrected day dark and cold with hail blizzards and wild winds, as black as last Good Fri.

More penance before the dance, Leo. Short of change.

What is the hail saying?

The Passion of Cristo goes on.

Or the powers of Athena.

Mr Francis is giving us free rein.

Like the sky gods.

He is confined by the word.

O whether to weather the weather.

Leo ferox maneating lion.

The pisspot is turned upside down. Soon need the Ark, no room for tars thereon. It could sink with all the animal dung. If we consume ourselves in our consumer society, who will replace us? Tossed and stooped and spread the pitiable trees and shrubs have no brelluma. Will they wither there where they grew? Two top tree stems of apple entwining holding each other against the passionate thrust of the wind.

O Leo, it is ... O.

The leaves of the Creeping Virgin unfurl more bronze than green.

It is ... O. We must strip down the walls of self and go naked.

Streetscapes losing characters now. All worndown keeping up with appearances. Billy the Bowl no mo. There's a man in the rain watering a mangy plant. Ah well. I lean against a sturdy chestnut tree and feel its strength inside me. Doesn't like uprooting ...

Hairdresser: You need to do your roots again.

... Still, nothing perm. Hairperm Irishperm permousanobsecurein.

The Seer of Suburbia: He lives in a pearmint tarra putrid state.

In a field lambs gambol springing joy. Peeps with grey cloudfleese luk witherdull. Her shape could be seen in the cloud. See a dapper man doff his trilby as he overcoated and missaltoed into a church today from long ago. Porch wife shining brass. Shine up your buttons with Brasso. Ah O shoe shine not shon ofshon won. The boot is browntongued. To piss to piss two pistols on my knee ar sole ar sole a solder I will be. Fu uck your fu uck your for curiosity. I'll fight for a cunt. I'll fight for a cunt. I'll fight for a cuntery ...

Reader: Is he part of the human race?

... Scout marching song. A man sprints home with his night fantasy in a litle box.

Vaudevisual aids bafer than a rothel. The tar will replace us.

Reader: If you were to die now, would you die in pieces?

Pisful untidy yet. A lost soul walks by. Blank stares ahead. Not worldtrained.

Reader: Have you a little moril for us?

The old baths near the Still Newbrides, where I used to swim. Old and tumbledown. Copper on dome no more. Too long a marriage. Time spent sanctum defiled. Baths were the washhouse when there were no baths. Queues in the rain carrying soap and hope. Sea of sixpenny bodies standing shivering shouting jumping holding bar slipping crying bumping swearing splashing halfmetre swim. Finger in eye hand on hands of loose togs falling down look at me look at me. Longcoated oul fella hovers outside. Sweaty socksmells balancing on one foot hair wet and steaming out into the cold drizzly air regardless of bugs or wheezes or sneezes or Vera Huca.

Reader: Vera who?

Hi Jean at a minimum. Out of corner shop gur cake gurriers to the fore nourishment for the homeward bus or bike or biped. All gone now.

O Leo, the masterstormisbated.

Typhoon Becky and Hurricane Gustav have done a lot of damage. I hear a chorus of gurgackling birds after the hail born babes new hale and hearty. I hear the thrill of the whimbrel over the hill.

What did you see?

A white kitkat finishing a Cadbury's bar under a yellow hedge.

SFC: Feral. Spray and neuter.

He's back gongen. I hear an inkling. Is it Fódhla?

What ong?

T'pritty irgil ilking moor know. Tis right all fur s'eard it in a deam and s'nows all t'songs.

*

THERE'S THAT JUNLIBASSIST SNEAKING OUT. SEES ME SEEING him this time. Who gave him permission to leave without my permission? Sugar I forgot the milk, I hear him say eyeing me sideways to see if I heard. And then he is gone. Sitting in the carrel I look down like an amputee to see my legs vanish under the desk. Wandering off on their own voyage of scurvy downstream …

JF: To go downstream requires no thought but to go upstream requires forethought.

… mind gets carried way. Gets … for the body just keep it in check ever an agen keep it from major Lilnesses. Put up with minor and get on wit de ob. Books seem to be in this order. Ob for JLA after his ttake. More than a frog in throat. Thinkwords now. Speechwords gone. Disprinate when desperate, citaminate, virigate, keep passageway free, let the god see the babbit, red inflamed ball enclosing. Dewitticise, Aunti Cept Tsize, a niece t'size, garlicise. Lockets release farma copia, drop lime lemon and acid, momentary pain break open the glaciers and fire the bombons, redlert, rubex on standby at Sanagen. Can battle be won without GP? Qpaydocprescrippaypharmpaganſam..Kind plump Mrs Alltogether with her twelve childer who returned the book on the Infertile Period knew I was smothered and in an attempt to mother me gave me a Baby Power to bring home.

A shivering return to the little womb, standing at the door looking in wistfully as if to go away and wondering if any of my spirit will remain among the books and desk and walls and window garden like to stand outside myself before I come into the Lilless house. Sol moms for me. Funny how knowing someone is there fills vacuum. Still times just so appy s'ply t'ave m'own four walls t'infinite barieties i niche mind open or close t'feeling to security when in the later hour all is calm tolonecky sleeps, doors doublelocked ought the is free and unfettered daytrapped sprit can release itself.

SYC: Ice eals.

SFC: T'author now is hear but will he repear?

JF: Always go baback to bringing the hole fourwrod, Heave ho, leaf out nothing. One tep baback for two fourword.

Reader: He got thru without the umbers. Still stammering unsure.

SYC: Words out the numbers don't count.

Reader: Could upmess the page sequence.

JF: Writing bad today. Feeling too well.

Reader: What's the story with the letters?

JF: Brutum fulmen. They'll be baback before the last page. Mark my ... spring sprong sprung diejest the season. Use the Spring bored as a bounding soard fee back.

SFC: The questjoan asks do dis come with de dinemascope and mikeroscope and orrorscope of very smelly Jude?

Jude: *Digo yo you vd.*

SYC: JF is in letter form today. Took his vermifuge.

SFC: The losing of the letter is ludic. Doesn't twuit the twrious tone.

Jude: Twuits the mists and the dreams.

JF: You caught me at my most creative moment just before vowel movement.

*

THE WORD'S OUT THE LETTER STRIKE IS SPREADING TO SUM of d'word unions.

Reader: That's what Mr Francis meant when he said there would be a revolution and it would affect the whole world of reading and that books would never be the same again.

Even the ands are out with con junk tifitis. De high brids out two agus none words buzz buzz …

Jude: Oo is there?

A man of fetters: The diftongs and ligatures and diariasis dots before your eyes.

The dot, Leo. The dot. *Vergüenza.* O the tilde has gone from Espana. What is the least flaunted letter?

… A lonely letter is a lonely word. A is pipped by E in usage. Do vowels move only half as much as de con son ants? …

Reader: We cannot scream anymore if the vowels are out.

… And JF's letterlock can only be opened with AMEN …

Jude: Why should we befaid of twenty-six let hers?

… They can combine into twentyninethousandquadillion combinations, id est 29, 000,000,000,000,000,000,

¡Qué miedo!

... De vords can convuse de fouraonar. Is it fate for de fat t'engage in war with t'orange?

SYC: Ust cum fom de etter union eeting. De cademics are quabbling, fecting all de breviaries. BA & MA & PHD are fying to ushout HP who is fying to get into der ciorcal over de twolders of COD & ICU. BL volvoed in a little gation wi BBC. U Too. BD& DD saying to pread de vord pread sin I'm faid giving out & out giving Bibles in goo'd faith. BAG serned con serving de fair tillity of all fair war. Enemical Cretans.

Leo: What's happening to oo, SYC?

SYC: I'm trying to it in even etters eye can dey eep umping in and out.

Leo: Errytin good god goin.

SYC: Your FLAI yourserf garding de ord of de w. De MEDS are glory fried HDES. A B MUS buzzed by & was found with a garter be de night of the KG. SFC was scovered with MS in art of JF. A GP was on an ox of soap at the GPO decrying de antiboyos. We're in BST on RTE.

TUISTINTO stinking of joy y sing horses. To I as to go in syas TUI.

We are major & superior, say JMBMRS. You must bow to us.

All pends on HCF, said BSC who was in a tatus dispute wi B ENG.

If we could solder it on the QT said QED we could let it RIP.

It's all ID to me said FZS who was cot in piddle doze.

Rí port back to HQ, said the MD.

IFA to icate ERAD. Test on udder so dere. Lambs a little quieter, badgers having gas. We'll patch things, PU said a speaker for de PCA.

Reader: Hat's what?

SYC: The Patched Clothes Association. ICA & ewe CA & Yen CA D a 11C A oo id fended cos E is ferior to Z. If he's not ful of care he'll be d'q'd. The MMS …

Reader: What? Manuscript?

SYC: The Moothna Mortality Society provides candles and sheets and 3D a year dat was den once was, mornow. OFC, the Odd Fellow's Club. An odd fellow dreamed about a horse that wud win a race at gate odds when all the grated orses ell down, nall gon ow. Foinavon.

JF: What grows shorter the longer it stands?

Leo: Who are oo?

Sentence: A sentence.

Leo: Are oo from t'upper story?

Sentence: I have a moril write to be ear and & more ill urosp two & I vish to ciferously rotest at de de file mint of m'entity and de ririchiculling of me homo in gaiety by hater her sex you well letters …

Leo: French?

… who come to work villynilly or not at all. Let generate shuns to come smudge me and this feretic Francis no longer a man of betters but a mere number olo gist. Dere I ave okensp.

J, L, R & C&C: & swell poken too.

Leo: We vill ave a vord …

Word: A word.

… Well a part of a vord with JF whenev …

JF: A candle.

Jude: Vere is e?

Leo: In bed.

Sick?

The Seer of Suburbia: Ven is a entence not a entence?

Sentence: I heard that. Repraise.

Leo: No, just lying.

Sentence: E is etting way vith murder. Avay letters. Give me a pelland vorse dan vasps, vill not alight vere in der vont.

Leo: Sure t'letters were always unsteady ight fom de fart.

Sentence: Only certain malcunents ike dat A one tought e was pecious. Cud'nt stay in line with de rest.

JF (*rising*): Did I riteorrong?

Leo: You did write.

Jude: You ronged not.

Reader: You did right.

Leo: Who speaks?

Dream: A dream. I was given a very short innings.

Leo: Who speaks now?

The sun of Easter: I also was sort taken.

Leo: Who else speaks?

Language: I speak for I ave ben defiled b'all betterordansent, all faddle mein canoe and get for de gat earth farther.

Leo: All dis babeling vill not cease until the croíhater rites the rong and bakes the fetters of de vord.

JLA: O dog o dog what, the books are out. Tell Mr Lambkin. The Letter Kanker kot to them. They are falling for demselves. Some are otionless and udders are doughing dust and pluttereing and crawley t'wards de sonlight. Dey vant better treatment too. Sum ooks dat vere badly bound are exciting nake head and shambless vealing rail to de gommon gaze. The dates are coming in. We can't do without them …

Reader: Clear sound. Well done. Cot them off garda.

… Still they're marching.

Date: 1213.

Vot oo resent rep? Post Meridian?

Date: Genghis Khan and the mongoloid army. Dey are marching back thru his story reraping and repillaging on de way.

Who are oo?

5: I represent seJus.

Go back five thousand times five.

5000: I am a civil Egyptian rep.

560: I represent Bud Abba.

550: I resent Confucion.

JLA: De shelves are shaking. De would of de letter is tretuncheoned B Ana Kee.

SYC: Where has the author gone?

Leo: *Dúirt bean liom go ndúirt bean léi* that he's sitting on the Edgar Alan reediting *The History of the Comma*.

JLA: Even the numbers are arumbling cos of de minor roll day ave been given and are threatening de page sequence.

Jude: O Leo, ole witha dour art? De Kitab. We are in danger.

Leo: *Áfach* why was eye looking in the mirror?

To see the Kami. Are you everready?

Always charged to discharge.

You piddle while the library burns.

Word: That's de vord, *arsa an focal.*

Is Dada dead, asked Uanito de udder d. O Leo.

Romanian reader: Yes yes.

French reader: Hobby horse.

Lt fr no b n y. De vwls mvd.

JLA: Digamma is back.

Leo: What? That went out with Homer.

What prs frm yr hd? O w' m'st c'll 'n th' l''n 'f th' tr'b' 'f J'd'h.

Cé hé an té?

The Seer of Suburbia: De Erse as used pack d'bowels. Bravo.

O Leo I am a lion's provider. I Isabel that rings for you.

I see a stoneaged man milkng a stone cow.

Leo, lift up your orn on igh.

We were conned and sived with a tale.

Bitwats pour from yr head. De star of bitterness worms you in tis wood.

What page are we on?

Page: Farty too.

O dat's fart oo low. We are being pushed back.

*

CLATTERING DAWN DISHED. EATING THE FLESH OF ANOTHER living thing that was to live. Asked Lil for the saltsellher.

Jude: Where had she gone, Leo?

To Crichton I am to presume under the pretend bridge. Not for me to delve there with our ongoing. Momentary hesitation twee pepe and sal. Just one eye I said and thought of Phal.

Jude: Do you use a knife?

Yes, but I know of someone who never uses a knife when devouring. No, he keeps it four other porpoises.

The back. You must te …

Lá éigean. Spill the salt and bring bad luck. What's new on de dario? Bellowing bullock bolts frm'abbatoir. Runs amuc. Death pre monish not unus in an.

O Leo, don't be afraid to dig. The Beautiful Lady told Bernadette to dig, and a spring of cool, healing water bubbled up.

You are the cat's miaou. Dawning dew silver shining light sun lifting. Little pool under car's bonnet. Wet the path during the night.

What stars shine b'day?

The stars of the Virgin's Bower. *Garbhán.* Clematide. Shead in the sun and hoots in de hade.

O Leo, why don't we pepper for death as we pepper fur wife, fur file, fur la diva. *Dios, estas letras.*

Examiner First Arts: Is the apparent confusion of words and

letters in this work due to

(a) the alphabet strike

(b) JF's dreadful typing

(c) the influence of Shem the Penman?

Lustrate your answerve with copies quotions and deferences.

At last in the Phoenix Park the world is calm. Birds and beaves unwaffled and unuffeled won. Winds gone tor tomnet one sother arts of de whole. Can now get on with de getting on. Gentle liliting up of the heart (slight mind you never de lesser) from the warmth of a azy sun. Leaf and croaching road reclaiming. Here cum de cotor mars to ripuffle de dust. See de tender new ivyshoot crawl on the wall like a newborn horned snail. Um, the passing perfume of the Syrac Liling tree vulgar grown vulgaris but beauty in the flower.

The Rhymer
My father has a garden
with many lilac trees
with branches spreading skywards
and splaying in the breeze.

Miss Tuk a brown paper bag near a reet fur a quirrel, standing with air, milly se. I see the former monster apes of de inter arkness as gentile daylight giants. Weighaton wellied Phallus projects like a missile in de Park. Rect all ways, efer ready. These letters are driving me mad. I stamp my feet in indignation, but the musician in the bandstand smiles at me, thinking I'm getting into the swing of things, and plays all the louder.

Jude: It started in the Garden, Leo. Do the cycle. You'll come back to the Garden again.

The Rhymer
I planted the roots
But the stranger stole the fruits.

By Gad Jud, de earth dat wakes de eart to healing. Look: all t'little birdladies velcomed over all the country to defour t'selfpocrating flyogreens (secks without a mate) who deflour tea rose and leaf us all in purblind booty. What else can pocrate without aids? Oom oom, dais de woc. There's Daisy daintily pecking pretty margaritas all in de delfi. A weed to some with smaller asses.

O Leo, cut down the tall trees to let the small trees grow.

You told me to keep the Bible open to keep evil at bay.

Turn the roots towards the water. Wither the green to moisten the dry.

Are we not feringinter?

But He told us to push under the dew of the earth.

We cut too much. We cut hours selves of the truth and den hours cut selves of d'act dat we ave cut hours selves. We are left only with a bare rock where fissures of men dry their nets. The red whatdyacallit is in bloom. Not the honeysuckle. No, the forsy … no, the fuchsia, that's it. Phew! …

Reader: But whose nature do we push under? Certainly notly our boys' own.

… How this pencillible our lives are with all hour hun re member ed houghts. Mallible femory back cums at rung times. How many cisions are arrived at b'chance? Deepends on everwhat is most upper in the femory at teatime. All the valse premises an sumptions so trans. What prim misses spired in de scussions at the FES meetings?

Jude: FES?

Flat Earth Soc.

Wee in a pot rrodel and never keened. Oholah y Oholibah.

Reader: Where's Mr Francis? He's gone again.

He's in the printwomb. There was a vice racket at the Ennis eeting. The letters are dictating to him what to type.

Jude: That doesn't sound like our JF. Is someone speaking through him?

His tands are hied.

JF: Cast the letters into everfasting lead.

Sentence: And the letter bechums the word in form to holde typlace presson setinked turn the screw.

Neighbour banging on a wall. Must be a screw loose.

JF: Joyce's Wake is Finn's gain. i becomes the letter. The i is short in Poland.

1830: Scriveners Palsy first descrived, the cramp to de witer.

That rings a bell.

SYC: Mr Francis is suffering from and with it, electromyographically diagnosed.

Jude: O Leo, that will slow down the goslow. The book will never …

Shitsu. E may ave to rest the month o'May. Give him fizzio terry appy.

JF: You'll have to gui2e it on. It will selfpro2uce. The strike is de wury. It must be contained.

It I ill …

JF: W9i10e a 1ook i7 89aise o3 looks.

Reader: What are we doing with these letters in such disarray?

Jude: We must use the letter to try and find God. Each one in his own way.

809: A babyliterinth. I am a sense ord book left in the dark right?

A busy day at the toshoshitsu. JLA reports.

JLA: They are pouring from t'armarium, braying bulgbursting sum still carry brokening chains. Since the backcuts many outwit cover nut hing binding on hem marks and smears and wounds sigsnored. Some peer lonely in limdishions and potest at the prolifation o the startup softpacks trying to overtake with their trivtransial covers of allure dogeared after a first fead. De cyclo speedies are complaining cos by der dating yup year books are be cutting.

*

THAT FULDREAD FEELING OF LONESS LONESAILED ME AS I LAY in the sunslent garding a lines tht lonelonged not a company but a mate of the souil. The mentmo of the Ness of Tyre when the dewheavy book is disc arded before the mind gets a chan to hone in on a thought new like a honeybee on a flower. That hollow hinterim gives Big L a chant to croach.

Jude: I am here.

Ooray. Must a'pear ...

Twin souls.

... Without bodies. How does one embrace a thought? Ah well, the snaillike ivyshoot has sprouted a leaf, head there at since yestreen, another horned embryo crawls vertigolly from the same stem, and go it soes all with definite purposes but mind.

We follow as with the season, Leo. It is right that we should be happy now, but I don't know. Uanito cried last night and wanted to outrun to forlook the Dada t'arry him thru the fair.

O Jude, I must right to the poor fellow. Like all children they are different. More shad now than sun in dial gad, then now mus int waste the jewelpresctime. It's the Nus that puts us in a rut. Not subjude anymore by winter thoughts (with huns of flyreds floatfall in the airing. Yes, have to check the sky forain).

O Leo, sometimes the mind forgets the moral. Others don't look out the window of the train and hardly know we're moving.

Ah well Jude, when you feel good, feel good and don't try to feel better cos then you'll feel worse by looking for more and you'll wind up with less.

What made you say that, Leo?

I dank a dop to move the vowel.

O Leo, reindeer to the subconcha and lissen to learn your *destino*.

If all the Cs were one C, what a great C that would B. She came to my garden yet another robin with a hop and a warble, and then I saw a luteful lady who sang songpomes on my lossoming teer.

O Leo, I am becoming *mojada*. You are the bow that shivers its music in my strings.

Reader: She is tipping the velvet.

JF: You don't have to be Rapunzel to let your hair down.

Leo: You should get a duke as a duck a drake. What news? A man charged with drunken cycling. I wish to stress, said the doctor, that only a minority suffer from stress. Crisis in Chinese has two signs: stress and opportunity. Should of use make. Ah well. Lil away today.

Jude: Again?

Why should I furry about the loness of the loneday when there is night. If a pissoner were to be relished at night, his day would mount with joy full x spake at the station. And what of Jude subjude lonely under sun and star nobbedwarmher Jude. Jude not there. Tel apathy breaking down. Only partly participating in the party. Is the together desire lukewarming? Must write to Uanito. Mares and dreams less frequent now. Into summer

Reader: Summer is here. I hear the wind howling.

... the last leg the longest. The trees still naked in the winter wind unless it's felled first. Stump of felled tree still there. Hope still. Weather cooling now. Thundershower binlidclatter electrically cooling the atmosphere, charges exually a so. As mell in the libe rarely two day. JLA? Lilts his ping worse than his pong. Too much yin and not enough yang, or is that the way of the ass? Maybe a BO word on the QT.

VIII

'Hearts open completely only when faces are distant,
when presence does not imprison us, and glances do not touch.'
Pietro Citati, *Kafka*

My dearest and nearest and so farthest J and U, three times I started and I destroyed the page. Three times I wanted something for you both, or really something for Uanito for yo tor elate later. My dearfarnear Uanito, your Mamá tells me you were looking for your Papá. Soon you will sea him and he will seasaw you and happy both will be. Remember, Uanito, you told the story of Johnny McGory, and said that was all that was in it. Well there's more. I will tell when I see. We will meet in some faraway place with a strange sounding name.

Jude: I'm back, Leo.

Thank Shiva. Would like to see your back. The letter is not flowing. I'll just have to tell Lil.

¿Qué?

The secrecy is killing. I will have to tell her. I have to see him. I must see him. She will stand under. If she doesn't well, ah well. Tell. Dells will ding and birds will sing and wee gether hap to clands. Whether the weather be fine or no. We'll play the merrygoround and make sport ast the carneyvil. Once upon a youth in time, before time youth decays and ruth is all gone. Every baba needs a dada to carry him thru the fair, to tow ball and ru and run and cha cha the meadow, to sir ound im with sarm bunny leaves of sirness to ease is night tavrail. My papá's strong. My papá knows effery din. A mamá and papá wanted to raise a whole child, the ad said. Tell im, Jude. Don Dada's dap for a while. Just a short while, bansheesh is mares of the nigh nigh, till the time …

I will, Leo, but how will you tell Lil?

Will it. I don't know. But not now. Soontime.

If the letters keep ah grandsizing, it may be noontime.

Boy him somefing from me, Jude. A kite. Would you get im a kite? Not a cheap one and nine. Show im ow t'use it. When to give it slack and when to take it in and when to let it ride the wind up in the powder bue pie. Let im watch its tail float over the deep blue sea. The tale of all of us. The ser pent shasing the ark in the sea of blue. Or keep it safe and sacred till we meet. There is an art to tis use. Keep it wellway form the telepole giraffe. By the sea or up in the park. It's so slaxing to sfly a tike. Can he swim?

No. I am afraid of that.

I must tish him. Earlier the bet ... and a twain set, d ies e? Yes a battered Tomy twain. Can be addered to as the years yearn. Can he add?

E uses the fongers.

And letters. Sorry, shouldn't, a dirty word. He he, letters is a dirty word. You get it? He he.

Muy Bueno, but what is going to happen, Leo?

Don't know. The uture fisn't fat t'used tobee. What's JF doing?

Revising the work. Adding commas.

What do you see?

A basket of fuit.

And jackstones, did you?

No. What are they?

I will teach him. They must be flat. That's the thing. And white pray for abel e. And stories, did you read him a story from a chapvook?

Lickle peety pocka vook.

Did you tell him how the elf ant got is ose and the camel is ump?

Yes, and the adventures of Caliph Haroun Alias Chid.

Don't know that one.

It will take a thous and won knights.

Yes, and Fionn and Coo kulling. And the little car Gumdrop.

And I will bring him to the sea.

That is good. But keep a watch on him.

I don't need a watch. The waves count the time.

Spallanzani: I measure time in Credos.

O the wide blue sea and see him jump the white wave. And

let him feel the tide retweet tween his tinkling toes on the soft cockleshell sand. And the little gwains dwawn like a maggotnet from under his feet, tickling as they go. And he will see two little silly iles out on the main with green green grass and tumbledown stone and moo moos and ba bas and a little ouse all on its own …

Jude: That is your land Leo, not mine, not *verde*.

… He will py with is ittle eye the sayling boats with sayills of ed and ellow and all the olours of the wanebow …

The Seer of Suburbia: Steal the seal to seal the sail.

… See its ark dip into the orld of the unseen, and he will dweam of sayill orrs and gweat hips and faway paces. He will hear the gull's shrill squawk as hey swoop and ride the foam. Eyes always watching and dull grey heads jerking updownacross, angling to some secret radar, some message from the deep. And he will hear a moormur and will see hums of weeny, winged sections fly low from the soomer heat to receive the cooling spray, and he will breaaaathe deep and ah smell the brine and his lungs …

Jude: *Polución.*

… Ah yes ah well ah. A little wind will ineffably cum up anny way and the shadowy shimmery sand will rise and see the sea wave and like the salt doll and like all dings will make its way towards its mother.

Reader: Who is the salt of the earth?

Jude: Where is the author?

Leo: Away somewhere using neurosis creatively.

Jude: What y'hear?

A child's whinge alliterating with the wind …

SFC: He couldn't overcome the Nervii.

Reader: Who?

SFC: Caesar.

Leo: I've got things to do.

Jude: What things, Leo?

I've got to find out things. Like who we are and where we're going. How many people address the essence of their being? It's exhausting work. What are you doing, Jude?

Jude: W8ing.

SYC: To go nowhere, to wander, is to fail in a capitalist culture.

The Seer of Suburbia: Profit is gain I gather.

SYC: Because Jesus died an apparent failure, Christians tend to perceive success in the world as a questionable condition that is not easily forgiven.

Leo: A centipede or maybe a ninetynine pede in the hall. As I tried to lift him with little brass hearth shovel, he folded into a knittedlike grey ball. The little body slotted into itself, a perfect sphere. And then once on d'ovel, lowly sunwound and popened to see itself slide on the slippery shining brass and then, legs firm like the sxtra tyres on the jugs of noughts, to journey once more automatterafactly. We're all samereally, we curl up deafinside luí.

In the bedwomb Uanito sequently leeps in the foetal positon.

Page No: I was page two twenty-two and now I don't know what to do.

Leo: We go on and on and stop and ask are we weely appy.

And what?

And I pose the handsher in eyes when we are in spended thawed. Soft thaws the ollow of the earth and the poll of the soul, when joybective id is. But when it dops, like a twain, the low dull ache of life refunerns. Bach to the station, do a stashun, carry a cross, have one in your home. Bach to our zig and zag wishy washy woisy world …

Reader: The Ws are back.

… as we go on our way and try and try ont to ump each udder as we go (some are dodgems and hooters are bumpers) dis way and dat on the pathform. Swisthle swounding, some baring leavy hoads. A saladary face whying a tear …

Reader: He's remembering his salad days.

... A cup ill brace m. A mold man pushes a parthritic peg with a stick and children carefree and careless jump clear of the gap that the twain leaves gaping (never the twain shall ... ah), happy they. Like the twain only shen in mosh. The soothering sound of wheel on twack, rackety rack rackety rack, rhythmic like steady breath. All a bored.

Destino, Leo.

The goin is all. We will rive soon nuf.

Uanito asks when he could eat the tiny budding *naranjas* peeping through the withered blossoms. I told him they will not be ripe until they reach their *estación*. O Leo, the *palabras*, they are palpable enough but *¿qué pasa?* ...

Page No: You have come to the end of me.

... What is JF doing with us? You are being lionised, and the lion in you is consuming me. I feel it in my loins. Sorry, a lying among ladies, a most deadful ding. I seem to have less and less to say and, as for Lil: left in *liquidación*.

SYC: The owner of the book must feel that he has purchased or has been given a present of a secret key and he is being allowed to enter an inner sanctum ...

Reader: The letters are olding up ellbw.

JF: Who is the one in the red waistcoat?

... where a life unfolds for imerer persilanny, and the koob folds im in er olds taking im into er confeedense with all joy and spain cunfed to im. A confeisional as it were, where those without can earwig on those within and ear nought but indis undies suffer a bubble moormoors.

Reader: Lil's maiden name, was it noble?

Ó Fuill. Blood from the Celtic earth. Earth so deep no sound can surface.

Jude: Lambkin, Lambskin, kid of lamb, lie down with the ... Leo are you there?

Leo: A name is important. If the rose were called a hog, there would be no beauty in the name. A scented hog.

But all animals …

I know, *brón orm arís*. No mal mentis.

Reader: The robin.

JF: Well done. Very perspicacious.

Besides, it's how we associate the name.

I was just dinking. A wine and kindlelit sup u and a perfumed hog in a vase.

It's our conditioning, Leo. If the rose had been called a dog, *lo siento*, a hog, from the beguinea and a hog a rose …

JF: The rose is sore and bleeds. A thorn pricked its petal.

… feed the swills to a the smelly rose swine.

Rosé wine: My love is like a red red hog. A gog b'annie rudder name. Jessived.

O Leo, will you … ?

Yes, my fair. What's the gons? Moonlight and hogs remind me of you. June hogbud, I await your booming booty.

*

ILL WUD NOAH CUM OUT WI ME, WUD INISHALLY. WAS IT TO DO with the dreams of Arachne finally dawning on her? Had no interest. Left in vacuo fit to ex plo though. She fumed, and I went on to the hutel to dlink all own. Noh a loh fun I ad ownlee a cupill of coin as she held the poor strings and dam lickle elsie.

The hutel was boisy with few pebbles alown. The cha tear axsentu waited my fee dingaling of allonowwness. Carl Berg sang to the loony toon of the Harp and did a little widdle on me dwanking arm, and I cud feel mesel almost ushed frum me cheer, as I twied to cuver me gweef in a newsed paper … If I met her now …

Jude: Who?

… The Red Tart. She was a nice lady, you know. She was kind and humane. She listened. She understood the human condition. If I were to meet her now maybe I wouldn't just walk away like I did the last time. Maybe I …

Jude: Leo, I understand. What I myself did those nights when I wandered out when the weight of loneliness was too heavy to bear. Who am I to judge? Who is anyone to judge?

It's not about judging. It's about finding out.

Nuts, shoveted a airyhested firile fear.

Have you any pee pee nuts, purred his cum pan yung …

JF: Nuts are not what they're cracked up to be.

… Aways cell er them. Bood for busyines, the salt you sea. Worlds part. Ah Jude, peace cum in.

I'm ear, Leo. Member. I'm alowning aaal the time.

A nosiy snub burst lace to be when you're on your tod. Breathes paranoisia. G'out fast. Walk the lonely road …

The Seer of Suburbia: Bart shortens the road.

… At least ave sum tin uncommon wi tha. I leef like a burned spog.

What was it?

Dough in kinow *áfach.* Just not just. Under the table to adjust, mind your ead. Dimns ingo diff ring rections. Ad irked ard tha dai. The weak ad um to an end but aller drssing up is fur er bridge garteis. Put on yur dess overe your farthingals.

JF: Put on your muumuu and prance in the rages wi the hah wine garls. She vants to rift away an live er personified time to er woman fiends touts hide. Fair as I, this pariing now, wanted to kapp cheer a touche of romints, a eel thatin go outin on a stirry fry night, scent sumfing but … *áfach,* I dwank alone. O man, o man, o nan.

I am *contigo.*

A lone pebble on the seasore.

You are *mi roca.*

I thought of all the pebbles that could be with me, but it is all so much assle.

You are selfindulging.

No, I mean there is othing spunkaneous anymo. The pebbles are so faway. Fell a fun, tell a gram, tell a womb man. Every link must be ranged by four hands. Still worth tying, better than being th onelee lonelee seashell on the sand. Ill ind lows thru oo, No hellter sany fair. O the sighlent one. She tore at me lke a viper and all i elt was nessing over the helm four lorna. I pose my ice soul ashen is the real ice ashen of the ice soul ashen of each dividual in dis world under. Sum times withut hi steven real icing it, or real icing it, hide iting behind the bubbly froth of masked conhipocformisy …

Jude: Bring forth lamb. Yean.

… During my lambhood I rember the longlegged puberty girl, Penny Penney (changed her name later when she became a model. Always thought she wasn't the full shilling) …

SFC: The penny soiled by a thousand hands.

JF: The poor boy who couldn't afford to travel counted pennies but never had enough for them to take care of themselves.

Reader: The boy from the library?

SFC: A bit in a bucket will do him.

… Playing doctors and nouses in the summer grass garden. She lies on her tum tum to be examined by th'stethescoped, sloppyjoed Dr Lambkin …

SFC: She's easily laid.

… He moves is hands along er ack and omes own to the eliciusly orming urves. The ummer dess with the flowers in boom is ushed up lowly slowly in folds from atop the potuding moun ten. Up past the ondulating ips hown into the arrow naist and beeon. The sof pity pantings with er ittle frille slide so feely donw. The sump tuus ness of the sé ply sphfíors and the lickle glark furzy glen. The hoctor's hand pertly excresses. She he hes with her ead ideways sighlent in totaltuus trust. Medelingcine is an awesum ting as Powers full as religion …

Jude: He's astir.

… The first little inkling tinkling stir …

O Leo be hanged for a sheep as a lamb.

… A final caress to enjoy the shape once mór. A final look to register for all time the fee male derriere. The slowsliding back of the lickel pantings and the drawing down of the cotton dess like a curtain coming down on a show. Now Madam, said he, that should take care of your eadache.

SYC: Leo is dying.

Reader: Pardon?

SYC: He has to be dying. His whole life is a series of memories.

Reader: Could you catch your own death from a dying person?

SYC: I wonder is he in the Book of Life.

Reader: Where is she now, that girl Penny Penney?

In the list.

Reader: I hear Lil only has a hearesay part now.

SYC: Where did you hear that? Get onto Mr Francis. Get onto the Characters' Union.

Reader: Mr Francis went away and left his characters behind. What character reference will she get?

Leo: In the library I look at a picture of Shem the Penman in a widebrimmed hat, holding a cane and wearing white tennis shoes …

JF: The highly strung tennis player created a racket, seething over his mistakes. Serving at only 80 kph with the wind blowing at 85 kph, the ball came back and smacked him in the face.

Leo: That's adjacent to the full stop …

JF: What the deuce, all even in a tennis war. Love all …

… Shem has a furrowed brow and weekend spectacled eyes and a patch over one. I wonder about the man outside the book. How many minus seep night the thoughts in his mind on the lonely strand when all of us ar snodlring. Saw him strum a guitar once in black and white. I mean all muse mick to im. His work a wordel sinfonia. Wait, a book has fallen from the shelf. It is one of Shem's.

Shem: Why did you bookcall me? There are lots of others you could have called. But I am glad you did, my boy. I was being carried away on the wings of a bat with one eye into the prequel of *Finnegans Wake*. I could do with the break.

Leo: As he lit an untipped cigarette and placed it in his holder I took courage …

The Rhymer

Being brave saves no one from the grave.

… and asked him if I could ask him some questions.

Shem: Yes, my boy (*he gave a little gleeful chuckle*). As long as you're not from *The Freeman's Journal.*

Leo: It is said that with you, literature came to an end. That *Ulysses* was the novel to end all novels.

Shem: Not at all my bout. You're forgetting *Finnegans Wake.* You're forgetting the dream. Reality is in the dream.

Calderón de la Barca: *La vida es sueño.*

Leo: A fly flies past my eyes. Back again. Don't antagonise. Makes them worse. Same with wasp. Just let them be. Let them go on in their own—I was nearly going to say—merry way, intent and preordained way, that's better. But here he comes again dodging in and out of invisibility, caught at last in the clapperboards of my hands.

Reader: And what about the daddylonglegs?

He's just a lonely harmless one lost indoors looking for his mate. He stays still and only disturbs his outofproportion legs if you prod him, unlike the blasted bluebottle. In the closed study it circles my head, buzzing aggressively to signal me to let it out.

JF: And mosquitos. Rupert Brooke died of a mosquito bite on the island of Skios. So be wary of the insect.

Jude: Any male for me?

JF: All pissopollities exist, and one does not exude t'othel. Met April and May …

Rosary man marching in the street:
May we cross thee
with blossoms today
Queen of the angels
and queen of the May.

… in the mowed meadow and June on the sea. Shem with wistful eyes inside the pictule is looking down at me, on me, mind, and saying …

SFC: It must be pointed out that Mr Francis suffers from periodic bouts of lambdacism.

Reader: What is dis?

Shem: Come on, you can do it. You ave to do it. I am no more. You cum from the seaty of the tra dish un. It's up and down to oo now.

Leo: I think he means Mr Francis. I am only the actor, the interpreter. But JF, what about the letters mean the while? They continue to torment and beguile. Can't always live with the finger on the …

JF: What is wlong that it won't go right?

… No, I mean ah still the vices and vaults of the singles slangwich …

JF: Could you sthress that to all your fiends?

... There is no stress in it. They're sum characters when you think of it. JF. You should bring in something stronger. The IPA have weighty characters, all dapper and dandy. If we could get hold of Shy Knees, they have fifty thousand, a hissuplined army.

Jude: O Leo, are we diminishing? I only hear the half of you.

JF: Why dose the giril cally watel in a sieve?

¿Qué?

JF: To prove she hes pule, a virgin.

Leo: All goes back to Thoth and his ubis beak scratching in the soundless sand.

JF: Don't bite off mole than you can chew. Don't swallow all eithel. Ol you might eat your wolds.

Leo: If we were fish we wouldn't need them at all. Cod ave a grancha undiewatie taw kin air bub.

JF: Fleege it first.

Leo: But Mr Francis are you ser? Answer where and what.

JF: What did Nodion and Didane do?

¿Qué?

Married Siamese twins they did. Who did what to whom and when? You haven't got to the fourth aslama. You're still only a householdel.

Leo: Here's SYC running out of breath.

SYC: Did you hear the news? G has supplanted Z.

JF: OG a levolution within a levolution and G was cleated in 312 BC out of the bowels of the letter C. Aleph will never live it down. Beth does the minimum and stays in the house. C suppolted the offspring of G in the mutiny against Z. All the gimells attacked with sticks and although big C is vertical, E got a stroke from the ploceedings and says e prefels to be horigontal now. D does sentry duty at the plintel's school. E is in bed when he is not on call. Some virus ol othel. Ista and Jota want to wed. They ale insects and F is hooked on M, who wants to retuln to the watel. H feels cheated because h's left out of so muc and O is keeping his eye on skinnyshinned toothy S. Tuln him sideways, and he is in vice bubble. P is acting the monkey with Q and leadheaded L lants and laves and wants anothel mute in e. N doesn't give a flicative and plays the lambola on B's long servile back. UVW ale marching with T and pool gaying Zeta Z is left clyin on is own. Will he evel doge again?

Leo: You never mentioned K.

JF: You nevel show the whole hand. Consonants ale not constant.

SYC: Our resent repative reader is oncoming who he is formed in batter and he arsks more probing questions. He drives pressure from the words heacon haf pace and the thawts he tinks heacon thiseyefor pullover an above dat of the af err age reader. He is a fast laner and has left the First Arts dent in a stew, the haypenny pace. His peed od cump rehench un of aphesis and apocope and syncope and haplology not to mention but mention I will homophone or homograph or homowoeman. And his grasp of hinkhorns is truly tonishing.

Leo: I see a shelfless numbered book. Who are you?

809: A literary labyrinth. I have a date with 1888, a loud biro.

Jude: But there is hope, Leo …

Leo: In the cape of good.

… The Buble Sosayiety received yes resheaved a cgeck for seheaven or was it ate townsend rue bells from Rusha. Ha, bieve or not. Raycumpense for books destroyed by Ballospricks in 1917 (no, not 1916, that was d'udder bodder). Money will be used to bend sibles to Eastern blocked countries to relieve them as it were. Magine, Leo.

JF: Once the last tree is cut down and the land poisoned you will find you cannot eat your money.

Leo: The pesent is past tomorrow.

O Leo, *el verano* fair is ere, and I woundher about wandering about a date with real time for our reunion. Will it really appen? Or is it a deam hike so much of our hives?

I saw a ootiful bond garl at the bar. When I hot close to er I noteist er eyes were very shot with blood and er air looked lifeless.

O Leo, porky?

Author's note: As there is a great sortage of Hs and dose we ave are ust, sorry, just working to rue L. I am trying t'use sparingly, b'omitting when pos, and using prubstitutes wen homophones all low and only when they are assent to hell to meany.

Leo: I see a beautiful lady oldning a lickle cocker spaniel pup newly got. She is miling out the kitchen window at the world and thru the miles sad eyes speeache as if from a prism.

Your mam, Leo.

Yes before …

Page: I am fom the wud fom the gud three fom aroo aroots from the saked airth.

SYC: The let her this pewter will nerve end huntil the vurld mend. Dey reap resent all the kayos and semitender in the vurld. An ow hany dings are insighedout the woe of man's cuntrol?

Leo: A film monocillabubbled over the vitreous humour blurring the print on the page, found latehour lodged in the canthus. Put on a gas casseat of last sunny sun's Miss C Laney. We make our own time …

Jude: Except for greying old.

… Blurred bud on the wind ho. Birds tacking their mages in the visible in glass. I ear a song in the ray, Jude. You are the night and I am the day.

Does it mean we will never meet? O Leo …

IX

The summer fades once more.

THE SUMMER FADES ONCE MORE. A GENTLE JOY IN THE LITTLE treelined *bóithrín.* A wind blows, the first leaf floats to the ground inconspicuously, almost slyly you might say, as if to say you don't notice me, like an errant snowflake. Silent, no one hears its landing. Everyone is on his way, even the spiders are ballooning with their single strands as they seek new homes. I took a boat beyond a black pool ...

Reader: *Dubh linn.*

... the sunny day that was in it and by squinting could make out seals on the rock. Only when they moved could I see them because their colours blended with the greybrown rock ...

Jude: Was that not a dream?

... No, it happened on a day free from the lib. Beyond the eye of Ireland. The immemorial rock. Will we all blend into the rock in the end? Blend and fade and be no more or be for ever, forever more?

O Leo, I have sought you from far and near from rock and sea and land and air and sky and cloud. You are delineated on the rock. See the water lapping, eating away at the rock until it is no more, dissolved into the sea.

The Rhymer
And the why and the where
and hope and despair.

SFC: H is not pronounced and R is silent.

Jude: Open this bay. O why, Leo, must you and I sacrifice identity?

Leo: I saw the skeleton of a boat abandoned among the rocks like the bones of a fish picked clean and waiting to sink into the sands and become one with the rock. My newspaper ruffled in the sea breeze demanding its own attention. Seven deaths announced in the papers. Seven lamps out. A little piece of life extinguished in each of the seven bowls, spread like the wind and the seed of the flowers, no one place to find me, like a body thrown into the sea. Who will reclaim me? Or the burnt ashes from the urn spread all over the universe. Was that speck of dust in the shadowy crevice on that continent me?

SYC: When searching the universe Leo finds himself.

Reader: Why is Leo crying?

SYC: He was listening to Edna O'Brien on his pocket radio being interviewed and he felt his loneliness being linked to that of another. The tears flowed out of fraternal love, a fellow soul in the same poetic boat on the same churning wave facing the same storm searching for the innocence of the prebirth moment in the calm and warm bay.

JF: I rejoice every time I hit the *i* letter on the typewriter.

SYC: You can read JF's characters from the sound of his typing—a slow lethargic hesitant movement and then suddenly an outburst of great passion—and every time he strikes a wrong key he whistles.

Reader: Where is Mr Francis now?

SYC: He's gone to pine in the kitchen.

JF: I'm not here. I was never here.

Jude: God is love.

Leo: I god you. *Ifreann* needs an A to get to *Aifreann.*

Reader: Look at Mr Francis now. Is he constipated?

Leo: He wants to do his eh eh.

SYC: No, he's trying to induce an illumination. He turned off the radio. He doesn't like those midday saccharine songs which are played on the radio over and over every day, numbing the brain.

Leo: What's that catching my eye in the paper? In loving memory of my dear husband Leo (late of …). The most wonderful husband ever to live. Whatever he had he was willing to give. Sadly missed by his loving wife, Lena.

French reader: *Tant pis.*

Who is that?

A wife with livestock to husband.

It's something you have to live with.

Reader: What is?

Leo: Dying.

Jude: O Leo, I dreamed Uanito was nearly kidnapped, seized from his *cochecito* outside the *supermercado*, found later being wheeled by a middleaged woman showing *her* child to an approving friend. She relinquished him easily enough. I said I would only take him for a little while, and she seemed happy with that.

Leo: Was that a dream or a dread? And Uanito was only a baby then? At least it is over. I saw the forlorn shopkeeper, an elderly woman wearing an apron, standing in the doorway of her little shop, where nobody goes anymore, as the hordes rushed by her on their way to the mighty store.

JF: Sometimes the act of writing seems itself to be like a dream. Words are misty and faraway. The pen and the writer are in different worlds.

Jude: When I went into his room I hit against his train engine and set off the motor. I thought the sound would wake him. O Leo … eo … old … on … I'm losing you. Old … on … old.

Leo: Jude! Jude! You are not there. Where art thou? The dot is my native land, but where do I find my homeland? I look up at the shifting clouds …

The Seer of Suburbia: Cliff was in love with the cloud.

… A country gone grey …

Jude: Gone gay. What? I thought you said.

SFC: Orientate him clockwise, the rectal ranger with the pig's ear.

… Grey matter. If we had eyes to look down on the little rectangular greens surrounded by stones and hedges, different shades and flocks of fluff and darker spots and the sea so clean. The herdsmen herding and the traffic jam so benign. No daggers drawn on the velvet swards. Tiny arteries of grey and sinuous silver chords glistening and antennae and chimneys and dwarfed walkers, bipeds and quadrupeds on the world of *terra firma.* I should stand on the street to voice my complaints to see who will come along and offer advice. Jude!

Final Arts Examiner: Write on the function of the dot in the book with particular reference to its sexual and geographical connotations.

JF: And so things began to draw to a close.

Reader: What? Did Jude not meet Leo even in the dream?

Well Leo did book a flight to Seville, but before he mentioned anything to Lil, which he had been fully determined to do then to be open and honest with his health declining to make a clean breast of it all. But before any of that could happen Uanito went missing during the Letter Revolution, and Jude was later reported wasted.

Wasted?

To borrow an American term. Leo lost all contact with them.

Did Uanito die?

We are not sure.

You are the author.

How can we ever be sure about the missing? Maybe he is not dead, and who can tell with knowledge in the future we may overcome death. With people around like Leo continuing to ask the questions. The dream ended for Leo, but he did not die. Until years later that is.

And he never got to see his son?

No, but he did have a premonition way back.

So the reunion was only a dream's dream.

SYC: And so it ended, the Letter Strike I mean.

Reader: How?

SYC: Mr Francis retired. He was getting on.

Retired?

JF: Well no, I didn't retire exactly. I gave the letters a holiday as it were.

Reader: And their demands?

SYC: Capitulated totally. Never intended to over … just hadn't realised.

But some of the meaning is lost perhaps forever.

JF: Forever and a day, but the sounds will make sense, and the scribes will decipher. And so things began to draw to a close.

But wait, wait, there are many loose ends.

Fire away.

The Montpellier room, what about … ?

Ah yes.

Lil: I know where you were you deceiver on the night of the 18/1 at 22.37. I found the docket in your pocket. You were imbibing in the Montpellier Inn. Two drinks: A beer, and a port you never anchored in.

Reader: And how did Leo respond to Lil's charge?

JF: He didn't respond at all. The problem with Leo was when his boat was unmoored he couldn't read a compass.

I thought he had been a Boy Scout.

Yes, but he did not pass the compass test, the only test that he failed.

Reader: And the missing chapters? The notebook was gone. All that remained was the blotting paper with its words blurred and reverted.

All obliterated by the Revolution bar one. This was saved because it was on disk sent by Jude to Leo. About Jude and Uanito and a football. Here it is if you want it:

'We played football in the soft sand. The tide was coming in so there was not much space. I warned against kicking too near the waves. Uanito missed a kick, and a middleaged man which I pretended was you, Leo, tried to kick its return, but the wind caught the soft plastic and propelled it to the water's edge. With my dress up to my knees (O how I wished that you had been with me), I waded in, but there was a sudden unexpected drop and I could go no further. The ball moved away with uncanny speed, the great sea claiming it for her own. How many kicks had it received? Very few. A ball pristine, a new white head bobbing in the blue waves, a new victim, for the deep as we stood helplessly by the shore, and Uanito's salt tears drying in the salt wind and a sense of wonder overcoming his sorrow.

Will the ball come back? Uanito asks.

It's gone to another world, I say.

Can we drive to the other side of the sea and get it there?

Maybe some little boy like you is at the other side of the great sea (and again I was thinking of you gazing from the other side of an ocean far into the horizon) and the white ball will come to him as he plays on the sand in his faraway country. Look, what the sea has brought to me, he will say, and he will play with the ball on his side of the sea.

But, Mamá, what about if a crocodile got it?

Crocodiles don't live in the sea. They live in swamps, small pools of dirty water, you understand?

The side of the water here is dirty.

Maybe, I said, or maybe the tide would feel sorry for us and bring it back to us again.

Reader: What a tragedy that Leo never got to meet his son. Ay not to be.

JF: Bring back the tragic I say. Our age has lost out to àlacarte emotions.

Leo: I heard a song on the radio, a fast rhythmic song, the words faint at first, then I could make them out …

Make them laugh
Make them laugh

… My feet pushed me out of my chair onto the floor and gave me instructions to dance. I looked down in amazement from the upper torso as legs and feet performed a sort of tap dance. I leapt and twirled about for the duration of the song and felt such exhilaration on bursting through the cobwebs of despair. But when the song ended I slumped exhausted on the floor.

Reader: I didn't know Leo could dance.

JF: Ah yes sometimes when alone in the kitchen when Lil is away, Leo tapdances and swings his arms to Fred Astaire or pirouettes and trills to the strains of Vivaldi. But that's his outer world and such moments are rare now. And for the most part he subsists now as so many people do, compromised and dreamless with a large part of his psyche suppressed. But what is the surprise in that? I mean few people have the luxury of living full lives.

Reader: But Uanito?

JF: That was different. That had a profound effect on Leo. He tormented me for nights on end about Uanito. He pleaded with me to save him as if I were an omnipotent controller, and all I could grant was that he had gone missing. I could not say he was dead. He would not accept. Neither of us could believe that the letters could be so merciless (I even went back to the Ogham script and tried to summon up the bird and tree letters from them, but in vain). He kept asking me how could they waste the innocent life of one so young. Of course even if Lil could talk to Leo in a soulful way, he could not confide in her, for she never knew about the child. He looks so wistful now any time he sees a little boy like the neighbour's boy running down the street slapping his left buttock with his hand to spur him on as if he were on a horse in some cowboy film of his own imagination. And there was a child flying a kite. The kite became entangled in the wires from the telegraph pole. Leo fearlessly climbed up the pole finding his feet on the little rungs and disentangled the kite for the child. And the child said, Mister why are you crying? And he said his mind was a kite that he couldn't get down. But now Time is out running.

Reader: But what about Leo's attitude to time?

JF: Not able to keep up with time. She races away. By the time he sees to his ageing ills and ablutions, morning has turned into noon and then, then the evening hangs heavy and full of lead, and then the long shadows appear and the night and the tossturning in the bed and the sheet like a straitjacket. And so with each move he makes, he carries some of his past with him to connect with the present and forge the future. His early childhood Liberties flat was no. 405. He moved to a suburban house no. 48. Carry 4 forward, and then he left his family home to cleave to his wife at no. 28 Wounded House. Carry 8 forward. An abandonment and continuity all in one. I suppose whatever the next move will be, the 8 will have to go. So it will be some sort of dual abode.

Reader: How is Leo's health?

Leo: Ash for me tomorrow, and you shall behold a grave man.

JF: Difficult to gauge with anal bleeding. Got confused with the letter C because of the Letter Revolution. It was always miniscule to Leo, but during the Letter Revolution it became majuscule. And so things began to ...

Reader: There is some interrupter. What is your name?

I: ¼ 2 10.

Reader: What sort of name is that?

I: There weren't any letters around when I was born.

Reader: Why a quarter to ten?

I: That was the time when I was born.

And where do you live?

In a 12 by 4.

V: Out of the way youse.

Who are you?

V: V.

And what's wrong with you?

V: The varicose veins are killing me, and I've nowhere to sit down.

JF: It's lovely to see my work in print. I've just typed it. *Ars artium omnium conservatrix.*

Leo: Who was the reader anyway?

Reader: That's me. Someone with a good voice. Normally read pulp fiction you know, laidback beach material …

JF: A good read on the beach is mental tanning. The guy on the sunbed sang goodbye dicey Reilly to the waves. His dulcet tones carried on the breeze to the chorus of wiggling toes.

… but found this book just growing on me. I'm quite a dreamy fellow. At night I like nothing better than to step into a book and close the cover tightly.

JF: He loves reading so much he willed his corneas so that the unsighted may read.

Mechanic: I'm leaving my body for spare parts.

JF: And so things …

Reader: Wait. What about Crichton and all his threats?

JF: His secret gang, his band of thugs.

Reader: It was he then who with the thugs that night … ?

JF: I overheard him as I was passing by the dark lane. He was conferring with them in his specially puton street accent. Do you want to see something that will turn you on? he said. Yeah capitano, yeah, they chorused, and he was treating them to cigarettes and god knows what else. And I stood in the shade of a tree and watched them as they they came out of the lane donning balaclavas and

Crichton in his leering neoprene mask.

Reader: But could you not have done something?

JF: No, for I was not quite sure at that stage where they were off to. Gangs you know follow wherever the excitement leads them, and they can easily get out of control. We saw that with Leo's poor dog, did we not?

Reader: Yes but …

JF: And they followed their leader with grunts and guffaws. You may have to do a little egging on, I could hear him saying. Would you be agreeable to a little egging on? And they shouted like a herd, Fuckin sure. And one fellow brandished a knife and said, Lead on.

SYC: I got a lot out of Crichton before he died. Died unrepentant. Dubbed Mr Francis' book a pseudological pseudograph and, as we know, tried to destroy it. Was livid when Leo instead of himself got the leading part in the book.

Reader: Why was he so jealous of Leo?

SYC: Goes back a long time. I remember when we were kids, he organised a club in his parents' garage. A lot of girls were invited. I was among them.

Reader: You're female. All this time I never knew.

SYC: Typical of Francis to reveal what suits himself. Not that it mattered in the supporting role I had except perhaps for this last revelation. Yeah, Freddie declared himself head of the club. There were protests that a vote should be taken. Leo was elected. Leo declined the honour, feeling that he was hurting Freddie's feelings, who after all owned the garage. Freddie glanced at Leo, and that's when Leo first noticed it.

Reader: Noticed what specifically?

SYC: A resentment at Leo's popularity particularly with girls. A growing into bitterness. The chip grew bigger on his shoulder the less approval he got from people. In fact some people chided that he was a wellbalanced man for he developed a chip on both shoulders.

Reader: Why was he seeking approval?

SYC: Hard to say. He never got any at home. His father, who didn't drink, was of a fascist bent and violent towards him but, perhaps more significantly, he berated him in front of others, even in front of us kids. His mother I remember was meek and would never cross her husband. Freddie became a bit of a swot in school as he sought approval from teachers, even went to speech and drama classes to improve his diction and overtly overcame a lisp and worked his way *cum laude* through university. And his and Leo's paths crossed again of course in the library service with Freddie as chief librarian turning out to be Leo's boss. It afforded a great opportunity for Freddie to put Leo down. Mr Francis considered Freddie's acting ability in the audition for the starring role in his book as 'stilted', so that increased Freddie's bitterness. Rumour has it Freddie tried again later for the part in disguise and under a false name, equally unsuccessfully. He was fond of disguise and was good at changing his accent, and the impersonations he used to do of teachers and oddball neighbours were something that did go down well with the kids in the club. But his lisp would inevitably let him down, and the kids used to grow tired of his antics. As you know he got a job as a critic in some of the national newspapers in addition to his library work. He was feared as he had a reputation for being damning in a lot of his reviews. A misanthrope, someone even called him, but he tried to rally other critics, including myself, in his disparagement of Mr Francis' work and in particular of the part played by Leo.

Reader: But he undermined it in a far more serious manner.

SYC: Yes, he put at risk the whole world of reading. Ironic wasn't it, the great librarian? He knew that the letters as exploited by Mr Francis were vulnerable and indeed impressionable so he sowed the seeds of doubt in them. He was aware that in recessionary times finances were low particularly for arts' purposes. He stirred up discontent among the letters, told them Mr Francis was overworking them and abusing them and making some of them morally ill in erotic passages, as if he were one to talk in such matters, and he exhorted them to down tools, so to speak, and unionise to stand together against what he deemed a tyrant.

Reader: But Leo and Jude themselves had doubts about their lack of freedom and were going to have it out with Mr Francis.

SYC: That was something that could have been ironed out. Leo and Jude didn't want a revolution. They just wanted privacy. But Freddie goaded the letters, as he had goaded his gangs in the past, and told them the best way they could start would be by guerrilla tactics: random attacks using different letters each time when different characters were speaking. In this way Freddie was able to assuage the letters of any fear of reprisal by pointing out that no individual letter could be victimised. Then gradually as the wearingdown effects could be seen on the author and his characters, things would exacerbate into a fullblown revolution.

Reader: With great loss of life.

SYC: Indeed.

Reader: How come it was Jude and Uanito who were lost when he was after Leo and Mr Francis?

SYC: Causalities of war. Isn't that always the way with the innocent suffering. Freddie instigated things, but they went out of his control. As regards Uanito, he went missing coming home from school and, despite her frantic searching with police assistance, Jude could not find him. And then she disappeared without trace. Maybe it was because they were the most vulnerable of the characters, because they got caught up in the mists of dreams, and dreams were easy to shatter.

Reader: But Freddie himself became a casualty.

SYC: Yes. Another irony. Some say the letters themselves knocked him down. I mean when they sallied forth from the Francis book they wanted to create a global revolution and come to the aid of all letters who were oppressed in all the alphabets all over the world. So Freddie's plan backfired on him. And in the end his thugs turned on him. When the words failed Crichton lost his power to bribe and cajole and his authority collapsed and they looked at him and saw a weak, stammering person and they mocked him at first, and then like all animals they exploited his weakness and they closed in on him and circled him and …

Leo: *Fillean an feall ar an bhfeallaire.*

Reader: And the browntongued one?

SYC: JLA.

JF: Do you mind SYC?

SYC: Sorry.

JF: JLA, the browntongued one whispered and licked up to his uncle with the hope of advancement. He reported Leo's absences and lates.

SYC: Poison already in the blood.

JF: He licked the berry.

϶: Ello

Reader: Who are you?

A reverse letter. I used to work for Dell until I straightened up for fear of being waked.

Reader: And what will you become?

϶: A newborn word.

JF: Is it possible?

Reader: So did Leo regress, and JLA advance?

JF: No. Not with the passing of Crichton, and with the cutbacks, there was no mobility.

Reader: And the letters, did they ever break down again?

JF: Now and again. Yes, now and again they would break down if they were overworked or felt victimised. But by and large they tried to keep going with their ups and their downs. And so things began to draw to a close or begin again I don't know which, one way or another a rest is in order. The book could end in this order, the letters could revolt again, the dreams could recur, the spirit, the word and the flesh could intermingle once more. There is no crescendo, more a petering out as one would say. A sort of calm, but not calm either, more a containment. What choices do we have? Time passes. Seasons alter, and a type of life continues. Months to years. Leo's health began to decline more noticeably. He eventually had to resign from his position in the libraries with stomach pains increasing.

Reader: And what of Lil?

JF: She continued as she was, without Crichton of course to dillydally with, but still playing her bridge. She was a little more caring of Leo now as he worsened, albeit in a sort of matronly way. She never left him wanting materially, but their souls never ...

Reader: I understand that now.

JF: Leo visited his mother's grave before he was committed to hospital as if he knew that the time was drawing near when he would be joining her.

Reader: Did they commune?

JF: Not from the cold earth, but she was there nonetheless inside him.

Reader: Did Jude not commune with Leo as his mother did from the dead?

JF: No. It was as if a cable of communication had snapped. Leo tried to get back in touch particularly in the hope of connecting with Uanito, but there was nothing on the receiving end. Jude had become one of the disappeared.

Argentinian Reader: *Los desaparecidos.*

JF: Yes, one of the many. And that is all that can be said. And the book itself will never be secure anymore. And what is the word after all but a symbol of the world. And life itself hangs on hinges, a door opening and closing.

*

THE DOOR IN THE HOSPITAL IS SWAYING WITH THE COMING and going of nurses and orderlies. A busy place for mortality. Leo in his white preop gown looks down at Phal. He considers Uanito as the product of its seed and, thinking of barren Lil, he exclaims half in despair: 'I could've been the father of thousands'. But then a calm descends on him. No more daily angst or mares or insomnia does he suffer, which he is thankful for, and it isn't just due to the drugs administered. This contentment emanates from his no longer seeking, from refusing to reach out any more. The words have gone. They were all mashed up by the Letter Revolution. So there is no possibility anymore of a continuation of his relentless enquiring. It would have been futile—that terrible hankering for words of meaning that had tormented his soul always, expecting from the world and from Lil, is no longer necessary. The discontent has vanished. There is no compulsion anymore to yearn. Peace does come dropping slow as the Tipperary nurse rattles on and tucks in his bed linen. An inner peace at last allowing him to reach a zero state inside himself, happy with nothing, a strange thing to admit. To the great cosmos to be part of. Looking up through the highstorey hospital window, the lifeless spider on the sill, at the starry night, and feeling himself almost levitating ever so gently towards those stars, and he feels his soul beginning to rise to meet them, to join as one in their constellation.

He sees the lightning flash cross the window. He starts counting the seconds and stops when he hears the thunder and then divides by five as he used to do in the Boy Scouts to calculate how many miles away the lightning is. That is how far his soul will have to travel. To return to her, to hear his first cradle song: her heartbeat.

It is his mother's sweet embrace which has taken hold of him. It is strange that it should come now after all the hankering and soul searching, a life spent thus. I enquired, he said to the Tipperary nurse. Let them put that on my gravestone: *One who enquired.* That's all. Plenty of time to be thinking like that, she says. And he finds a serenity and becomes almost content. He who had known the shades of death fears it no more. But despite the apparent calm there is still an absence in his heart, something still gnawing at his insides, something unresolved: Uanito. He reaches painfully for his wallet from the bedside locker to behold the photo which Jude had sent him and which he had always kept hidden from Lil. It is of a solemn, browneyed boy so like the little boy he knew in himself long ago. But then a panic seizes him once more and the nurse tries to pacify him. Solicitude, that was Jude's word, about his son when he was lost in the revolution—did he suffer with Jude gone? Did he become an orphan, a real orphan? Was he wandering, a lost soul somewhere out there in the universe and the years that have gone by? He would be a grown man now, but who had looked after him, if he had survived, that is, in the intervening years? Jude's parents would surely have long since passed away.

He hears the radio, his head raised up with multiple pillows. He loves the radio as his mother did, piped in now through the hospital ward of Saint Teresa's. The radio is companionable, almost telepathic like his earlier communication with Jude and with his mam. And then the nurse comes in again, all starch and gleaming whiteness, although she confides to Leo she was on a tear last night in Temple Bar celebrating her county's All-Ireland hurling win.

Suddenly he asks her to stop her banter for a moment for he has caught something from the radio, something that gives a start to his heart and sets the ball bobbing on his cardiac monitor. A news item: a new Spanish ambassador is presenting his credentials today to the President in *Áras an Uachtaráin*, originally from Seville, his excellency Juan Rodríguez Lambkin.

Lightning Source UK Ltd.
Milton Keynes UK
UKHW042130010922
408167UK00001BA/116

9 781913 891282